The Hollywood Unmurders

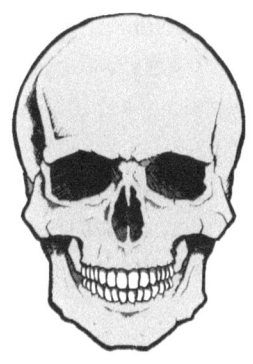

Other books by the author

Fiction

Support Your Local Vampire Kitty-Cat
An innocent vampire kitty-cat and his human partner fight for their lives—er, undeadness?—against the mob and a vigilante vampire-killer gang.

The Summer Boy
A murder mystery wrapped around a coming-of-age story set in Texas in the 60s.

Gundown
A speculative thriller that explores a real-world solution for gun violence.

Final Fire
A speculative thriller—a madman creates a plague to wipe out most of humanity.

Nonfiction

Mastering the Craft of Compelling Storytelling
Coaching on fiction craft and narrative technique for writers of all levels.

The Hollywood Unmurders

THE VAMPIRE KITTY-CAT CHRONICLES

RAY RHAMEY

Ashland, Oregon

 The platypus breaks all the rules—it's the only mammal that lays eggs, is venomous, has a duck bill, a beaver tail, and otter feet—and it does just fine, thank you very much.

It can be the same for novels that don't slip tidily into genre pigeonholes. Platypus authors take readers on unique paths to entertainment, truth, and enjoyable reads.

This book is a work of fiction. All characters, organizations, and locales, and all incidents and dialogue, are drawn from the author's imagination and not to be construed as real.

The Hollywood Unmurders Copyright © Ray Rhamey 2025. Manufactured in the United States of America. All rights reserved. No part of this book may be reproduced in any form or by any electronic or mechanical means including information storage and retrieval systems without permission in writing from the publisher, except by a reviewer, who may quote brief passages in a review. Published by Platypus, an imprint of Flogging the Quill LLC, Ashland, Oregon. First Edition.

ISBN 978-0-9909282-5-6

Book and cover design by Ray Rhamey

Acknowledgments

A big thankyou to Aaron Dawson, attorney, for helping keep the trial sequence true to form.

Thanks to Captain Patricia Sandoval of the Los Angeles Police Department for information on the Hollywood station and police procedures.

And thanks to the invaluable insights and corrections contributed by my beta readers: Donald Maass, Judy Brennerman, Kristin Oakley, Barbara Russell, Elizabeth Gelb, Ann Chapman, Gary Bayer, Tony DiMeo, and at least one other whose name I have lost. Oh, and my lovely wife, Sarah, too.

For Sarah, Abby, Molly, Becky, Dan, Julia, Beth,
and the cats we have loved.

Bob
Alex
Sally
Isaac
Olive
Casey
Oscar
Rocky
Rugby
Skunk
Fraidy
Gracie
Peanut
Pepper
Xerxes
Floppy
Frisbee
Mittens
Wrigley
Lancelot
Sylvester
Alabama
Guinevere
Strawberry
Ryder Parsnips Revenge

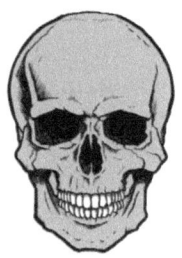

1: Patch

I hate to admit this, but there are times when my tomcat modus operandi—I-am-an-independent-entity-who-doesn't-give-a-meow-what-you-think—is a tad shortsighted. Like tonight, when Meg let me out for a prowl.

She tousled my fur as she opened the front door of our apartment and said, "Be careful, Patch. They say a coyote never met a cat it didn't like." She ran her hand down my spine—*mmmmm*, what was she saying? "And I'm pretty sure even vampire kitty-cats are on the menu."

What did I do? Roll my eyes.

So now a giant hunchback coyote over by the *W* in the "HOLLYWOOD" sign has me hunkered down behind the *H*, straining to hear movement. That serene full moon up above has turned into a spotlight aimed at me, and there's new meaning to "snack attack."

Although we cats are not inclined to admit a mistake—ever—well, I was wrong, Meg.

And, yes, a giant hunchback coyote, three times as big as any coyote I've ever seen.

I wouldn't worry if it were a dog—why get your tail in a knot about a creature that has devoted eons of evolution to drooling?

But this is a toothy carnivore with an appetite for fillet of cat. Oh, I'll have my revenge—noshing on me will give him a terminal case of indigestion. Unfortunately, by then I won't be in any condition to say gotcha.

Being undead isn't much of a life, but I'd like to hold on to what little I have.

The silence is making me crazy, so I slink low, belly to the ground, and peer around a post.

He isn't there.

Uh-oh.

I scan the rocky slope below, an arid holdout of the old desert in the middle of L.A.'s artificial lushness. Rocks. Bare dirt. A lonely scrub oak. Chaparral bushes. No giant coyote. Maybe my orange-white-black calico colors are as good for camouflage as I hope they are.

Something cracks behind me, sounding entirely too much like a dry twig snapping. I whip around and there the coyote stands, gazing at me from four feet away.

So much for camouflage.

He's huge, all right, but not a hunchback—he's wearing a brown knapsack that blends with his fur. That's a bit peculiar, even for Los Angeles.

Hoping to look too big and dangerous to mess with, I arch my back and puff up the fur on my spine and tail.

He sits and licks his chops, no doubt considering which part of me to take a bite out of first.

So much for puffery.

He stands and takes a step closer. I'm beyond tense, mere seconds from incoherent screeching and utterly losing it to uncatlike panic. I take a deep breath and focus on looking cool and indifferent, thinking that thinking that will calm me down.

He tastes my scent once more with a deep inhale.

I am not calming down.

Another lick of his chops, languid this time, as if relishing the fine dining experience to come.

I begin to understand what food feels like.

Goodbye, Meg.

Then his blue eyes twinkle, he winks, and he turns and walks away.

Blue?

Winks?

Walks away?

I scram for home, flinching at every sound and shying from every shadow as I race down the hill.

At last, lights are ahead and I'm not far from the apartment. Just as I start to feel like I've made it, a coyote jumps out from a bush and lands in front of me. It's not the giant coyote, just a normal-size eater of cats. I skid to a stop, arch my back, and hiss. The coyote circles me, and I turn to keep facing it.

It launches at me, jaws wide. As I scramble to dodge his attack, the giant coyote soars in from behind me and clamps his massive jaws on the coyote's neck. The giant lands and then flings the coyote through the air. It hits the ground, yelps, and limps away into the night.

I run.

Paws rustle in dirt off to my side—it's the giant, ten feet away, pacing me. I speed up. He stays with me but comes no closer all the way back home.

When I get to where Meg and I live, a two-story courtyard apartment building with a swimming pool in the center, he follows me right in, firing up a bark storm from the yappy little doggie in the window that lives across from us. I head past the pool, darned glad that Meg leaves our door open a crack when I go out so I can nose my way back in. I'm also a little proud that I haven't panicked and run like mad.

Well, I do hurry, just a little, right at the last.

Okay. So I run like mad.

After I'm safely inside, I peer out. Standing right on our doorstep, the coyote eyes me, and then his ears focus forward—Meg is humming somewhere inside our apartment. He peers in, searching. Facing the coyote, I crouch and brace myself, poised to spring, claws blazing. I give him a mighty hiss. Despite his gleaming fangs, if he tries to mess with my associate, I will rip his—

He snaps his gaze back to me, he winks, and then he trots away. He leaps from the edge of the swimming pool to the diving board—must be twenty feet away—then springs off of the board to land on the other side. When he reaches the corner of our building, he gives me a last look and then ambles out of sight. The varmint knows no fear.

I, however, know great relief.

"Patch!" Meg scoops me up and pushes the door shut with her hip. She strokes my head. "You've been gone a long time, and I was worried that you'd run into a coyote."

As if on cue, a coyote howl slices through the room. Meg says, "See? That sounds like it's right outside the door."

Tell me about it. A shiver quivers me from head to tail.

I mentally shake my head at myself—I'm on the verge of self-pity, an emotion unusual for cats. I mean, we've been hailed as gods, and rightly so. Maybe a good tongue bath will take my mind off woe-is-me; I'm a bit dusty from my outing.

Meg deposits me on the couch and I turn to the task. As I tidy myself, my gaze slides over to the front door, and that coyote comes to mind, licking his chops—and winking. As I contemplate his mysterious behavior, the doorbell rings.

Meg peers through the peephole, then gives me a shrug. When she opens the door, a sandy-haired, lanky and lean man wearing a rumpled brown suit looks down at her—I'd say he's twentysomething, about what Meg is. He smiles, and I wonder if he would do that if he knew he was standing just outside a vampire den. Lucky for him we've recently had a helping of V1 juice, the type A-negative with the rich red color and a nicely meaty aftertaste. There's no stopping an attack when the blood hunger frenzy takes over.

The man holds out a badge. "Los Angeles police, ma'am, homicide. I'm Detective Nicholai Silver."

Meg scowls at the badge, and I join her at the door to back her up, my hackles rising. Ever since I was tried for murder back in Illinois, I tense up whenever the police come calling. But I stifle a hiss. It wouldn't be smart to draw attention to myself. Besides, I was found not guilty, so why worry?

"You are Megan Murrow, right?" She's still wearing her crimson jumpsuit, her uniform with "Meg" stitched in white above one pocket and the V1 juice logo on the other for her delivery job with the American Vampire Association.

Meg's voice tightens. "Yes." How does he know her name? We've only been in L.A. for a little while, living a very quiet life, not doing much more than her working and me being bored in this apartment.

He gives her a smile. "Nice to meet you. Call me Nick."

She nods but doesn't smile in return. "I'm Meg."

Nick glances at me and then says to Meg, "Can I have a minute of your time?"

"You said homicide?" She gazes down at me and arches an eyebrow. "As in murder?"

Give me a break, Meg. Will you never let that go? It was self-defense, the judge said so.

Nick the cop turns his gaze back to me—his twinkly blue eyes seem to have a knowing smile behind them.

If he winks at me—

He winks at me.

The only thing that comes to mind is this: *holy shit.*

I have to tell you, the human invention of levels of expletives is pretty cool. Cats had only variations of "meow" until we hooked up with people. As I'm sure you know, life offers many occasions that call for the use of expletives.

Something smells wrong about this. I study him, take in the scent coming off of him. Hmm. There's something about it that's not regulation human. But definitely not vampire.

Nick turns his sparkly blues back to Meg. "Murder most weird. And I can use your help."

Meg is always nervous around live people, as I suspect you would be too if they had tried to drive a stake through your heart. I think she would pale if she had any circulation. Her eyes widen. "My help? Why me?"

He smiles again. "It'll only take a minute to explain. May I come in?"

Good luck with that, dude. I look forward to his quick departure so I can get back to taking a bath. A good thing, too, because deep down I know this guy is trouble looking for a place to happen.

Meg is silent a beat longer than she usually takes to say no, so I zero in on her face to see what's going on. Her expression is soft, her eyelids flutter a couple of times, and there's a teensy grin at the corners of her mouth.

It widens into a smile.

Wait. What?

She takes a step back and opens the door wider. "Sure, Detective Silver, er, Nick. I'd like to help."

Uh-oh.

2: Meg

Meg glances down at Patch. Sure enough, he's wearing the WTF expression he gives her now and then, and this time she doesn't blame him. What is she doing, inviting a cop into the apartment? They're vampires! Although she doesn't believe it's literally a crime to be a vampire, people do think vees do disgusting things that are criminal, such as sucking blood out of their fellow breathers.

Sure, feral vampires run around in the dark and puncture jugulars, but Patch and Meg and the vees they know don't. Not that temptation doesn't pull at them when they're running low on blood and on the hungry side, but they've got V1 juice.

She knows the risks of being around a breather. When blood hunger overwhelms you, anything with a heartbeat within reach is a goner—Patch, her innocent victim from the bad old days, being a prime example.

So it doesn't make any sense to risk exposure by inviting a cop in, but whatever animal magnetism is, this guy has it. Woof. She's never felt it before, doesn't even really know what it means, but this is like standing next to a crackling fire in a fireplace on a winter night. Woof.

She'd like to shake his hand, but by now hers are clammy. It would not go well for him to learn that she's room temperature, not a normal 98.6.

As if haunted by her former life, her body remembers being embraced, and it ... desires.

What can it hurt to talk to the man? Besides, she wants to be a good citizen, and she has nothing to do with any murders. At least not here in L.A. She glances at her kitty-cat killer. He's such a sweetie. Currently, he's giving her that locked-in eye-contact stare that means he's pissed. She is going to have to come up with a double helping of scratching behind his ears. Not a terrible penance to pay, and his purr is so soothing.

Meg looks up and settles her gaze on Detective Silver ... er, Nick. She could go swimming in the blue of his eyes ... oh gosh. She's staring. "Who was murdered, and how can I possibly be of any help?" She gestures him inside. "Come on in."

Patch steps in front of the detective's feet, putting himself in perfect tripping position. Patch is seldom this rude; in fact, he gets along with most breathers as long as they pet him. And they do—he's a fine-looking cat.

Maybe he doesn't like a fireplace on a cool night, but she does.

She did.

She would if she could.

The detective steps over Patch, which provokes a miffed "mrf" from her friend, who then ambles toward the bedroom. Nick pulls a manila envelope from his inside coat pocket and points at the logo on her jumpsuit. "You work for V1, the juice company, right?"

"Technically, it's the American Veggie Association, and yes, I deliver juice on the night shift." Ha. The "night shift." Vees call themselves the Night Shift. "But I'm done for tonight."

"Been doing this long?"

"A couple months. It's part-time, but it covers the bills and gives me time to work on my writing."

His eyebrows rise. "You're a writer?" He smiles. "Let me guess—you're working on a screenplay."

This guy is good. She nods and says, "What makes you think that?"

"You're in Hollywood. Everybody here is working on a screenplay."

"Okay. Now it's my turn." She aims a finger at him. "A crime drama, right?"

He grins. "For me, it's more of a reality show." He holds her gaze for a long moment, then shakes his head and takes a small notepad from his pocket. He leafs through to a page, then looks back up at her. "A V1 van has been seen in the victim's neighborhood on a number of occasions. I checked with the A.V.A., and your route includes his address. We're talking to everybody who has had contact with him."

"It's somebody I know?"

The detective's eyes narrow, laser in on her when he says, "Flint Ascot."

"Oh, no!" Mr. Ascot? Who would murder that nice man? Besides, he's a famous star.

"He is on your route, correct?"

"He used to be a regular customer." For the veggie version of V1 juice, that is. "But not anymore. I don't know why."

The detective's gaze doesn't let up. He's pressuring her. She doesn't know what to do. Patch rejoins them and rubs against her legs. When she looks down at him, he says, "Mrr." It's not quite a growl, but he's not happy. She's not either, but she can't show it. She fakes a yawn and checks her wristwatch. "It's almost nine ..." Maybe he'll take the hint.

Detective Silver nods. "It's late, I know." He stuffs the notepad back into a pocket and opens the flap on the manila envelope. Then he stops and gives her a really pleasant smile that takes the stare out of his eyes. "Y'know, seeing as how you work for V1 and all, I sure could use a bottle of that juice right about now, it being late and me feeling peckish from—" He grins down at Patch.

Oh, my, who uses words like *peckish* anymore? She can't help but smile.

He seems to be talking to Patch more than to her when he finishes. "—doing a lot of running lately."

Patch whips his head around to look up at the detective. "Mrrr?"

Coming back to her, Nick says, "Can you sell me one?"

"Well, I'm not authorized for sales, I just deliver."

He shrugs. "That's okay, I—"

"But sometimes there's, er, damage. Let me check." She heads for the kitchen and Nick follows, trailed by her personal undead version of Grumpy Cat. She can almost hear a sigh from Patch, which she's certain she would be hearing if he were breathing.

After she flicks on the fluorescent ceiling light and tries not to cringe at the impact since she's role-playing a normal breather here, she gets a bottle of V1 juice out of the refrigerator. It's the alternative version marketed under the name American Veggie Association, made with a blend of red and gold beets, which makes it a one-vegetable drink, and it's the same color as blood.

It has the same label, except for the ingredient list. It even has the same number 1 logo with blood oozing out from under it. She likes the slogan, "Number 1 with vampires." It's like hiding in plain sight. One of her customers for the veggie version throws vampire parties and they drink their "blood" spiked with vodka.

If people knew what vampire life, so to speak, is really like, they wouldn't be so eager to join in.

She twists the cap and breaks the seal. "Oh, look at that. The seal is broken." She flicks a glance at Nick and he smiles. The ghost of a tingle rushes up her spine and ends with a quiver at the back of her neck. She takes off the cap and hands the bottle to him. "This should be disposed of. Can't deliver a damaged product, can I?"

He grins and reaches for the bottle. "Maybe I can help. Join me?"

She shakes her head. "Just had some."

Patch utters a little "Mrow," and she swears he rolls his eyes at her the way he did when he went prowling. She has a feeling the word *disdain* was coined by someone who lived with a cat.

Nick tilts his head back and drinks down most of the veggie V1, his Adam's apple bobbing, and gives a sigh when he's done. "I never thought I'd like beets, but this stuff is good." He gazes at the "bloody" label and then directly into her eyes. It's like he's trying to see inside her head. "Funny stuff, the vampire shtick, don't you think?"

Is he probing her? About vampires? *Calm down*, she says to herself, *you're being paranoid*. There's no way he could know. She shrugs and points to the envelope he holds in his other hand. "You were going to show me something ... "

"Ah! Yes, of course." He sets the bottle on the kitchen table and pulls a photo out of the envelope. "Your customer, right?"

It's the handsome face of 2010 Shadow Hill Way in Beverly Hills, also known as Flint Ascot, formerly a weekly case of veggie V1. His star had been slipping until he had a masterful face-lift done. She'd read in *The Hollywood Reporter* that he was in the middle of shooting his big comeback movie, *Murder at Midnight*.

She shakes her head. "*Former* customer. I can't believe he's dead. Really?"

Nick nods. "Not just dead, murdered."

Oh, no. Such a sweet man. "How ... " A shudder ripples through her, and goose bumps prickle her arms. She's a vampire, not a ghoul, so she says, "Never mind."

"You'll see it in the papers. It's gruesome—" He gives her a quick look as if he's watching for something, then turns back to the photo. "His skeleton was found in a tanning bed two nights ago. Had to identify him through his dental work. We don't know the cause of death yet."

Sorrow fills her throat. "He used to come out and give Patch a scratch behind the ears when I delivered his juice."

Patch stands, puts his front paws on her thigh, and she shows him the photo. He inhales, gives a little hiss, and drops back to the floor. Patch loves his scratches behind the ears, and Mr. Ascot was generous with his.

Nick brings her back to now. "Have you delivered to him recently?"

A shiver makes a run. "No. He discontinued our service a month ago, shortly after his plastic surgery. But the last delivery I made, he seemed fine. I was sorry to see him leave us."

Nick pulls a newspaper clipping from the envelope and shows it to her. It's from the *Beverly Hills Courier*, and there's Mr. Ascot with a bandage on his forehead. The headline reads, "Flint chipped in action scene."

Nick taps the article. "Got a deep cut just above his eyebrow. Says here he was going to see some doctor about it."

He runs a finger down the page. "Doctor Lovely." He cocks his head at her. "Weird name. Is he for real?"

She knows the name well, and Doc Lovely comes by it rightfully. "He sure is. His grandparents, Jade and Max Lovely, were America's favorite leading man and leading woman for twenty years."

Nick's eyebrows rise, and he nods. So he knows who she's talking about.

She goes into the living room, fetches the latest copy of *The Hollywood Reporter* from the coffee table, and takes it back to the kitchen.

As she pages to an article about the doctor, she tells Nick, "Doc Lovely is *the* plastic surgeon to the stars, huge in Hollywood. He's a perfectionist, and his work has been touted as fine art, mostly by the stars he has remodeled. Mister Ascot's redo was hailed as a Lovely masterpiece."

She finds the article on the doctor and puts the magazine on the counter. The headline reads, "Perfectionist perfect again." It's the story on Flint Ascot's surgery, but also features a number of the aging stars he has renovated. She taps a photo. "That's Doc."

What she can't tell the detective is that Doc Lovely is a saint down at the A.V.A. He comes into a building full of vampires, even though he's not one himself, to do pro bono reconstructive work on vampires' nonhealing wounds. He's also one of her best customers—five cases of V1 every week, and not the veggie version. Since the blood can't be for him, he must be helping vampire clients outside of the A.V.A.

The detective takes out his notepad and scribbles in it. "Thanks. Very helpful." He puts his notes away and takes out his cell phone. "We have surveillance video from the Sun Shine tanning parlor taken at one o'clock the morning of the murder." He taps the screen and turns it to her. It shows a blurry black-and-white video of Flint heading inside the parlor. Someone wearing a white hat, a jaunty feather in its hatband, guides him by the elbow, but it doesn't show enough to make out body type or even if it's a man or woman, much less a recognizable face. There's a white square above Mr. Ascot's eye—a bandage? The two go inside.

Nick says, "Any idea who the person in the white hat could be?"

All she can do is shrug. The lives of the rich and famous don't have much to do with her. Although she can hope. Maybe her script meeting with Disney tonight will get her a contract to write her—

"And then there's this." Nick takes a bottle from his side pocket and puts it on the table next to the V1 bottle. Except for the labels, they are twins—clear glass with a wide mouth for easy drinking and pouring, a sprinkling of bas-relief droplet shapes molded around the top. But the label on this bottle is a lovely sunrise with "Everlast Elixir" printed on it. "Have you seen this before?"

She shakes her head. Why is he asking her about it?

He gives her that penetrating gaze again. "It was found inside the tanning bed. In the skeleton's hand. The residue in the bottle tests positive for blood. Type B-negative. Ascot was O-positive."

B-negative is one of the most popular V1 flavors. The fun she'd been having with Nick sinks into the pit of her stomach.

"In fact, we found a partial case of these bottles of blood in his refrigerator."

She can't help but glance at her refrigerator, also loaded with bottles of blood. Could Mr. Ascot have been a vee?

That's crazy. She's sure she would have known. And Patch certainly would have—he can smell a vampire a block away.

Nick hands her the Everlast Elixir bottle. "There's something else." He points to the ceiling. "Hold it up to the light."

She holds it up so light shines through it. There's an image underneath the Elixir label. It's faint, and it takes a moment to make it out. It's a V1 label, oozing blood and all. And there's the slogan "Number one with vampires."

Uh-oh.

3: Nick

As Meg studies the bottle and the cat glares up at him, Nick gets a little tingle in his belly for the second time since she invited him in. Damn. Wow. He's standing in a vampire den. Talk about good luck. Who knew when he got the impossibly dull assignment to check on a delivery van driver that a little Google search would turn up these guys?

The place is an ordinary apartment, nothing creepy about it. The living room is on the dark side, though, with only one lamp in it providing light, and not a very bright light at that, maybe a 40-watt bulb. A little disappointing there's no obvious vampire vibe, but the main feature is the bloodsucker in front of him.

She's intriguing, he'll give her that. He tracked down old CNN video about her from when she lived in Bloomsburg, Illinois. She was holding her cat in her arms. They were running for county sheriff as vampire candidates, right out in the open. When he saw that, he wondered why, if there are a bunch of vampires in a small Illinois town, he never hears about vampires in L.A. There must be some. And there's the Death to Vampires League crazies who go around hunting for them.

Meg lost her election in Illinois by a few hundred votes because the polls closed before dark and her vampire

constituency couldn't come out to vote. She was defeated, but she sure didn't look like a loser. Or an animated corpse.
Or a murderer.
Yet.
Oddly, this place and person of interest feel ... normal? As if this is an everyday human being and her cat. But then, he'd had no idea what a vampire den would be like, had he? Or what an actual vampire would be. Despite the fact that there's no record of this creature doing anyone harm—though that's not so true for the cat—he still came prepared. He's fairly sure he's strong enough to drive the wooden stake tucked in his jacket pocket into her heart without a hammer. He can just shoot the cat, although he's not certain that ordinary lead bullets will do the job.

What fired up his hunter instincts when he discovered these vampires is that the bottle found in Flint Ascot's hand sure seems to say the murder victim drank blood. Quite a lot of it, considering the stash in his refrigerator. And who drinks blood besides vampires?

But Ascot was a famous star with a long Hollywood career. How could he be a vampire? Besides, vampires are murderers—and that makes them Nick's prey. Although, he will confess, the carnivore side of him has lapped up fresh blood more than once. But never from people.

Patch looks up at Nick as though he'd like to get a little taste of him right now, so he gives the cat another wink—Patch blinks and cocks his head, looking a little confused. Nick should feel guilty for screwing with a kitty-cat's mind ... but he doesn't. Mostly because cats are *bestia non grata* to him—it's a personality issue. They might taste all right, although he's never gone there. But their look-down-their-nose-at-you attitude irks him, and this cat is no exception. So he adds a little grin after the wink. The cat shakes his head as if to clear it. Ha.

Nick takes in Meg while she examines the bottle. If he'd ever thought about what a vampire would look like, it wouldn't have been her—no big fangs, no bloody eyes, nothing like what you see in vampire movies. Her pixie-cut blond hair frames her face nicely. In person, she's tiny, but her strong chin and right-in-the-eyes gaze make it clear that it wouldn't be a good idea to get in her way. There's a firm set to her mouth that turns sweet and warm when she smiles. Her eyes are about the same blue as his. She's more than pretty, and that, along with the strength she radiates, tugs at him ...

If he were a normal person and she wasn't a vampire, he'd want to hit on her. But he's not normal and vampires are way too creepy. Or should he say "crypty"? Even if she could interest him, between her "condition" and his, any connection with a ... a *thing* would be impossible.

But he can't help but wonder what her skin feels like. Cold? Cool? Room temperature? Soft? Hard? Dead? He knows how dead feels, thanks to his last murder case. Maybe he should offer to shake her hand when he leaves and see what it's like. But even the thought of shaking a deadish hand is repulsive.

Something about her feels a little off. It nags at him ... No, it's not something, it's nothing, a lack, a preternatural stillness. He focuses all his senses on her face ... studies her neck ... her torso— Ah, she doesn't breathe. There's no rise and fall of her chest. Except, now that he thinks of it, she inhales just before she talks. A check of her furry roommate shows no breathing there, either. Makes sense, he guesses.

She turns the Everlast Elixir bottle around and around, shaking her head. She looks as mystified as he is by the V1 label underneath the Elixir label. But he's puzzled about a lot more than the labels—like why are there traces of blood in a bottle that says it's for vampires? That makes sense only if there really is such a thing as vampires. Which, according to his research, is what Meg and Patch are. The victim was one of her customers, but other than the residue of blood in the bottle, there's no clue that he was a vampire. And vampires don't star in movies, as far as he knows. So what is Meg's and Patch's involvement with what he thinks of as the toaster murder?

He plans to keep that handle to himself; the captain wouldn't like him being flip about a homicide victim. The captain. Does Nick dare tell him that there are vampires right here in L.A.? Naw, not unless he's looking to have desk duty for the rest of his life. Not unless he has evidence.

Maybe it's because his coyote senses are still heightened after his run down from the Hollywood Sign with Patch, but a subtle aroma of blood in the room teases him. Inhaling deeply and swiveling his head, he searches the kitchen for the source. It seems to be coming from Meg.

He steps closer and draws her scent in. Yep, there's blood in it, much the same as he got from Patch earlier. The cat sits nearby, green eyes lasering him, radiating kitty-cat hostility. He's glad he doesn't live with the animal, and he's sure not going to turn his back on him.

But then, the cat is at her side, clearly ready to defend Meg from an intruder on their lives. *Their* lives. Together. Kind of a miniature, unnatural monster family.

Listen to him, talking about unnatural. Because of what he is, there's no "their" in his future with anybody, woman or beast.

Enough! Focus, Nick. A deep breath settles him ... but only until it tells him there's another source of blood scent in the room besides Meg and Patch. Well, he's a detective, so he investigates.

He steps deeper into the kitchen. "Nice roomy kitchen you have here. Wish mine was this big." He feels a little silly saying this, since her kitchen is about the same as the one in his apartment, the equivalent of a closet with appliances, a table, and a sink.

"Wow, yours must be *really* tiny." She puts the Everlast Elixir bottle on the counter. Her expression seems guarded now, her eyes not so wide, her mouth no longer wearing a little smile, her lips pressed into a thin line.

She backs away from the bottle. Her glance at Patch is a bit too quick to be anything but nerves. Why is she tensing up? The Elixir? She admitted delivering V1 to Flint. Why did the Elixir have blood in it? How is she involved? Whose blood does he smell?

Flint Ascot's?

When he gets to the end of the counter, the source of the aroma is evident: a roll of candy that looks like red Life Savers with one end of the wrapper open. But what he can see of the name isn't Life Savers. He points and says, "That looks tasty. What flavor is it?"

She quicksteps over to the counter, snatches up the candy, and buries it in her fist. Her shrug looks stiff to him. "Oh, it's a promotional gimmick from the A.V.A."

He raises his eyebrows.

Meg opens her hand. The label reads "Death Savers."

Okay, that's on the queer side. He leans closer and reads "Condensed Type AB" in the ingredients. He raises his eyebrows even higher. "Really? It's blood?"

She chuckles, but it's a strained, tight little sound. "That would be silly. It's a spoof, that's not a real ingredient. They just made it blood-*flavored* to go along with the vampire theme for V1 juice."

Blood-flavored candy doesn't even appeal to the carnivore side of him, so he shakes his head. "I'll pass."

She exchanges looks with Patch, and he can see her relax a smidgen, her back not so rigid. Patch says, "Mrrr."

Dropping the roll into a drawer, she says, "Me, too. It tastes as disgusting as it sounds."

"I noticed some pieces are gone."

Her eyes widen, then her gaze flicks off to the right the way people do when they lie. She makes a sour face. "Oh, yeah. My boss said I had to try it and tell him what I thought. All I could stand was a lick. Patch didn't like his piece either. Now that I think about it ..." She fishes the roll out of the drawer and drops it into a trash basket under the sink. Her smile is too quick, too rigid when she says, "Ewww."

This is all a bit too bloody for coincidence, so he sticks a finger into the neck of the Elixir bottle and curls it to lift the bottle without touching the sides where she handled it. "Well, this bottle is kinda strange, isn't it? Why would this happen? How did it happen?" He eases it into his jacket pocket. There should be a good number of her fingerprints on it.

She shakes her head, her blank expression saying that she has no idea. Then she laughs, a bitter little burst. "Reuse?"

"Ha! Good thought." She gazes directly into his eyes, and he doesn't think she's hiding anything. Other than her blood candy and the fact that she's a vampire. He can't fault her there; he has his own hidden, er, qualities.

She looks at her watch. "Oh my gosh! I can't be late for my script meeting. I gotta change and get going." Meg extends a hand toward the living room.

"A script meeting?"

"In Burbank, and it'll take me a while to get there." She turns for the front door. "Please?"

He's impressed. She hasn't been here long and she's already taking meetings with a studio. "Sure. Many thanks for your time." He digs a card out of his wallet and hands it to her. "Please call me if you think of anything that might help me with Mister Ascot's murder."

He gathers up Ascot's photo and the newspaper. A confession would be nice.

She takes the card and leads the way, turning off the kitchen light as they leave the room. She strides to the front door and opens it to the night.

When he steps outside and turns back to her, Patch walks up and stands beside her, giving him the evil stare that cats do better than anybody.

She says, "Good luck, Detective."

He knows she can't mean that. She's mixed up in this somehow, and he wants to see what she does next. He leans over her—actually, he towers over her. Is he trying to intimidate her? You bet he is, and it has worked with other perps. "I may have more questions. You don't plan on leaving town, do you?"

She lifts her chin and drills him with a back-off look, and he retreats a step. Her gaze moves to somewhere distant, and then she drops it to Patch.

She scoops the cat up, hugs him to her chest, and looks Nick in the eye. There's a wistfulness to her whisper. "No problem. We don't have anyplace to go."

Her expression is that of someone who is lost.

He's seen it before.

In his bathroom mirror.

She closes the door in his face.

4: Patch

I should have given Meg a nudge when she invited the cop in to warn her that he was trouble. What worries me most is his ability to suss out the pack of Death Savers. The aroma of blood from it was so faint that I could hardly pick it up, and I knew it was there. There's no way a normal breather could do what he did.
And what else did he sense? And how can he do that? Humans have a paltry sense of smell compared with animals such as, let's say, coyotes. Yeah, that's the extra note in his scent—canine.

Anyway, the cop is gone. Meg squats down so we see sort of eye to eye. "Hey, big guy, it's time to go sell our movie to the Disney producer. We'll head out in a minute, okay? He wants both of us there."

Doing a movie about me—I mean, us—could be cool, and helping Meg prepare for the meeting to pitch her movie by researching cat flicks has been fun. We watched *That Darn Cat!* and a bunch of Sylvester the Cat cartoons. She even found an old horror movie from the 1950s, *The Cat Girl*. And last night we watched the movie version of the musical *Cats*. So I say, "Mrow."

Her quick smile warms me. "Oh, great!" She rushes into the bedroom, I guess to change out of her V1 uniform.

Humans got the short straw there, being furless and having to wear clothes. My fur wardrobe is simple and classic: form-fitting and always stylish.

We go a lot of places together, and she's adapted a car seat for her old Miata convertible as a safe perch that lets me see out. I know she gets lonesome, and I don't mind keeping her company. I don't *need* to, of course. Also, I look good in a sports car.

She's back quicker than a cat after a mouse—ahhh, the good old days—wearing jeans and a Grateful Dead T-shirt. The woman does have a droll sense of humor. She drops a new roll of Death Savers into her purse and scoops me up.

Two steps out the door, she says, "My stuff for the meeting!" She sets me down, rushes back inside and then back out with a notebook and a file folder. "Sorry, Patch, just nervous. My whole future depends on this." She adds, "*Our* whole future."

When we take off, I look out the rear window to see if that creepy cop is following, but I don't spot anyone. I'm glad to see the last of Nick Silver, Detective.

When we drive up to the gates at Disney, a handful of protesters holding signs mills around in front of an arch that displays a silhouette of Mickey Mouse's head. Chanting slips through our open windows: "Death to Vampires. Death to Vampires."

It's the L.A. chapter of the Death to Vampires League with their oxymoronically stupid notion of death to people who have already mostly done the death thing. Some protesters carry signs with the universal "no" symbol superimposed over a cartoonishly evil vampire sporting impossibly long fangs that drip blood. Other signs read, "Mickey, say no to vampires!"

We thought we'd left the Devils behind back in Illinois, but no such luck—the infection has spread. Meg eases her car through them, heading for the guard at the gate. I tense up because most of the mob carries long, sharp wooden stakes and mallets in custom sheaths. The stakes are more like stilettos than the old-fashioned wooden things people once used to tie down a tent. One protester, a towering redheaded man who has to be six three, walks a bloodhound on a leash, the dog's tongue hanging out of his mouth, dripping slobber. Dogs are such animals.

As we near the big guy and the bloodhound, maybe twenty cat-lengths away on Meg's side, the dog lifts his nose and stops. He swivels his head toward us, his long ears swinging. He steps closer, pulling on his leash, sniffing. Then he bares his fangs and lunges at Meg, baying, his teeth glistening. The dog tows his big minder toward us, and I stand in my cat seat, claws out, crouching to attack. Or run like hell.

Meg sees them coming and taps the car horn. A gap opens in the marchers ahead of us, and she guns the car to zoom up to the gate. Left behind, the big redhead pulls the bloodhound back and glares at Meg. He mouths words at us. I think he said, "My dog knows what you are." He pats the stake in a sheath on his belt. A shudder runs from my ears to the tip of my tail.

Meg stops beside a guard who looks a lot like Geppetto from the *Pinocchio* movie. "Meg Murrow to see Mister Harvey Flem."

The guard runs a finger down a page in a book on a shelf beside the booth, then nods and looks up. "Welcome, Ms. Murrow." He gestures her in. "Take a right and go all the way to the end of Mickey Drive. He's in the Team Disney building."

Meg points back at the protesters. "What's that all about?"

"Oh, word got out that the studio is doing a vampire movie, and that brought out the crazies."

Great. We're here to talk to a producer about the kind of movie that brings out crazies, including a gigantic nut with a bloodthirsty dog that wants to kill us.

We find the building and then the underground parking across from it. Meg pops a Death Saver in her mouth and gives one to me to chew on. It wouldn't be cool to go into a blood-hunger frenzy and do terrible things during the meeting. One Death Saver isn't enough to send us into the usual stupor. In fact, it can be a pick-me-up.

She says, "Well, Patch, let's go get 'em." She gives me a scratch behind the ears, which feels good with that extra bit of fresh blood in me, and gathers me into her arms. "This is our big chance. I could work at home, we could have a nicer place, and be safe." I like safe, though our place is plenty nice enough for me. Cats don't take up a lot of room. In fact, sometimes smaller is better with us. I like boxes.

We go into the waiting room for the producer's office, Meg clutching me to her chest, holding the skin on my neck in a death grip; good thing it's loose. Disney characters—Goofy, Mickey, Scrooge McDuck—smile out at us from frames on the walls. Luckily, there isn't a cat character—the only good animated cat is Sylvester, if you ask me, and he's not Disney. Disney's had some cute felines, but no real leading cat. The Siamese in *That Darn Cat!* was a one-hit wonder.

It's about time Disney had a cat star. I give myself a lick and exude my natural kitty-cat charisma.

A woman at the desk smiles at us. "Hi, I'm Jeanine, an associate producer. Are you Meg?" She moves her gaze to me and winks. "And Patch?" Her voice is on the deep side. She's broad-shouldered and has a hint of a mustache.

Meg nods. "That's m-me. Us."

Jeanine pushes a button on her phone and says to it, "Ms. Murrow is here, Mister Flem." Her voice is musical and kindly when she hangs up and turns to us. "Please have a seat. And don't be nervous—you'll be fine."

"Thank you for being here so late."

Jeanine waves that off. "Clocks don't matter much in the movie biz."

Meg perches on the edge of a chair and swallows hard, but I feel her body relax, just a bit. "You're a producer?"

"Associate producer."

"Sounds way better than secretary."

She shrugs. "So far, that's all I am, though. Mister Flem hasn't let me assist on any films yet."

"Have you worked for him long?"

"Long enough." She glances at the door and lowers her voice. "He's not always the most pleasant person, but this job is a great place for learning a lot about producing movies." She smiles. "That's my goal, to be a producer. I read your treatment, and I love your vampire kitty-cat story." She shrugs. "I know I could do great things with it, but ... Well, I'm sure it'll be just terrific."

I don't feel all that reassured now. The way Meg's grip tightens again, I don't think she does, either.

The door to Flem's office bangs open, and a slender, pretty, thirtysomething woman stomps out, crying. With uncommon grace, she performs a dance-like move, wheeling and hurtling back to the doorway, where she rages, "You're wrong! I'm not too old! I'm not!" She wails and storms past us, face wet with tears, her fists clenched.

The woman's face and her smooth flow of movement are familiar, but from where—

"Patch!" Meg whispers in my ear. "That's the dancer who was the white kitten in the *Cats* movie."

She's right. If ever there was a human who could have been a cat, it's that one. Meg and I both loved what she did as a dancer.

A fortyish, bulbous man, rolls of fat beneath his chin and straining at the bounds of a Hawaiian shirt, steps into the doorway. The sparse whiskers of his beard stubble might look good on someone else, but Central Casting would call this guy for a wino-with-a-shaving-disability gig.

He smiles and comes to us. As Meg stands, cradling me, he says, "Ah, Ms. Murrow and her kitty-cat." He extends a hand for a shake, but Meg shrugs and glances down at me, busy filling her arms. Even if she hadn't been carrying me, she would have found a way to dodge the handshake. Breathers don't respond well to room-temperature flesh.

Flem says, "Of course" and pats me on the head instead. Not a smooth move—head-patting is not welcome to a cat. Gives us headaches. You want to pat something, go find a dog. There's nothing in their heads that could ache. But I play nice and just look up at him.

His gaze slinks down Meg's body and back up as if he's looking at his favorite confection, and I stifle an urge to leap from her arms and bury my claws in his face—Meg needs this gig, and I'm here to help. He gestures us into his office.

Jeanine gives us a discreet thumbs-up. It's good that she ... he ... who cares ... thinks we're going to score here.

5: Meg

After Flem's vertical stare oozes up and down Meg's body, she clutches Patch a little more tightly when she swerves around Flem's belly to go into his office—and he reaches down as she passes him and squeezes her butt. "Welcome to Disney."

She wants to drop Patch and slap the creep ... but she smothers the impulse. That kind of thing happens, doesn't it? Especially in Hollywood—the #MeToo movement made a dent, but only a dent. Well, his grope is simply the price of getting to write her movie. It's nothing that hasn't happened to other women.

Two chairs are set close together in front of a desk the size of Rhode Island, its surface holding only a Starbucks coffee cup and an iPad. After setting Patch in one chair, she's moving toward the other one when Flem stops her with a question.

"You're really a vampire? Our scout assured me that you are, and the cat, too ... but you don't look like one to me." He grins and wriggles the fingers of the hand that got friendly with her butt. "Didn't feel like one, either." He licks his lips.

Fighting back nausea, she sits in her chair. "That may be true, Mister Flem—"

"Call me Harvey."

"But I am a vampire, Mister Flem. And that's why it's important to tell my story—" Patch glances at her and she strokes him. "Our story." She sets her notebook and file folder on the desk—Flem frowns at that—and opens the folder to take out the treatment for her movie, *Gnaw Me*.

He holds up a hand to stop her. "We'll get to that. First, show me your teeth."

She gives him a wide smile.

He shakes his head. "No fangs? We'll have to do something about that if anybody is going to believe you're really a vampire." He turns his gaze to Patch. "And this is purportedly a vampire cat, right?" He leans close and almost pokes Patch in the nose with his pointer finger.

Sitting in his chair, Patch inhales and gives Flem a huge hiss, showing his fangs in great, gleaming detail. Inwardly, Meg cheers her kitty-cat partner.

Flem flinches back. "Heh, well, those qualify as fangs, I suppose." Patch stiffens and rises to a crouch; he looks like he's tensed to launch himself at Flem's sweaty face. She suspects he'd like to give Flem a demonstration of his fangs in action. She presses down on Patch's back, and he quiets and sits on his haunches.

Flem scurries around to the other side of the desk and plops into a leather executive chair. "But that messy fur, all those splotches and colors. We'll have to do something about that, too." He points at a *That Darn Cat!* movie poster on the wall. "I'm thinking Siamese."

Patch draws in another deep breath, but before he can hiss again, she scratches under his chin. The hiss cuts off, he lifts his chin to enjoy, then gives her a look and settles down. If a cat could show emotion, she's sure she'd be seeing pissed.

Meg shrugs. She knows movies take liberties with ideas. Getting to do a script is what's important. "Well, whatever the casting, it's the story that counts." She flashes on the dancer who had shouted into Flem's office earlier. "Oh, I was wondering why that dancer from *Cats* was here."

"Oh, Margo. She wanted in on this project to play your role, but she's way too over the hill. You were saying?"

A dancer? From a musical? To be her? As lovely as she is, the dancer wouldn't be a good fit for her story. "I see a *cinema verité* approach to tell the gritty truth about vampires in America, about the dark side of—"

"Whoa!" He holds up a palm to stop her. "Gritty? Truth? Dark?" Goose bumps prickle her skin, and a sinking feeling invades her gut.

Flem says, "No, no—around here we do *happy*. And I'm happy to be producing the first Disney happy horror movie. Maybe a musical, sort of a *Glee* or a *La La Land* crossed with the highest-grossing vampire movie ever, *Twilight*." He peers at her. "Your skin doesn't sparkle like the *Twilight* vampires."

She looks at Patch and shakes her head, and he says, "Mrrrah." This is crazy. She's a real person and Patch is a real cat, even if not totally alive anymore, and they've gone through real suffering. And their story is going to be a happy horror musical? "But—"

Flem cuts her off with a wave. "That's what I pitched to management to get you your up-front money, and that's what we're doing. The boss loves it. If you don't want to write it my way ..." He gestures at the door. "Don't let that hit you in your cute little butt on the way out."

All she can do is sit. She realizes that her mouth gapes open, so she shuts it. If she had blood in her veins, it would be boiling.

He scratches his belly. "Before you go, write me a check for the advance we gave you. You have to provide an acceptable treatment for my approach to earn it, and if you don't, well ..."

Holy crap. She's got no way out. The move out here to pursue movies ate the advance money. All she has is her job at the A.V.A., and driving a delivery van barely pays for blood and rent.

Meg coughs out, "Yessir. You'll get a happy story." She can't look him in the eye.

"One more thing. Our contract calls for you and kitty there to help promote the movie when it comes out. To that end, you need to maintain your current pert appearance." He glances at the hand he'd used to fondle her and flexes his fingers. "Are we clear on how things are going to go here?"

She learns right then that it isn't easy to hold a smile and nod when what you want to do is projectile vomit. But she manages a nod.

"Good." He scrolls to a calendar on his iPad then looks up at her. "Bring me a treatment day after tomorrow, same time. Remember to keep it kid-friendly if you want to keep this gig."

6: Nick

It's been a couple of hours since Nick followed Meg and Patch to the Disney Studios and came home, and now dawn lightens the sky. *Disney!* He is truly impressed. But now he's so wired by discovering two vampires who might have ... well, he doesn't know what they might have done yet. *Which leaves him with* a frustrated need to do *something*. It drives him to *shift* form and take another run through the hills of Hollywood to work it off.

It's never easy to do the *shift*—he loves it and hates it. He loves the result, but the transformation sucks. He parks his car at the Brush Canyon hiking trailhead. Nobody thinks twice about an empty car here. He takes off his jeans, briefs, T-shirt, and flip-flops and stuffs them in his knapsack, slips it on, then lies down on the back seat, leaving one door open, his feet sticking out.

He triggers the *shift* by focusing on the sensation of running free in his coyote form. It doesn't exactly hurt when his bones soften into something like modeling clay, but there is a high level of ache. And he's totally vulnerable while it happens. Luckily, it takes only a minute for his body to rearrange itself and grow fur. The effort leaves him panting.

Scrambling out the open door and then pushing it shut with his head, he feels strong and trots away from his car.

He likes to loosen the knots in his mind by scaring fat cats and pampered poodles in their yards.

Back at his car an hour later, he's tired, but his mind feels clean and clear. He *shifts* again and puts on his clothes to head back home; a shower and bed are all he can think about. Then, naturally, his police radio comes to life with a raspy squelch. "Dispatch to Silver, code one-eighty-seven. Dispatch to Silver."

He's technically still on call because he forgot to sign out, and duty demands an answer. "Silver here. You got a body?"

"Sort of. Dog-walker in Lake Hollywood Park called it in as 'I think it's human remains.'"

That sounds creepy. "Roger. I'll check it out."

When he gets to the park, the medical examiner's van and a couple of squad cars are already hogging most of the parking spaces, so he makes one, his car half on the lawn, half off.

The rising sun over the hills to the east casts a moving line of light that's already most of the way down the few trees on the west side of the park. It'll inch down and illuminate everything soon, but it's still dim over most of the area. High on the hill above the park, the Hollywood Sign, already catching the sun, gleams white.

He spots a streak of yellow at the south end of the park, grabs his flashlight, and jogs toward what has to be crime scene tape staking out one of the biggest trees in the park. On the way in, he passes a "Caution Rattlesnakes" sign on a gate, a reminder that this is a desert. He's thinking there's more dangerous stuff out here than a rattler or two.

The park is mostly a field of grass surrounded by trees and picnic areas. He jogs closer to the scene; a couple of uniformed cops mill around, heads down, searching the area, flashlight beams twitching back and forth.

A coyote howls in the distance, and the feeling of running free and unfettered tugs at him. But he's on the job. *Stifle.*

He's maybe ten feet from a bloody mess on the ground beneath the tree when a cloud of blood scent envelops him. His limited human senses supercharged from his run as a coyote, he gets a peculiar nuance about it that he's never encountered in fresh blood. A dark, musty undertone. Then it strikes him—it's the scent he caught from Meg and Patch.

The odor of vampires?

When he gets to the remains on the bare ground beneath the tree, he understands what the caller meant by "I think." The corpse, if that's what it is, is a circular mass like a giant red hockey puck that looks to be about two feet in diameter and a couple of feet thick. A femur gleams white in the red muck along with other big bones, a rack of ribs in pieces, and a crushed human skull, all mixed in with what looks like hamburger meat.

Next to the whatever-it-is stands the stocky shape of Manny, a sharp though chubby guy who's the medical examiner assigned to the Hollywood station—they work well together. When Nick gets closer, Manny gives him a smile, his teeth gleaming white in the midst of his cocoa skin color despite the low light. He kneels near the object, holding a flashlight and probing with a metal rod.

Closing his eyes, Nick draws in a deep breath through his nose to see what he can pick up. Besides the funky blood smell, there's human sweat, a cologne that smells too good to be anything other than expensive, and a hint of latex. When he opens his eyes, Manny is shaking his head. Nick says, "Hey, what do we have here?"

Manny shrugs. "I wish I knew. It does seem to be the remains of a body, somehow crushed into what you see. But there should be a lot more blood besides what's left in the flesh and on the bones." He aims his flashlight beam at the dry dirt surrounding the thing. "Something like a gallon and a half that ought to be here isn't."

Nick runs his flashlight beam across the remains, and something glitters at him. Taking out his pocketknife, he crouches and clears away bloody flesh to find a ball chain. He slips the blade under it and lifts. A pair of dog tags dangle from it. "Check this out."

Manny comes over, holds one of the tags with a gloved hand, and reads, "Markham, Andrew S. There's a serial number, his blood type was O-positive, and he was Christian. No clue to where he served." He drops the tags into an evidence baggie and seals it.

Breathing through his mouth to keep the stench of blood down, Nick studies the heap of flesh and bones. There's a sleeve of a T-shirt; the toe of a running shoe, maybe a size eleven, sticks out; and a femur protrudes from what looks like part of a pair of jeans. Everything is colored blood red. It's as if something just took the victim and mashed him with a giant potato masher. Even though the police photographer will be covering this, Nick takes pictures with his phone. "Any idea on cause of death?"

"Who knows? Was he dead before he was somehow compressed into this? Did the crushing kill him? I don't think there's any way to know. I do think this was brought here rather than done here—otherwise we'd be seeing that gallon and a half of blood soaked into the ground." Manny shudders. "I hope the crushing was postmortem. I don't want to think about what he suffered if it wasn't." He gazes into the woods around them and shakes his head. "This is the work of a monster."

Voices approach from behind. Nick turns to face a uniform cop and a guy with a beagle on a leash coming up. Behind them, the line of sunlight is halfway across the park now, moving toward the crime scene, which should help with searching. The cop signals him, and Nick says to Manny, "I'll be back."

When he gets to the officer, he introduces himself and learns that Patrolman Jenkins was the first responder on the scene, and the man with the dog is Stan Fields, who found the remains.

"Tell me what you know, Officer Jenkins."

The cop's voice is shaky, and he keeps his gaze on Nick even though it tries to drift to the remains behind him. "The forensics team is searching the grounds. We might have a little luck here ..." He aims his flashlight to show tire tracks in the dirt. Although most of the park is grassy, the earth is generally bare beneath the trees. "They'll be getting impressions."

Stan speaks up. "I think they're from that van."

Jenkins's eyebrows climb his forehead. Looks like he's surprised at this info. So Nick asks, "Van?"

"Yeah. Black van. It was how come I found that." He points behind Nick. "The van nearly hit me and Roscoe here when it drove across the lawn toward the street. It was moving pretty fast, got me to wondering, so I backtracked it here."

He glances at the bloody lump on the ground. "Kinda wish I hadn't."

"License plate?"

"Naw, too dark, gone too quick. Van was plain, no sign on the side I could see." He scratches his head. "There was a bumper sticker that glowed, though. I didn't catch it all, but I saw the words *death* and *vampires*."

Speaking of vampires, they're not far from where Meg and Patch live. Nick pictures the last time he saw her, so tiny, Patch clutched to her chest. She's so alone, with nothing to protect her other than a cantankerous cat.

That and vampire superpowers. He needs to do more research into what she's capable of, violence-wise.

The tire tracks aren't all that sharp; the dirt is mostly dust, likely too dry for a good impression. He thanks Fields and Jenkins and walks along the tracks, following indents in the grass all the way to the street. Nothing but ordinary litter, candy wrappers, and a beer can. No tire marks on the curb or street. No help.

As he makes his way back to the crime scene, the sunlight beats him to it, and Manny yells, "Holy shit!" He stumbles back from the disk of remains. Nick runs to him.

Where sunlight hits the meat and bones, wisps of vapor and smoke rise, but there are no flames. The bloody meat part of the remains darkens from red to black to gray ash and then falls off the bones. They stare. Then Nick remembers to get his phone out and video what's happening. By the time the sun finishes moving across the remains, all that's left is a circular pile of broken, crushed bones and clothing on a bed of ash.

No, wait, there's something else. A bit of wood? It's closest to Manny. Nick points. "What's that?"

By getting down on all fours and reaching, Manny is able to drag the thing out. When Nick joins him, he holds a slender wooden stake, maybe two feet long and tapering to a lethal point. At the top, where the stake is broadest, three letters are stamped into the wood. "D.V.L." The Devils? Had they actually killed a vampire?

Manny raises his eyebrows. "Cause of death?"

Uh-oh.

Back at Nick's apartment, he Googles "vampires sunlight." There's no single answer about the effect of sunlight on the undead. Some sites say that it only weakens them, others say it burns them up, leaving only ashes and a skeleton. Another search verifies that a wooden stake to the heart is the recommended tactic for killing a vampire. Nothing says why, but that's the gospel. Of course, a stake to the heart would kill a non-vampire, too.

Ashes and a skeleton were all that was left of Flint Ascot in the tanning bed, but there was no stake. The victim in the park became ashes and bones only after sunlight hit it, and there was a wooden stake. Ascot was indoors, the other victim crushed to pulp and left outdoors in a public park. It's possible that the one in the park was done in by the Death to Vampires League, but there are no clues connecting the Devils to the toaster murder.

Vampires? Really?

There's only one thing to do. Shower, get some sleep, and then report this to the captain. It won't be pretty. He should never have made the case against Vernon Memmer, the Napkin Killer, after the captain told the press that Memmer was not a suspect.

Even worse, Nick used the help of a psychic to track Vernon down. The captain is, he guesses you could say, less than open to such shenanigans, as he characterized Nick's actions. Nick spent six painful months on desk duty after that.

But Vernon won't kill anymore, so it was worth it.

It's past noon by the time he reports in at the Hollywood Community Police Station. After dropping off the Everlast

Elixir bottle Meg had handled at the lab for fingerprinting, he goes to his cubicle and emails a request to meet with Captain Numm. While he waits for a reply, he prints out pictures from his phone of the tanning bed skeleton and before-and-after photos of the pile of bones in the park. The captain won't look at things onscreen, claims it's bad for the eyes. Nick also prints out articles from CNN about vampires campaigning for county sheriff in Illinois. There's a photo of Meg holding the cat. She is kinda cute.

But she's also kind of a killer, isn't she?

Finally, the captain is available and Nick goes to his office. It's tidy and ultra-neat, a contrast to Nick's helter-skelter cubicle. Other than a mug of coffee, an empty inbox, a full outbox, a pair of file folders, and a pen, the captain's desk is clear. Two chairs are lined up precisely in front of his desk, centered, with each exactly the same distance from the desk and each other. He likes his detectives and cases to be just like his office. Nick's afraid he's a disappointment to him. The feeling is mutual.

The captain waits in his chair. He reminds Nick of a steamer trunk turned into a human—broad, boxy, and sturdy. He takes Captain Numm through the pictures of the skeleton and ashes in the tanning bed and the captain nods. He knows about this one, but it doesn't hurt to remind him.

"Last night there was a second strange murder that I think could be related." Nick shows him the bones in the park, first the giant red, bony hockey puck. "Manny thinks the remains were dumped because there was not enough blood on the scene. And when the sunlight hit it, this happened."

He puts down the after photo, the pile of bones and ashes once the sun had torched the meaty parts of the corpse. "The second sunlight hit this, everything but the bones cooked off."

The captain gazes at him flat-eyed, giving him no clue what he thinks of this. Nick's obligated to take the leap, and he does. "I did my research, Captain. And there's only one thing that explains what happened to the body in the park and maybe the one in the tanning bed."

The captain raises his eyebrows, then lifts his coffee mug, peering at Nick over the rim as he sips.

Mentally holding his nose, Nick leaps into the void. "You're going to think I'm crazy, Captain, but what happened to those bodies is what happens when sunshine hits ... vampires."

The captain sprays his desk with a burst of coffee, but then, instead of blowing up, he smiles. It's the kind of smile where the eyes don't join in the fun. The last time Nick saw that smile on him was when he shackled Nick to his desk for six months.

Then the captain laughs. And laughs. Shaking his head, he says, "I've thought there was something off about you since you got here, but this takes the cake. Ha! The fruitcake!" He erupts into another bellow of laughter.

Nick spreads printouts of articles from *The Bloomsburg Times* about Meg and Patch. "There are vampires, and I met one yesterday who is, in fact, a person of interest in this case." The captain scowls at the growing clutter, but he's got to pay attention to this. Nick taps an article headlined "Vampire candidate and cat campaigning for sheriff surge in polls."

The captain focuses on it and his scowl deepens, but there's no stopping now. Nick adds another printout. "Here's a picture I downloaded from a CNN story." A photo of Meg and Patch goes onto the desk.

To the blank expression on the captain's face, Nick says, "Look, Captain. CNN and the local newspaper reported on vampires in Illinois. They're real." He taps the photo of Meg and Patch. "I interviewed this woman yesterday—she's connected to the Flint Ascot murder, I'm sure of it."

The captain snickers and shakes his head. "Fake news. You know what Senator Grimes says, especially about CNN."

"But—"

"That's enough." The captain shoves the printouts toward Nick. "I don't have time to waste on fake news and even faker vampires. A vampire cat? You have somehow detected a creature that does not exist? You've gotta be kidding. What's next, a vampire parakeet?" He squints at Nick. "I'm thinkin' you have no business being a cop, much less a detective. Never have, as far as I'm concerned."

Nick doesn't dare bring up the Memmer case he broke behind the captain's back. "But this is real!"

The captain grins, and then his mouth turns down, a grimace that holds no mirth, only malice. "Tell you what, you bring me a vampire and you can keep your job. If you don't, well, I hope your patrolman uniform still fits." He takes a tissue from a drawer and wipes up the coffee spray.

He pokes Nick in the eye with his gaze. Nick feels like a mouse facing off against a snake. The captain says, "Yeah, I like that. Bring me a vampire." He taps the photo of the pile of bones. "Not this. A *live* one. Dismissed."

Back in his cubicle, Nick's mind spins its wheels. There's nothing solid about this case to work with. All he really has is suspicion and speculation. He doesn't have actual proof that Flint Ascot was a vampire. How can he prove that? And, although there are reports from Illinois that say Meg Murrow and her cat are vampires, she could have been putting on a publicity stunt, maybe just claiming to be a vampire to promote her writing or something. Her connection to Ascot through her delivery route is tenuous at best. He checks the route sheet the American Veggie Association gave him, and it confirms that she stopped delivering V1 juice to Ascot four weeks ago. Nonetheless, it is a link.

He pins the printout of her photo on his corkboard, hoping to work it into some kind of pattern with the other random pieces of this murder he's posted there—a crime-scene photo of the skeleton corpse with an Everlast Elixir bottle in its hand, the blurry shot from surveillance video of somebody in a white hat apparently escorting Ascot into the tanning parlor.

He studies Meg's image for signs of vampirism—she doesn't have visible fangs, but maybe they come out when she's going to bite someone. But aside from that, he finds himself liking her smile. It hadn't been creepy interviewing her. She seemed like a normal person, a vivacious young woman whose only flaw, as far as he can see, is owning an irritable cat.

Normally, when he meets an attractive woman, and Meg is more than simply attractive, he imagines a relationship—having lunch, conversations at a coffeehouse, spending time together. He never goes further than imagining, of course. Sooner or later what he is would come out, and then any relationship would be as dead as Flint Ascot.

But still, he can imagine that it might be fun to get to know Meg, maybe talk screenwriting with her. Assuming she isn't actually undead, that is. He should have shaken her hand so he could have—

The email alert on his computer dings. Good, it's the lab report on the Everlast Elixir bottle he showed Meg.

Her prints match some they found on bottles of blood from Ascot's refrigerator that were labeled Everlast Elixir. She's connected.

More than that, her fingerprints on the bottles say that she lied about not recognizing the Elixir bottle. Anger flares in him at the betrayal. Then he reins himself in. What's with this anger? This isn't personal. Of course criminals lie to cops. It happens all the time.

Still, he's stuck with feeling personally screwed over. Well, he can let off some of that steam when he arrests her on suspicion of murder.

The captain is going to get his vampire.

6: Patch

Meg hasn't talked to me about our meeting with Flem, and it's a good thing, too. It's taken a whole day to get the slimy taste of it out of my mind, but at last I'm ready to settle into a quiet evening snuggled up to Meg while she reads.

She comes into the living room with an e-book reader in her hand, the cover of a mystery on the screen, and heads for the couch beneath the living room window, comfy in her gray sweats and a blue tank top. I hop onto the couch and stand on her favorite spot before she can sit. I give her the "I'm hungry" meow, hop down, and trot to the kitchen.

Meg follows me. "Good idea—let's have a little dessert before we kick back and relax."

She turns on the kitchen light, and its fluorescent flare floods the room. Places where the light reaches my skin itch with irritation—thank goodness for fur. Meg nukes a cup of V1 for herself and a bowlful for me. Soon the metallic aroma of warm blood issuing from the microwave makes my mouth want to water even though it can't.

Meg sets my bowl on the floor and I dive in, so to speak. My tongue comes alive as blood washes over it. It brings a tingle and the heat of life all the way down my throat to my gut, a peristalsis of warmth and bliss. Soon it starts my heart to pumping, and for a little while, I have my old self back.

It's never long enough.

Finished, we head for the living room, soothingly dim with only the lamp on. Meg settles in next to me on our Goodwill couch and, of course, creates a lap into which I, of course, immediately curl up. I'm fairly sure that laps are the reason we cats first decided to hook up with human beings way back when, people being the only place we could get them.

Soon we sink into the deep lassitude that comes with taking in a meal of blood, leaving us with all the get-up-and-go of pudding. I'm a pool of pleasure as the blood permeates me.

After a few minutes, we come out of our stupors. The blood has enlivened us, powered up our senses. Meg scratches behind my ears and under my chin. Ahhh. My purr kicks in and a teensy smile curls the corners of her mouth up. Mine, too. If you think a purr sounds good, on the inside it feels like what you hear, only ten times better.

Meg reads her e-book, and as time ticks away, the warmth in her fingers fades until they are back to room temperature. My body does the same, and my skin returns to numb. I still feel her stroking me, but it feels as if it's from a distance.

Her little smile flatlines, her face becomes chill and still. My purr dies out and we are back to being forever undead. You might think that immortality would compensate for this tepid existence, but even if we were able to fly *(we can't)* or could turn into bats *(we can't, but who would want to?)*, not a day goes by without my wanting my life back.

Then she puts the book down. Lucky for me, the scratching doesn't stop.

"What did you think of Detective Nick, Patch?"

It doesn't take much thought to take in a breath and give Nicky a hiss. Besides the fact that he was harassing us about something we didn't do, there's something amiss with the guy. I don't think the hint of canine in his scent was from a pet. A certain giant coyote comes to mind.

Meg says, "I kinda liked him for a while there. It felt like we were connecting when we talked about writing."

Twisting my head to look up at her, I wish I had eyebrows I could arch. Connecting? Really? With a breather?

She shakes her head. "I know. That's impossible, of course, to have a relationship with a breather."

I say, "Mrf" and put my head back down. Apparently, she got my point. Then she protests.

"But then there he was, radiating a sense of warmth." She holds up her hand and examines it. Her voice is sad when she says, "Oh, Patch, I so miss touching. And being touched."

What, I don't qualify as touchable? She picks up her e-book, and we subside back into undead. I'm thinking of dozing off when a burst of yapping from the dog across the way demolishes the quiet. One of these days I'm going to catch that thing outside its apartment and—

The doorbell rings.

Meg moves me off her lap to the couch and goes to answer it. When she swings the door wide, there stands the cop, a uniformed policeman behind him.

Uh-oh.

She smiles. "Oh. Hello, Detective Silver."

"Ms. Murrow."

His voice is stiff, hard. Her smile fades away. "Are you having any luck with your investigation?"

"I am, ma'am."

My, aren't we being formal.

Then he takes a pistol from inside his coat and says, "Please raise your hands to shoulder height and back into the room."

WTF? I roll off the couch. Meg backs into the room, her hands up, and the detective steps inside. He aims the gun at Meg's chest with one hand and grips the handle of a cat carrier with the other. His backup cop plants himself in the open doorway, his hand resting on the butt of his sidearm.

I take a deep breath and growl. And back away.

Nick says to Meg, "I'm placing you under arrest for suspicion of the murder of Flint Ascot." He sets the carrier down and aims the gun at me. "Ms. Murrow, I need you to put your cat in there."

She starts to lower her hands, but he says, "Keep 'em up."

"This is crazy. I haven't done anything." She glances at me, her eyes wide. I don't get it either. I wish I could reassure her, but I'm linguistically challenged. She turns back to the detective. "I really haven't."

He recites her rights, and then dips his hand into a side pocket and pulls out a pair of handcuffs. I've seen enough *Law & Order* episodes from the vantage of Meg's lap to know what comes next.

I crouch, take a deep breath, give a yowl, and launch myself at the cop's face, paws up and claws out.

Meg shouts, "No!"

The cop is quicker than I've ever seen a human move. While I'm on my way through the air, he drops the cuffs, grabs the carrier handle, and swings it up just in time to bat me across the room. I crash into the wall and slide down. With dregs of fresh blood still in me, it smarts a little, but I can handle it. Back on my feet, I look up at the black hole at the end of his gun barrel, his mean little blue eyes right behind it.

"Do that again, cat, and I'm going to find out what lead does to a vampire kitty-cat."

Simultaneously, Meg says, "What?" and I say, "Mrow?"

"Yeah, I know about Bloomsburg." He sets the carrier down and opens its door, then retrieves the handcuffs. To Meg he says, "Hands."

She holds her hands out, he takes her wrist, stills and glances at her face, and then, one-handed, cuffs one wrist and then the other, never taking the gun off of me.

Chin up, Meg stares him in the eyes. "There's no law against being a vampire. And I don't have anything to do with Mister Ascot's death. I told you, he stopped buying from the A.V.A."

"It's your fingerprints. All over blood-filled bottles of Everlast Elixir in his refrigerator. They were relabeled V1 bottles. I'm taking you in."

"That's just not possible."

He's taking her in? That could be a death sentence. Well, not exactly death, considering our undead natures, but you know what I mean. And she says it.

"I'll die."

He shakes his head. "I doubt it. You're not alive, anyway."

She shakes her head. "Without the right ... food, I'll end. It's messy."

"Not my problem. You shouldn't have killed Ascot."

She fires up. "What happened to 'innocent until proven guilty'?"

"Okay, I'll give you that. You seriously want me to tell them you're a vampire and need to drink blood?"

"It's not just *my* problem. Without my food, if anyone is near me when the blood hunger hits, I'll probably kill them."

He laughs. "With what? Your fangs?"

"We go berserk. And we become very strong. The A.V.A. says it's because the vee-bug in us supercharges when the pain hits."

"The American Veggie Association knows about vampires?"

"The American Vampire Association."

He gets it. "I'll recommend solitary. You can talk to them about your special diet." He looks to me. "I need to take both of you in."

The cop pushes the carrier my way with his foot. I back up. No way I'm getting in there. He says, "Ms. Murrow, put your cat in the carrier."

She stands straight and as tall as a tiny person can, her gaze leveled at him. "Never."

He points the gun at me. "I will shoot it if I have to."

That's my cue to skedaddle. I dash into the bedroom. There's a tear in the fabric on the side of the bed's box springs, and I zoom inside. I turn around and face the opening, my claws ready.

It doesn't take long for the detective to detect the hole. His eye appears, and then his hand enters and gropes my way. I bury four needle-sharp claws in the back of the hand, and he yelps and yanks it out. I know from experience that he'll be bleeding from deep grooves ripped in his skin. As a side note, his blood smells delicious, but it doesn't make me crazy since I had supper not long ago. I do lick my paw, however.

He says, "Fine. You want to stay here, fine. You won't be opening any doors to escape, and I'll get you sooner or later."

Footsteps move away. I ease out of the springs, sneak to the bedroom doorway, and peek. They're in the kitchen. He says to Meg, "I told you to stay put."

"Just tidying."

"Come on. We're going."

"You can't leave Patch here. He'll ... end."

As miserable as being undead can be at times, I don't want me to ... end, either. I've seen what happens when the vee-bug needs blood and can't get it. Your body eats itself. Ugh.

"It's no loss. He's not material to the case."

"God, how can you be so cold? Apparently, I'm not the only one who's mostly dead."

"Get moving."

"All right, but let me take a couple of rolls of Death Savers with me. They could save my, er, existence, and maybe the life of someone else."

"Candy? You want candy?"

"Since you know who and what we are, you won't be surprised that they're condensed blood. A few can keep us going for a fair amount of time."

He shrugs. "Sorry, they won't let you take anything inside. Let's go."

They move toward the living room. Meg's voice comes my way. "Patch. I'll come back. Somehow."

After the front door clicks shut, I trot to the couch, leap up to the back, and look out the living room window, the curtains open since it's nighttime. The detective pulls Meg along by the arm, followed by the uniform, who lugs the empty cat carrier. The yappy dog across the way erupts when Nick passes by its door. They're soon out of sight.

And I'm locked inside the apartment. There's plenty of V1 juice in the refrigerator, but no way to open the door. Or the bottles, even if I could get to them. I go into the kitchen, hoping for some way to not end up totally dead.

I smell blood above and leap up onto the counter. There, hidden behind a couple of empty V1 bottles, is an open package of Death Savers. They weren't there before. *Thank you, Meg.* I'll let them sit until the pain strikes and then try to nurse them along.

The jaws of a terrible trap are closing on me, and there isn't a thing I can do about it.

And I don't even want to think about what Meg is facing.

Courts operate in the daytime.

They'll take her out into sunlight.

If she survives the night.

7: Meg and Nick and Patch

Meg's hands still cuffed in front of her, she follows a jailer at the Hollywood Community Police Station, Nick trailing behind her. The guard, a burly guy who rolls his shoulders as he walks, stops in front of a cell door.

Nick gestures at the woman in the cell next door. She sits on her bunk and watches. He says, "I wanted solitary for this prisoner."

"That cell's occupied," the guard says. He glances at Nick. "Crazy guy who pees on anybody within range."

As the guard opens the cell door, she eyes the bars. If her body was still able to wet her pants, she's sure it would now. Nick says, "Hands."

She extends her hands and he takes a wrist. The claw wounds on the back of his hand have stopped bleeding—he kept blotting them with an old KFC paper napkin on the way here.

Way to go, Patch. Give him something to remember us by.

When Nick touches her skin, his gaze flicks to her face, just as it had when he handcuffed her at her apartment. Back then, she was a little bit warm from a fresh helping of V1. But now, after the trip here and the hour it took to get booked, she's almost back to room temperature. She shrugs, and he drops his gaze, maybe to avoid hers, keys the cuffs, slips them off, and gestures at the cell. "You'll be here for a while, and then transferred to the Van Nuys jail in the morning."

"Morning" isn't good, it being a lethal time of day for her to be riding around L.A. in a patrol car. She steps into the cell. When they shut the door, metal clanging on metal, she grips the bars and says to Nick, "You son of a bitch. You've killed me." Not precisely accurate, but close enough to count.

Nick's formerly friendly and charming face is stiff as a hangman's. What had she been thinking, *fireplaces*? He's all business, keeping his distance, his gaze freezer-cold. He says, "And who have *you* killed?"

She'd been forced to kill animals when the blood hunger first took her back in Illinois and before she found the A.V.A. and V1 juice, but she has never killed people. When she was a newbie, there were a couple of rats that hadn't survived her need for blood, and then she turned Patch into a vampire instead of killing him. Which, now that she thinks about it, is a form of death—like a paler shade of death. Dead lite. Still, totally dead is not the same as undead, still able to have an of-sorts life. She gives Nick the stink-eye. "No one. Never. You're wrong about me."

He shrugs. "Funny thing, I never met a criminal who was guilty. I follow the evidence where it goes, and right now it's knocking on your door." He turns away.

He's a few steps away when she whispers, "It's like melting."

He stops. There's a hiss of air intake. She tells him, "That's what happens to ... us. I've seen it. He screamed until he couldn't anymore because his vocal cords had ... had—" She can't finish it.

Nick just stands there, his back rigid, then walks away.

Her voice echoes off the concrete walls when she calls to him. "At least help Patch. He's just a cat. He hasn't done anything to anybody." Well, except to that yappy little dog back in Illinois. But the judge ruled that was self-defense.

He keeps going. Bastard. The guard gives her a puzzled look, then follows Nick Silver, asshole, out.

She knows the bars are not closing in on her, but it feels as if they are.

She's not ready to finish dying.

~

Back in Nick's cubicle, the sting of the gashes Patch carved into the back of his hand has calmed with the application of ointment and a bandage, and he's thinking a cold beer is in his near future as he leans back in his office chair and stretches. Only one more thing to do—send his report on Meg's arrest to the printer. He'll drop it in the captain's inbox on his way out to his preferred microbrewery. It's Friday, so he's thinking he'll add a late-night Reuben sandwich with onion rings to a tall, cool ale at the Brewhouse. He clicks on Print.

In the morning, he'll give Meg's apartment a thorough search—he's got the keys, and her fingerprints on blood-filled bottles will get him a search warrant. He can't help a little grin at making a solid, evidence-based arrest that puts him closer to solving Flint Ascot's murder. He doesn't know what Meg's role is yet, but the forensics say she's involved—her prints plus the fact that Ascot had blood in bottles. And then there's evidence that she's a vampire. And that Ascot might be.

Thank goodness he has a "live" vampire in custody, the hurdle the captain put up for him to keep his job. Maybe the captain will believe him now, though he doesn't have any idea how to prove she is a vampire—unless to take her out into the sunlight, and then she wouldn't be a live vampire anymore.

He has to admit that, other than body-temperature issues and not breathing, she seems like a perfectly normal person and a hardworking young woman. And Patch is a normally insufferable cat. Although her situation is well deserved—you get what you give, and vampires give death—the law should protect even people who are mostly dead. And, as she pointed out, it's not against the law to be a vampire. It's just the killing part that is.

He wonders if he'll find the cat melted down to his bones in the morning.

Melted. If he's right about those remains in Lake Hollywood Park, what he saw there is what will happen to Meg. A quiver shoots up his spine.

Maybe he should have let her have some of those Death Savers. He could have smuggled some in.

Nope, the care and feeding of prisoners is not his responsibility.

Except maybe he should have told someone that she's a vampire and might be needing to, er, feed in a disgusting way. And avoid sunlight. But he did include her nature in his report. Everybody knows about vampires.

It'll work out. There's no reason to feel bad about it.

At the Brewhouse, one bite into an amazing Reuben sandwich, juice running over his fingers, his phone buzzes. It's his medical examiner buddy. He answers, "Hey, Manny. This better be good."

"Hey, Nick. I'm looking at a new one-eighty-seven that's an awful lot like the tanning bed murder you're investigating."

Another toaster murder? But Meg has been in handcuffs or in a cell since— He tells Manny, "I'm on my way" and then signals for his check and to get a box for his sandwich and onion rings. Thank God for microwaves.

~

Meg is alone except for the woman imprisoned in the cell block with her, and it's quiet. The woman curls up on her bunk, and her soft snores soon flutter through the silence. Stepping to the floor-to-ceiling bars, Meg strains to hear any sound of guards approaching. No shuffle of footsteps, nothing. Eyeing the cell floor, which is far cleaner than she had expected, she lies down on her back, then sprawls her arms and legs as if she's fallen. If anybody should be good at playing dead, it's a vampire. Whatever they do with her, they won't just let a corpse lie in a cell. They'll take her somewhere else, and maybe she can escape.

She needs her "body" to be discovered before the blood hunger hits—and before the melting part starts. From deep down, a soft *blood-blood* whispers into her mind. She hopes the Death Savers she left in the kitchen will keep Patch okay until she can get to him. That asshat of a detective, locking a helpless cat up to die a terrible death. When she gets out, she just might see to it that Detective Nick Silver learns more than he'd care to about vampires, starting with a little nibble. Let's see how he likes it.

Her flesh cold, her pulse nonexistent, she lies still and hopes someone notices the dead person in the cell soon. Real soon.

The other prisoner turns on her side, facing away from Meg, and stops snoring. Maybe she can encourage the woman's participation. Meg draws a deep breath and yells, "Hey!" The word ricochets off the hard walls.

Sleepy startles awake. "Yeah?"

Meg slits her eyes and watches the woman sit up, glare woozily around, then settle on Meg. "Hey, what'choo doin' there?" She stands and comes to the bars separating them. She's still a good three feet away. "Hey, you okay?"

When Meg doesn't answer, the woman stares for a long moment. "Hey?" When Meg doesn't respond, she bellows, "Guard!"

She has to call two more times before the cop who locked Meg up strolls in, a drowsy look on his face. "What're you yelling about?"

Sleepy points at her. "She don't look too good."

The guard's dozy look trades places with a dropped jaw and bulging eyes. He grabs his keys and hurries to her cell. She shutters her eyelids the rest of the way and lies as perfectly still as only an undead person can.

Her cell door clangs open, and fingers check for a pulse in her neck. She stifles a grin when the guard says, "Oh my God!" He jumps to his feet and runs out. Unfortunately, the door swings shut behind him.

Still, she's on her way out of here.

But to where? And will it be soon enough? Before the blood hunger and worse hit?

Blood-blood.

Shut up.

~

The flashing red and blue lights of the light bar on top of Nick's car clear traffic in front of him, and it doesn't take long to get to Deep Tan Tannery in yet another Hollywood strip mall. When he gets there, Manny waves to him from the back of the lobby.

Manny reaches out to shake but stops when he sees the bandage on Nick's hand. "What's with the hand?"

"Encounter with a violent perp. No big deal. Let's see it." Manny leads Nick down a hall and into a tanning room.

The scene looks a lot like the Flint Ascot killing, ashes and a skeleton in a tanning bed, but there are crutches propped against it. A dress folded over a chair looks expensive. This time, though, there's no Everlast Elixir bottle.

Manny says, "All I can tell you right now is that it's female, but not a young woman, and there's a fresh fracture in her right ankle. No apparent cause of death, just like the other one."

He signals to a thirtysomething blond woman whose dark roots are showing, standing outside the door. "This is the manager, Virgie Jones. Cleaning staff discovered the body and then called her."

When she comes over to them, Nick gives her a sympathetic smile and says, "This must be hard on you, ma'am."

Virgie wrings her hands. "Nothing like this has ever happened. Nothing like this has ever hap—"

"Do you have surveillance cameras, ma'am?" She gets a deer-in-the-headlights look for a second or two, then nods and leads him to her office, muttering, "Never. Never ever."

He finds footage of a middle-aged woman limping in on crutches. The view is from behind her, so her face doesn't show. Helping her along, opening doors for her, is what looks like the same person in the white hat who walked Ascot in to his demise.

This time the image reveals enough to see that it's a man, but the quality of video is so poor that that's about all he can tell. At least the time stamp shows when it happened—hours after closing. At eleven-thirty.

"They broke in?"

"Anybody could—the lock's been busted for a month."

Eleven o'clock was when he'd seen Meg Murrow being locked in a cell. A cell where, if what she says is true, she could "end" by ... *melting*. Because he wouldn't let her take any of those Death Savers with her.

The forensics team arrives and starts taking photos and samples, dusting for fingerprints. He goes back to Manny, still beside the tanning bed. "There's nothing much for me until your report and forensics come in, so I'm going to run an errand."

How long does Meg have left?

Once outside, Nick runs for his car.

~

The Death Savers Meg left for me are long gone down my gullet and *blood-blood* is starting to pulse in my mind. I know I should keep still to make what blood I have left in me last longer, but pacing helps keep the pain away.

For now.

For the eleventy-leventh time, I put my paws on the living room window. Can I break through it if I get a good-enough running start? Can I build up enough speed to get over the coffee table and the couch?

I go back to the kitchen. I know which drawer Meg keeps the Death Saver supply in, but so far the knob has been impossible for me to hold on to. I jump and try again. No go. If ever having an opposable thumb would be handy, this would be the time.

Blood-blood.

The pain creeps through me.

BLOOD-BLOOD!

8: Nick

As Nick runs around the corner to Meg's apartment, a *thump* sounds, like a soft something hitting a hard something. He gets to the door, key in hand, and the thump is a lot louder when the cat hits the front window right beside him. He recoils a couple of steps as the cat rebounds. The window has small cracks in it. *Thump*, Patch hits the window again, and a crack spreads.

Nick dashes to his car and grabs the cat carrier. Back at the front door, he slips the key into the lock and positions the carrier in front of him, its door open. Seconds after he slips the key into the lock, the cat hits the front door, *thump!* It vibrates with the force.

He unlocks the door, and one good shove sends it flying open.

Patch glares up at him from a few feet away, braces himself, and then charges, his eyes wide, frenzied. He leaps, his jaws wide open, sharp fangs aimed at tearing into Nick's neck. Nick lifts the carrier, and Patch zooms into it and crashes into the back wall. Nick smashes the door shut.

Claws hook one of the air vent holes on the side and tear out a piece of the plastic. Patch is impossibly strong—Nick couldn't have done that. Another piece tears off. At this rate, he'll be coming after Nick again real soon.

Running into the kitchen, Nick yanks open drawers until he finds a dozen rolls of Death Savers. He sets the carrier on the floor to open a roll, and Patch hits the door, bending the little metal bars and scooting the carrier forward half a foot. The creepy thing is that, despite his fury, the cat is completely silent.

At last, Nick tosses two Death Savers into the now entirely too large hole in the carrier side.

The carrier stops moving. At least the cat is calming down. The sound of chewing emerges.

Opening the refrigerator, Nick finds two groups of V1 juice bottles, three in the door and a carton holding at least ten on a shelf. There's nothing else, not even water. The label on a bottle from the door tells him that it's beet juice, the same stuff Meg gave him when he was here before.

But a bottle from the box on the shelf declares the contents to be 100 percent AB bovine blood.

They drink cow blood? Actually, that makes a lot of sense. And Meg did say she had never killed anyone. It looks like the A.V.A. hasn't either.

A soft "Meow" sounds from the carrier. He bends down and looks in. Patch sits there, calm as can be. He lifts a front paw and pushes at the door, then eyes the bottle in Nick's hand and licks his chops.

Okay, for her sake he'll help the cat out, but it has to be quick. Finding a bowl in a cabinet, he pours the contents of the V1 bottle into it, puts it on the floor in front of the carrier, and lets Patch out.

The cat hurries to the bowl, but then pulls up. He gives Nick a look, not a friendly one, then leaps onto the counter and butts his head against the door of the microwave.

My, aren't we picky?

But he's a cat, after all. Nick heats the blood for thirty seconds, which is enough for its rich scent to swim through the air. He confesses that the smell of blood appeals to his alternative self.

Bowl and cat back on the floor, Patch laps up blood. With him distracted, Nick conducts a search of the apartment.

So here he is, in a vampire den, and what deep, dark, nasty things does he find? A coffin full of dirt, perhaps? Skeletons under her bed? A black cape? Bat guano?

No. There are a young woman's clothes, not expensive but tasteful, and a couple of purses. The bathroom has body wash, shampoo, conditioner, toothpaste and a toothbrush, but no medicines of any kind, not even aspirin. Makes sense.

Crime novels fill a bookcase in the living room. Her taste is close to his, and he spots an author he hasn't heard of. When he samples the first page, he's immediately drawn in. He wonders if she'll let him borrow—

He shakes his head and puts the book back. Ha, sure she'll let him borrow her book. He could take it, of course, since she's locked up, but that would be wrong.

The cat has finished drinking and sits, purring, his fury over. Holy shit! If Patch was that crazed by his need for blood, what's happening to Meg? Is she melting right now?

Rushing back to the kitchen, he jams a half-dozen rolls of Death Savers into a pocket and grabs a couple of bottles of the V1 cow juice.

His stomach growls and he takes one of the beet versions too; he hasn't had a chance to finish his Reuben sandwich.

On his way to the front door, his phone buzzes. It's Manny again.

"Something new?"

"Yeah, but I don't think you're gonna like it. I got a call from the Hollywood station. Female prisoner found dead in her cell. *Your* female prisoner."

Dead? How can that be? "Ah, was she like, heh, melted?"

In the kitchen, Patch cocks his head as if he's listening.

Manny chortles. "Melted? What have you been smoking? No, according to the report, just no pulse, room temperature. No rigor mortis yet, so the death wasn't all that long ago. No signs of violence."

Patch follows him toward the door. Nick says to Manny, "You on your way?"

"Need to wrap up here first. She's not going anywhere."

He yanks open the front door. "See you there."

Patch zips out ahead of him. Nick locks up and trots to his car. The cat keeps up with him. Nick kicks at him, but the animal dodges easily. "Get lost."

He stays with Nick. When Nick opens the door, the cat leaps into the car and then scrambles under the passenger seat. "Oh, no." He hurries to the other side and opens that door. "Listen, your owner is in trouble and I've got to get moving." Why is he talking to a cat? "Get out."

Patch glares at him.

"Okay, we'll do it the hard way." However, as he starts to reach beneath the seat, the bandage on his hand and a hiss from the cat remind him that he has a nasty souvenir of what it's like to grab for this particular cat when he and his claws are looking at you.

So he gives Patch a little wave. "Hey, fine with me."

He uses his light bar to speed to the station. When he gets there, he unbuckles at warp speed, flings his door open, rolls out, shoves the door shut, and locks it. He waves at the seat Patch hid under. "Enjoy yourself, cat, I'll be back."

When he turns to go into the station, he sees that Patch is now sitting on the pavement a few yards away, watching him. *How'd he do that?* He knows Patch's face isn't physically capable of smirking, but he's sure he is doing just that.

Fine. He runs into the station, hoping he's not too late.

9: Meg and Nick

Meg forces herself to be still when the cell block door bangs open and Nick's voice echoes off the concrete block walls. "We have to move her." The pain of blood hunger is ramping up, and it's hard to keep from going into attack mode. Imagine an explosion deep inside you and the shock wave expands outward, but you've got to hold it in or it will blow you apart. Jeez, she can't even grit her teeth—that might show. Playing dead is a lot harder than she thought it would be.

Two sets of heavy footfalls come in, and then the door to the cell next to hers clatters open. Nick's voice comes from close by. "Miss, we need for you to go to an interview room so we can talk to you about what happened to ... her."

Her neighbor gives the same answer as when Meg was "discovered" by the guard. "I don't know nothin'. Was sleepin', woke up, and there she was. Looked dead to me."

The guard chimes in. "Me, too. She was cold as a fish."

Nick says, "You folks leaving right now would be good."

Two sets of footsteps fade away and a door shuts. Meg's cell door opens, and she senses Nick kneeling beside her.

Blood. Blood-blood. She forces herself to be still. But there's all that warm, fresh blood inches away ...

He says, "Are you really dead?" He touches her bare arm. "So cold."

Underneath her lids, her eyes roll toward where his face should be.

"I saw that."

Cracking her lips open just a skosh, she murmurs, "Alone?"

He sighs. With relief? "Yeah. We can talk."

Opening her eyes, she looks up into blue ones that frown down at her. *Blood-blood.* "You'd better leave. The blood hunger I warned you about is coming on."

Before he can answer, a door opens and more heavy steps enter the cell block. Nick says to someone, "Manny." She slits her eyes, sees a chubby brown man entering the cell, carrying a black medical bag. She clamps her eyes shut.

Her cell door opens again. "What we got here?"

"You tell me."

Fingers touch her neck and press where the artery is. Manny says, "Yeah, room temperature and no pulse, that means pretty much dead."

The pain swells. It takes all of her will to keep from grabbing his hand and biting it.

Blood-blood.

~

Nick stands back from Meg's "corpse" while Manny takes photos from several angles, scowling the whole time. He lifts one of her hands and lets go. It plops to the floor, lifeless. "No lividity or rigor mortis. Nick ..." He shakes his head. "Something weird here. When did you book her?"

"About ten o'clock tonight. She was in the cell around eleven."

"One hour ago." He takes a long thermometer out of his bag. Nick looks away when he rolls her to her side and pulls her sweatpants and panties down.

A minute later, Manny examines the thermometer and says, "Her internal temperature is seventy-four. Considering the temperature in here, which is about seventy-two, at one and a half degrees per hour it should have taken seventeen hours for her to lose that much body heat. Not one."

He's not about to tell Manny that room temperature is her norm.

Manny shrugs, restores her clothing, rolls her to her back, stands, and puts the thermometer away. "I'll call and get her taken down to the morgue." He rubs his hands together, relish written all over his face. "It's a mystery, but I'm a medical detective. Maybe an autopsy will explain this."

Nick doesn't think even a vampire can handle being autopsied. He's got to get her out of there. "You let me know when you're going to do it? I'd like to be there—maybe a half hour's notice?" He wants to make sure he gets to her before Manny does.

Manny nods and takes off. He's out of the cell block and they're alone before Nick touches her shoulder. "He's gone."

She shudders and looks up at him. "God, that was embarrassing. I haven't had my temperature taken that way since I was a baby."

He raises his eyebrows. "Modesty? From somebody who's mostly dead?"

"Hey, we don't stop being people."

After seeing the ordinary way she lives, he thinks that's true. Then she clenches her fists and her voice shakes when she says, "Considering what you've done to Patch and me, I would not ordinarily tell you that I'm about to go into a blood hunger frenzy and gnaw a hole in your neck. It would serve you right."

"Thanks. I think."

"But I'm trying to play dead here, and it occurs to me that if they come for me and find your bloody corpse next to me, they might suspect something."

He loves dry humor, and this is Saharan. "You think?"

She grits her teeth and then says, "So you'd better run for it."

Having seen Patch in action, he doesn't want to be around when she goes berserk. The cat was supernaturally strong, and she's a lot bigger than he is. Nick opens a roll of Death Savers and slips one between her lips.

She sighs. "Ohhh." Meg closes her eyes as she chews and swallows. "More."

After two more, she looks up at him and nods. "Thanks." Then she frowns and sits up. "Oh my God. Patch!"

"He's okay, I got to him in time."

"You saved him?"

He shrugs. Then tosses a grin at her. "Well, it was more a matter of self-defense, but yeah."

She lies back down and resumes her "dead" position. "Can you go back and feed him again?"

"Nope." She frowns up at him. "He's right outside, in the parking lot." He glances at the bandage on his hand. "Hitched a ride with me."

She relaxes.

"So here's what to expect. They'll bring in a gurney, zip you into a body bag, and take you to the morgue."

"What was he saying about an autopsy?"

"It's standard procedure."

She sits up, her gaze darting side to side, looking panicky. "How do I get out of here?"

He holds up a hand. "I'm sure we'll be able to get you out of the morgue before that happens, not much security there. I assume it won't be a problem if they refrigerate you?"

"We?"

"I got you into this, I'll get you out. Uh, refrigeration?"

She chuckles, shakes her head. Then she scowls. "You mean they'll put me in one of those refrigerated compartments?"

"You can open it from the inside. It's a safety thing. So far, though, no corpses have gotten out."

She frowns at him. "I'm not exactly a corpse."

That gets a one-shoulder shrug. "Not exactly." He gives her the open roll of Death Savers plus a couple extra. "Take these."

Meg eats two more pieces and puts the rest in a pocket. "I hate you, but I have to thank you. And for helping Patch, too."

She resumes her "dead" position and closes her eyes. "Go away."

10: Patch and Meg and Nick

To a cat, the idea of being restricted in ANY way is super-galling ... but once Nick goes inside the police station, all I can do is hide out in the parking lot, crouching low under his car whenever headlights pull in or go out. I've tried to sneak inside when people go through a cat's most exasperating nemesis, a door, but no go. Did get kicked. That guy's lucky the door closed before I could sink my fangs into his leg.

Was I crazy for leaving the apartment and coming here? Hmm.

There's nothing there for me without Meg, is there? Hmm.

Am I a little panicked?

Hmm.

Okay, maybe a little. But when Nick took rolls of Death Savers and bottles of V1 with him, I figured he had to be taking them to Meg. Which means she's here. Behind that expletive door.

But so what? First—and second and third—this threatens what I have left of life. I am a critter known for independence, though, so I could just move on. Live in the wild, feed off of whatever I can catch. Squirrels, birds, mice, rats ... Ewww. Not appealing to a city kitty used to gourmet cat food in his previous life, and then there's the hassle of hunting when all I need now is for Meg to open a bottle.

Meg.

Is she okay? Did Nick get the blood to her in time? *Whack*, it hits me that I might not see Meg again. So, what about that, mister independent kitty-cat?

I don't want it to happen. We started out in the normal cat-human relationship as associates, but darn it, I really like Meg. I'd say we're more partners than associates, if not closer. But I don't know how she feels about me.

Hmm. She does stroke my back when we snuggle on the couch. And talks to me.

And she promised to come back for me when she was led away in handcuffs. I've got to help her if that's even possible anymore.

What's worrisome is that Nick hasn't come back out with Meg. WHAT IS GOING ON IN THERE?

Headlights turn into the lot and a blue-and-white van backs up to the door. The driver gets out, opens the doors at the van's back end, and pulls out a narrow table on wheels. He takes it inside, and once again I'm too late to follow inside and hunt for Meg.

In about the time it takes me to lap up a bowl of V1 juice (entirely too long), the guy and the wheeled table come back out, this time with a cop pushing one end. There's a lumpy black bag on it, big enough to hold a person. The driver opens the van doors, and the cop takes a clipboard from on top of the bag and hands it to him. "Okay, sign here for one Megan Murrow, deceased."

That's Meg in the bag? I creep closer, slinking under a row of cars and then under the van.

The driver says, "What happened to her?"

"Nobody knows. She was found dead in her cell. She was a murder suspect."

Dead? That's a problem. But, *actually* dead? The only way a vampire can truly be dead is after the sun does a number on us or lack of blood destroys us. Or a wooden stake in the heart, which is actually a loss-of-blood issue. None of those endings would lead to a body in a bag. A skeleton, yes, but not a body. There's hope.

"Huh. A murderer gets dead. Maybe a little bit of irony there?"

Irony? I guess so. An undead person becoming dead after making another person become dead. This vampire stuff is mind-bending at times. The cop says, "Yeah. Be seein' you."

I watch the driver's feet move as he shoves the table into the van and then closes the doors. I scoot to the front and jump up on the bumper. If I hook my legs into the grill, I can stay with her. I hope. The van starts up, and out we move.

Hang in there, Meg.

The van takes a sharp left and my hind end swings free. I focus on doing my own hanging in.

~

As near as Meg can tell from what she hears, the gurney she was put on in the jail cell has now been unloaded from a van and wheeled into some kind of room.

But since then she's just sat here. Lain here.

If she doesn't get out of this bag soon, she'll start screaming. Running out of air isn't a problem, but the pitch-black dark is driving her nuts. It brings back the horror of burying herself in the ground during daytime when she was first changed and couldn't get to her apartment.

Metal clinks on metal, the sound the key made when they locked her in, and then there's a *click*. Two sets of footsteps come in, one of them the clack of high heels on linoleum.

Thank God, somebody is here. Be still. Be still.
Ignore the need for blood.
Be still.
Blood-blood.

The footsteps stop beside her. The zipper opens above her face. Ahhh.

The red of light coming through her eyelids is like a sunrise in her mind. She can hold still. But the hunger stirs. She wishes she'd eaten a couple more Death Savers on the way here.

A man wheezes noisily when he says, "This is her"—*wheeze*—"just brought in from the Hollywood station."

A woman says, "Prep her as usual, Steve. Bag her clothes, don't wipe her down until after the exam and autopsy, you know the drill."

Holy shit. She forgot about the autopsy part.

Steve wheezes. "I do, I do."

The high heels exit and a door latch clicks. Steve unzips the bag the rest of the way. "Hey, a young pretty one." *Wheeze.* "Been a while."

His touch is gentle when he lifts her body and limbs to slide the bag out from under her, leaving her on her back on the gurney.

"We need privacy for this, don't you think, pretty lady?" *Wheeze.* Footsteps retreat, a *click* from the direction of the door. Locking it? Footsteps back.

A large hand grips her breast, then the other one gets the same treatment. "Not real big, but nice enough. I bet they're perky."

Damn right they're perky. You'd think a morgue would be the last place for sexual assault. This is truly disgusting. The hands leave her breasts, and fingers slip under the bottom of her tank top and lift.

She opens her eyes and glares straight up at a jowly face littered with white whiskers, sort of like Santa gone homeless. She sucks in air and her perky breasts rise. Steve's watery gaze widens.

She says, "Hands off, creep."

One big wheeze and his eyes roll up until only white shows, and then he crumples like a leaky balloon. She swings off the table and drops to the floor, one foot somehow unfortunately landing on Steve's round belly. He oofs but doesn't stir. There's going to be a bruise. She grins.

Her hands tremble as she digs out a roll of Death Savers and pops a couple into her mouth. The shakes go away and she's about to sneak out the door when it hits her—she doesn't know where she is, though it should still be nighttime. She doesn't have her purse, either, so how does she get home? Steve moans, and the solution wheezes at her.

Kneeling next to him, she searches his pockets and comes up with a wad of cash. She takes thirty—no, fifty—bucks and stuffs the rest back in. Since the door's still locked, she takes a minute to track down a pen and a scrap of paper, then slips an IOU into his pocket. She doesn't sign her name, but she can track him down later to redeem it. She may be a vampire, but she's not a thief.

She gazes at his whiskery face and then his greedy hands. Although she's grateful for the loan, she's still pissed about the groping. The guy needs to chill out.

A wall of stainless-steel doors gleams at her, and she smiles.

She opens a refrigerated compartment. The interior is chilly but not freezing. After checking that the door can be opened from the inside, she pulls out the shelf and, with some serious lifting, manages to heave Steve onto it. *Sweet dreams,*

Wheezy. For a moment, imagining his terror when he wakes up in cold, absolute darkness stops her. Does he deserve that? Yeah, he does—she's surely not the first "corpse" he's fondled. Besides, he'll know how to get out.

Going to the door, she opens it a crack and listens for sounds of people. Nothing nearby, so she slips out and starts toward an "Exit" sign at the end of the hallway, striding along as if she has legitimate business there.

Manny, the medical examiner who did rude things to her in the jail cell, rounds a corner ahead of her and comes her way, possibly on his way to autopsy her. She lowers her gaze to the floor and hopes for, well, nothing to happen.

Out of the corner of her eye, she catches his quick glance checking her out, and then he's past.

Two more steps and he calls to her from behind. "Hey."

She lowers her head and keeps going.

"Hey, lady. I need to see your pass."

She ignores him. His footsteps hurry her way.

"Or I'll have to call security."

Okay, she's a writer, a natural liar, er, storyteller, and she should be able to get out of this. Putting a look of grief on her face and wishing she could produce tears, she turns to him, takes a deep breath, and sobs. "Oh, I'm so sorry. I just saw my twin sister"—she points back to the morgue door—"in there. And I'm not thinking too straight." Another sob, hand over mouth.

He stops in front of her. "I'm sorry to hear about your loss." He bends down and peers at her face. "Wait a minute. You're that dead woman. Megan Murrow." He leans back and shakes his head. "No, that's not possible."

Sob. Big shuddering breath. "I am Meg Murrow, but the woman in there is my identical twin, Myrtle." She points at the morgue door again. "There's been a terrible mistake." Then she starts backing away from him, heading toward the exit. "Listen, I need to go, this is making me crazy."

Manny reaches to take her arm. "We need to get you to security first."

She flinches away; it would not be good if he touched her room-temperature skin. "I'll go with you, but I have a thing about germs."

He nods. "Yeah, me, too. Follow me." He takes his cell phone out, hits a number. "Nick? I'm maybe a half hour from that autopsy. Got to take care of the deceased's twin sister first." He glances at her. "Yeah, here at the morgue. Amazing resemblance. Even wears identical clothes."

~

Nick had had no choice but to call the captain and tell him about the prisoner's, um, death before he could leave. Naturally, the captain came back into the office even though it's past one in the morning. Nick is sure it's not actually possible that he sees steam coming from the captain's ears, but heavy heat is radiating from the gaze of death coming at Nick from the other side of his desk. Nick ends Manny's call and turns back to the captain. "Sorry, sir. That was Manny. But it was about this case."

The captain sits ramrod stiff. "Let me get this straight. You arrested a vampire on suspicion of murder in the Flint Ascot case."

"Yessir. That's all in my report." He doesn't know where this is going, but he's sure it isn't going to be a place he wants to be.

"And it was a live vampire who walked in and was put into a cell, right here in my station, correct?"

"Yessir. It was what you wanted me to do."

"And now you're telling me that the perp is a *dead* vampire?"

"Yessir. According to Manny's examination. That's what he said."

"I thought vampires were already dead."

All Nick can do is give him a blank look and shrug. "According to my research, they're actually *un*dead."

"Not all dead?"

"Yessir."

"But this one is?"

"Yessir."

The captain's face reddens from the neck up. When the wave of color hits his hairline, he stands up and bellows, "Are you fricking kidding me?!?"

He has a thing about using *actual* cusswords. "Nosir."

The captain scowls. "I want a look at the ... remains?"

Nick shakes his head. "Manny sent her to the morgue for an autopsy." *Oh, please, Meg, figure out a way to escape.* He doesn't think he'll get out of this in time, and he doesn't want to be responsible for her ... he doesn't know what to call it. Not death. Mutilation? And then what?

The captain says, "If you were any more incompetent, you'd be bait on a fishhook." He takes a deep breath, and his voice is calmer. "I want to see this ... this ... figment of your imagination. Now." He leads the way out the door. "You drive."

When they clear morgue security and start for the hallway leading to the autopsy room, Meg's voice comes at Nick from the supervisor's office. A rush of relief ... and happiness? ... rises to tighten his throat.

He steps to the open door, the captain right behind him. She sits beside the supervisor's desk and she's saying, "I don't have my ID with me because I panicked and came straight here and left it at home."

When he steps in, her eyes widen when she sees him, and then she looks back to the supervisor. Manny stands to the side, his arms crossed, attention focused on her. Meg goes on. "I'd been calling and texting my sister all day and she never answered. Finally, I called the Hollywood station to report a missing person." She shudders.

"They told me that there was a deceased person with my name who'd been taken to the morgue. I just dropped everything and called a cab." She puts her face in her hands. "And I found Myrtle. Dead." She wails. It hurts his ears. But she's convincing.

The captain steps to Nick's side. "You arrested the woman and you got her name wrong?"

Time for some tap dancing. There must be a way ... He holds up his hands. "All she had on her was a credit card in the name of Megan Murrow."

Meg is quick. "Oh! I gave it to Myrtle because she was going out to buy food for my cat. She's—she was visiting here from Idaho." She shakes her head. "If only I had gone instead. It's my fault."

But the way the captain grits his teeth tells Nick he isn't letting go of this. He turns to him. "Your report says the suspect was a vampire."

Manny's head whips around, and he stares at Nick.

Meg sucks in a breath. "That's crazy! She's—she was as normal as I am. There's no such thing as vampires!"

She's a wonderful liar. He almost believes her. "That's my conclusion, and I'm sticking to it."

Manny unfolds his arms. "A vampire? Really?" He looks to Nick. "You didn't tell me that."

Meg shoots Nick a look, but what can he do? "That's where my evidence points."

"That could explain her core temperature reading being so low." Manny rubs his hands together. "Listen, can we finish up here?" He glances at the door, practically vibrating with his desire to get to the autopsy room. With a vampire to examine. Nick can't blame him. But he's going to be disappointed.

Meg is looking away from Nick, her shoulders hunched. She must be terrified, but she's handling it fairly well. He says, "How about this? I take Ms. Murrow home and verify her identity. She's shaken, and I can clear up her part in this now." He steps closer to her and offers his hand. She gazes into his eyes, then slips her hand into his and stands. She's as cool as he expected, both physically and mentally. He lifts her hand, then releases it. "She's clearly not a dead woman."

The captain stares at Meg. She faces him. "Please?" There's grief in her voice. She's either one helluva actress or there's some pain going on in her.

The captain stabs a stubby finger at Meg. "This isn't going to happen again."

She crumples and her voice breaks when she says, "Oh, God, how can it? She's my only sister." She squints at him. "Or are you saying that I could be next?"

The captain's eyes widen. "I didn't mean ... I meant ... I mean ... Of course not. I'm very sorry for your loss, miss." He nods at Nick. "Take her home, take good care of her."

Damned if he mightn't have a heart in there somewhere. "Yessir."

11: Patch

When that traitorous detective and the boxy man arrived in the morgue parking lot, I was too far from the door to dash past them when they hurried inside. But I'm ready now, behind a bush a couple of cat-lengths from the door. I seem to spend a lot of time hiding these days, and I don't like it. But Meg is in there somewhere. I don't know if I can help her, but—

Footsteps approach from the inside. The door swings open ... I zoom through it and past two sets of legs. A guy shouts, "Hey!"

Claws slipping on the waxed floor, I slide and scramble down a hallway. From behind me a woman's voice cries, "Patch?"

I stomp on the brakes, do a one-eighty, and skid to a stop. Meg? And Nick?

Meg drops to her knees and holds out her arms. "Patch!"

I have to confess that my ever-cool kitty-cat heart warms at the sight of her. I launch into a run ... but then, halfway there, my natural dignity kicks in and I slow to a saunter, stopping to sniff at something nonexistent on the floor now and then. Can't have associates thinking that we need them.

But, what the hell—I bound the last three feet into her arms. She hugs me to her, and I give her cheek a lick. Generally,

I'm against public displays of affection, but this warrants an exception. She's not dead, at least not all the way. I add a little headbutt for emphasis, and she smiles.

Nick steps in behind her. "We'd better get out of here before they discover that 'Myrtle' is gone."

Why is Nick here? With Meg. Who is Myrtle?

"Right." Meg springs to her feet and follows him out into the parking lot, holding me tight. I must say that I don't mind.

When we're driving away, with me snuggled into her lap, Nick says, "How did you get out?"

She tells him about refrigerating a creep named Steve after his hands got a lot too friendly. I think how she handled it is funny, but Nick scowls. "What a slimeball." He glances at Meg. "Too bad you can't testify against him, I'd put him in another kind of cooler."

Then his phone rings. He checks the screen for who's calling, puts it on speaker, and sets it in a holder on the dashboard. "Hey, Manny."

"You won't believe this, but the corpse is gone."

Nick wriggles his eyebrows at Meg. "It escaped?" Meg covers her mouth and smothers a laugh. Not a bad line.

"I wouldn't say that, of course, but it's not here. We did find the attendant in one of the refrigerated compartments. He's babbling about the corpse opening its eyes and talking to him. He doesn't say about what."

"Well, after being refrigerated, maybe there's a little hysteria going on. Which doesn't explain how he got into the cooler, though."

"The guy says it had to be the talking corpse that did it after he blacked out."

Now Nick snorts a stifled laugh. "Yeah, that explains it."

Meg gives him a thumbs-up and grins.

Manny says, "It's a mystery Captain Numm is determined to solve. He's called in a forensic evidence team to dust for fingerprints and find whatever trace evidence they can. He wants to interview everyone in the building. Considering his mood, I think we're lucky he hasn't locked us down."

Nick winks at Meg. "My, this is a puzzle, isn't it?"

A tinge of sadness quiets Manny's voice. "I sure was looking forward to doing an autopsy on a vampire."

The corners of Meg's mouth turn down in a moue of disgust.

"Wait a minute, the captain just stuck his head in ... He wants to talk to you."

The captain's voice is gruff. Definitely not friendly. "Silver?"

"Yessir."

"I want you back here ASAP to work on this missing corpse. You got that woman home yet?"

"On the way there."

"Keep an eye on her. I have a feeling she has something to do with this."

Meg clenches my fur and murmurs, "Oh, crap."

"Will do." Nick sticks out his tongue as if he has a bad taste in his mind. "But what if her ID checks out?"

"I don't care. Sooner or later, I'm bringing her in for questioning. Something's not right about this. I'm currently thinking it'll be sooner."

The detective gazes at Meg for a moment, then turns back to driving. "Gotta go, sir."

"Is she a vampire, too?"

"She says she isn't."

The captain mutters, "Numb-nuts," and then, "Over and out."

Nick ends the call. Meg says, "That doesn't sound good."

"It isn't. The captain is a bulldog, and he's not going to let go of a missing body mystery—thanks to me, a missing *vampire* body mystery."

"He'll figure it out when he brings me in for questioning." Her eyes widen, and she looks at him. "It'll be daytime, right? Maybe I—" She gazes at me and strokes my head. "Maybe we ought to run for it."

I'm good with that. What with creepy Disney producers, giant coyotes wearing knapsacks, and entirely too much police interest, I'd be fine with seeing the last of Tinseltown. Put it in the rearview mirror. I mean, could things be worse somewhere else?

Don't answer that.

When we park in the apartment parking lot, Meg gets out with me. The detective comes around from the other side and hands a key to Meg. "Your key."

Meg takes it. "We're free to go?"

"For now. I've searched your place, and you're good. I do need to check your ID like I said I would." He pats his coat pocket. "I've got a couple of bottles of your V1 juice, too. I imagine you'll want them back."

"You're going to check my ID? Really?"

"I'm a cop. I said I would. I follow the rules."

She grins. If I could grin, I would when she says, "Like helping a corpse escape from the morgue isn't against the rules?"

He has the sense to keep his mouth shut.

She leads the way to the apartment. "All I have is an expired Illinois driver's license."

He frowns. "It's illegal to drive without a valid license."

"Yeah, but I can't get one."

"I don't see the problem. You're driving now, and you can get a valid California license."

"The DMV is only open in the daytime."

His eyes widen, then he nods. "Ah." When we reach the door, he stops and adds, "You know, the captain isn't going to stop until he finds a body."

"And, since Myrtle is missing, I'm it." She squints up at him. "Would you do it? Take me in if he says to?"

His answer is immediate. "Yes."

"I haven't done anything wrong."

He shakes his head. "It's about the rule of law. I've wanted to be a detective since I was a little boy, and I've finally achieved it. I'm good at it, too. But a part of that job is doing what the captain tells me to do no matter how I feel about it."

"If it's daytime, I'll—"

He holds up a hand. "I know. I've seen ..." His eyes go blank for a moment as if he's watching something scary in his mind. He clenches his teeth. "Maybe a way can be worked out."

"Maybe?" Her volume goes up a number of decibels. "MAYBE?"

He holds his hands out, pleading. "I took an oath."

That gets him a glare. "Let me guess. To serve and"—she yells, right into his face—"*protect!*"

That staggers him back a step. Meg squares her shoulders and gazes into the distance. "Maybe we really should run for it." She shakes her head. "But that can't happen until payday, which isn't for a week." She gives Nick a look. "All I have to do is not be arrested."

Nice shot, Meg. All he can do is stare. She goes inside, sets me on the couch, and heads for her bedroom. Nick comes in and puts the V1 in the refrigerator and returns to the living room.

She comes out of the bedroom with her purse. "Who invited you in?"

He points at the kitchen. "I just brought in the—"

"You are not welcome in this house." I've heard Meg angry before, but nothing like this. A boiler is about to explode, but she keeps her voice low—and right on the edge of KA-BOOM. "Look, I know you helped me tonight, but you also put me in a situation that could have ended what little existence I have."

She comes to me and scratches behind my ears. Though my skin is numb this far from my last feeding, the pleasure is still enough to make it hard to follow along. Then anger soups up her voice again.

"And you caused Patch who knows how much pain. So get out. Oh, I know you'll be back to haul me in for your precious captain, and you'll try to look sympathetic while sunlight does away with me. Unless, that is, I can get out of here before that happy event."

"Look, I'm just doing my—"

"Your duty, yeah, I know." She takes her wallet out of her purse, fishes around in it, and holds out a card. "My driver's license."

He makes a show of studying it. Takes a picture of it with his phone. Then nods. "Okay."

"Don't let the door hit you in the ass on the way out."

I take a breath and add a hiss to punctuate his exit. When the front door closes, Meg collapses on the couch beside me. As she runs her fingers down my back—mmmmm—she says, "We're screwed, Patch. We're totally screwed."

She does have a way with words.

We stay like that for a few minutes, and just as I'm sinking into contentment from her back-scratching, she stops and sits up. "And we have a meeting with Disney at nine o'clock tonight." She ruffles my head. "I have to do a synopsis of a happy, funny, musical story about people who've had their lives ripped away." She takes her laptop off the coffee table, opens it, and gets to work.

I will never understand how humans can even think that way, much less spend millions to make a movie out of it.

It's time for some serious licking. I recommend it.

12: Nick

Nick slams his apartment's front door. That went well. The only way it could have gone better would have been if Meg's door *had* hit him in the ass on the way out.

Where does she get off with that attitude? He saved her life—er, her undeadness? And that jerk of a cat's, too, who is a public nuisance for sure.

Maybe a beer will cool him down, so he gets one from the refrigerator.

Of course, he also nearly killed them.

But then, they're vampires, and vampires are killers.

And he's a good guy. But he feels like a bad guy, although not because of the cat.

Those two are bad guys. Allegedly. All right, so he doesn't *know* that they actually are. They do drink blood, but not from humans.

But then—

His phone buzzes. He's glad to be pulled back from a whirlpool of confusion. It's Manny. Nick can't help but sigh—the world is piling on. "You're still working? What's the captain up to now?"

"It's not the captain. Remember the Deep Tan Tannery case? I'm sending you a link to an article in *The Hollywood Reporter* from day before yesterday."

Nick hangs up, grabs his laptop, and logs in to his email. The link is there, and he clicks it and goes to the site. The lead article online shows the lovely face of a star actress he fell in love with as a boy, her flaming red hair framing her cherubic face, a face he remembers seeing in her last big movie, must've been ten years ago.

The headline reads, "Stella Golden injures ankle in dance rehearsal." Holy crap. She's making a comeback after her long career starring in romantic comedies sputtered and died out. As usual, she blamed it on the refusal of Hollywood to cast aging actresses. He agrees with her. He reads on.

"The actress put on a brave face after a fall while rehearsing for her new musical comedy. 'I'm not worried—we can shoot around the dance until my ankle heals,' she said.

"Her director, Stevie Spiel, confirmed that, saying, 'A fractured ankle won't stop a talent like Stella's.'"

Their female skeleton at the Tannery has a fractured ankle. Skimming the rest of the article, a familiar name grabs him.

"Ms. Golden credits her resurgence to Doctor Adonis Lovely, surgeon to the stars. When asked about the star, Dr. Lovely said, 'She is so agelessly beautiful now. One of my finest achievements—almost perfect.'"

Nick calls Manny back and asks him to confirm the identification of the victim as that of Stella Golden. Manny has already fired off a request for her dental records—there should be plenty, since her teeth in the photo are unnaturally perfect. Then Nick calls the captain to ask him to get them a search warrant for Stella Golden's home. "Captain, it looks like we have another toaster murder, and I need a new search warrant."

He says, "Say again? Toaster murder?"

"Oh, that's just a handle that came to mind."

The captain clears his throat. "What about that woman from the morgue? The twin."

Thank God for the captain's current obsession. "Her ID checked out. I don't think she has anything to do with anything." Which is a lie. His cop side won't let go of her fingerprints being on those bottles of Everlast Elixir.

Muttering about being sleep-deprived, the captain says he'll secure a warrant in the morning and hangs up.

Nick hits his bed and collapses. It's not a good sleep, though. Meg keeps popping up in dreams. First he's in coyote mode, chasing her, and then she's chasing him. And she has long, shiny fangs. But when she catches him, she pets his head and he wags his tail. He doesn't know if this is a dream or a nightmare.

The next morning, he meets the forensics team at Ms. Golden's home. It turns out to be in a manufactured-home park. It's a spacious double-wide with vaulted ceilings, lush carpeting, and high-end furnishings, but still ... a movie star in a trailer park? Seems un-American.

A storage shed in the carport holds a sixteen-cubic-foot stainless steel refrigerator full of bottles of nothing but Everlast Elixir. No food in the house. They send a bottle out for analysis and fingerprinting, but he's fairly sure he knows what they'll find.

In her kitchen, they discover an empty Elixir bottle by the sink. The scent of blood emanates from it. He holds the bottle up to the light. The V1 label is underneath. They send that to the lab, too. And he asks the lab to check any fingerprints against Meg's.

He always feels like a voyeur when he goes through a victim's things, the detritus of their lives. But then, he's their advocate, in a sense, looking out for their rights. A twinge of guilt pings him. It could be that he was a little loose with Meg's rights, sort of, maybe.

Not maybe, *was*. He dragged her into jail before he had more than the skimpiest circumstantial evidence. Where was the good guy when he did that? Had he let the captain pressure him?

He scours Stella's dresser, closet, and a desk in the living room. Nothing but mementos of her career, ordinary correspondence, photos of two kids who must be grandchildren, and a handful of bills. He pages through them, and three are overdue. So she has—no, had—trouble paying them. There are invoices from the Body Care Salon, Fantastic Hair Care, Lovely Care Products, Caring Psychologists ... She had a real need for care. Well, not anymore. He adds the businesses to his notes and decide he's done in there.

Leaving the interior of the house to the forensics, he checks out the exterior. There's no front yard to speak of, but the backyard, although small, has a shade tree beside a cozy patio with a table, chairs, and a big umbrella over the table.

An older woman appears at the low fence bordering one side of the yard. "Hey, you. What're you doin' snooping around Stella's place?" Her voice has the low rasp of a heavy smoker. Or a longtime breather of L.A. air.

He pulls out his credentials and goes to the fence. "Detective Nicholai Silver, ma'am. Homicide. I'm conducting an investigation. May I ask your name?"

Her eyebrows rise and she puts a hand to her chest. "I'm Marjorie. Oh, my. Don't tell me something has happened to her. I mean, besides breaking her ankle. Poor woman."

With the cramped lot that the double-wide barely fits on, there's not a lot of privacy here. What has the good neighbor seen? "When was the last time you saw Ms. Golden?"

"Night before last. She hobbled out on her crutches and was having a drink on the patio there. Looked like a Bloody Mary. It was after it got dark. She used to sit out there in the daytime, and it was bourbon then, but she said she'd turned over a new leaf and wanted to stay out of the sun. Me, I'm sticking with bourbon." She winks. "At any time of the day."

He takes out his notebook and adds all but Marjorie's drinking preference. "Have you noticed any suspicious people around lately?"

She shakes her head.

"Strange cars?"

She gazes at the street and frowns. "Late the night I saw her, there was a black van I've never seen before parked on the street. My cat got out and was hiding under it. A real hassle to get a pootie out from under there."

A black van? He thumbs back through his notes to be sure. Yep, black van at Lake Hollywood Park. "Did you see any bumper stickers on the van, Marjorie?"

She shrugs. "Coulda been one, but it was dark. I don't know, I was chasin' the cat. What happened to Stella?"

"That's what I hope to find out." He hands her his card. "Please call me if you think of anything more, especially about that van."

She nods, and he leaves to knock on more neighbor doors. He's not surprised when no one has seen anything. After he checks in with the forensics team and learns they haven't found much, he heads for the office.

13: Patch

Meg says to me, "It's such a pleasant night. Let's put the top down." I know she's not exactly asking me for permission, and she doesn't need to—the first time I rode with the top down, I liked the wind in my face. I think that I look cool with my fur streaming in the breeze, and it kinda feels good, so I give her an affirmative "Mrow."

When we arrive at Disney a little before nine o'clock, the Devils with their signs are back, marching in a circle in front of the gates. Meg says, "Maybe going topless wasn't such a good idea."

This time, besides the signs declaring death to vampires, there's a table displaying merchandise. Red caps are inscribed with "Make Vampires Dead Again," and a row of sharp pointy stakes looks downright threatening. The vendor holds a stake up and cries, "Be prepared! You never know! Have your stake ready! Only ten dollars." The vendor switches to waving a bumper sticker that reads, "Spot a vampire? Text *vamp here* to 385." Waving a stake again, he shouts, "Be ready to call our vampire patrol, they're ready 24/7 to take out undead monsters."

Meg knots her brow and looks to me. I crouch down in my car seat. She rolls up her window and mine and starts easing through the jam. It's slow going, but we're making progress when the huge, red-haired Devil we encountered last time, the guy with the bloodhound, spots us and trots our way. He's wearing one of the red MVDA hats that clashes with his hair. His dog goes berserk again and lunges at Meg's side of the car.

This time the big guy lets the dog go, and in an instant its paws are on her window and its mouthful of sharp teeth bites at the glass, leaving streaks of slobber.

The big guy comes up and raps on the window with a big ring on his finger, its ruby-red stone clacking at us. He shouts over the crowd, "I know what you are." He slips his stake out of its little sheath and aims it at us, mostly at Meg. "You're next."

He raises a gigantic hand and is reaching over the window glass, his fingers heading for Meg's head, when a gap opens in the crowd. Meg ducks and guns the car through the opening, coming darned close to clipping the guard when she screeches to a stop in front of the gate. It's the same kindly guy we saw before, but tonight he scowls at us.

"If you're going to drive like that, little lady, I don't think I'm going to let you in."

"I'm sorry, sir." She glances back, and so do I. The big redhead is scratching his dog's head and laughing at us. She turns back to the guard. "Those people scared me. I'll be careful."

He looks out at the rabble of Devils. "They scare me, too, miss." His scowl turns to a smile. "Who are you here to see?"

After Meg gives him Flem's name, he waves us in. Meg says, "I sure hope those nuts are gone when we leave."

I second the motion with a hiss.

Jeanine is on duty at her desk outside Flem's office when we arrive. She is stylish in a yellow summer frock, and her smile is sunny. "Oh, it's so good to see you again." Then she glances at Flem's door and lowers her voice. "I wish more than ever I was a real producer. I love your original story idea. So gritty." She shrugs. "But the biz is the biz, and musicals are making money these days." She presses a button on her desk phone. "Meg Murrow and Patch are here."

Harvey Flem opens his door. He looks much the same as before, still whiskery, still bulbous, still pushing the boundaries of a Hawaiian shirt, this one more red than anything else. He looks down his nose at me, and the corners of his mouth turn south. "How charming. You brought your kittycat again."

I don't think he means it.

Meg, holding me with both hands, says, "He's my partner. And he's half of the story."

Flem leads us in and then flumps into his chair behind his desk. "We'll see about that. Let's hear it."

Meg sets me in the other side chair and takes out her notes. "We open with Patch walking through a cemetery at midnight. It's creepy and dark. Suddenly I—well, a vampire woman—bursts out of the ground and grabs him. She bites him and he's turned into a vampire kitty-cat. Sort of the origin story, if you know what I mean."

His eyes are heavy-lidded, lizardlike. "This is supposed to be a fun musical."

She smiles. It looks a little pasted-on to me. "Yes! And that's why more vampires rise out of the ground around me—the vampire, that is—and Patch. They dance and sing a song called 'Needing You Till I Never Die.'"

I'm trying not to be judgmental, but ... really?

She looks to me. "It's about the hope for an eternal relationship. I see it as uplifting and setting the tone of the story."

Why is it her eyes look sad?

Flem leans forward, his façade of boredom exchanged for a flicker of interest. By that I mean greed. "Dancing vampires. That sounds happy."

"Oh, but then danger arrives when a giant, seven-foot vampire attacks Patch and is about to kill him."

Flem says, "Vampires can be killed? I thought you were undead. Immortal."

Yeah, we can definitely be killed. It's ugly, and permanent.

"Yes, there are ways to, well, end us. And that's about to happen to Patch in the story."

"Okay, a little violence never hurt a children's movie. What's next?"

Meg beams. She never beams. "We get happy again! Patch is saved by Vampires Anonymous. The V.A."

I'm guessing she doesn't want to give away the existence of the actual A.V.A.

Flem leans back and rubs his belly. "All right, that sounds happy. But where's the music and dancing?"

"The next number comes up at the end of the murder trial."

"Murder? In a kids' movie?"

"Sure. What about Bambi's mother?"

Flem laughs. "Sure. What was her name? Venison?"

I don't think Flem catches Meg's shudder. She lifts her chin the way she does when she's in a fight, but then tacks on that smile again. "Oh, Mister Flem, what a joker you are."

As Flem preens, she goes on. She strokes my head and says, "Patch is tried for murder for killing a yappy little poodle."

Flem's eyebrows rise, and then he grins. "Why was he even charged?"

My sentiments exactly.

"Yes!" Meg says. "And, sure enough, he's found not guilty because it was self-defense. And then the courtroom bursts into a big dance led by the Latina judge."

Flem nods. "Good idea, sticking a token Latina into the story. What's the song?"

"I think we should adapt that famous lyric 'He had it comin'', from the 'Cell Block Tango' number in *Chicago*, a terrific musical."

Flem nods. "Sure. Why be original when you can rip something off?"

I'm a little amazed at Meg's imagination. She's taking what really happened to us and turning it into fun.

She turns a page in her notes. "And then romance enters the picture."

"A vampire romance? Is there mutual sucking involved?" The grin he gives is creepy, and then he licks his lips.

Wait a minute. She's not going to tell the story of—

"A vampire kitty-cat romance." She strokes my head again. "Patch meets a lovely Siamese named Queenie and they fall in love. There's a love song and dancing beneath a full moon."

Here's what I mean by turning what happened into fun. What really took place was that there was no rendezvous with the Siamese of my dreams because Meg grabbed me. The story she's telling now is what would have been. Oh, if only ...

Flem shrugs. "Okay, that's kind of a romantic twist, and the kids will love two romantic cats. Teaching cats to dance, though, could be a problem."

Meg shudders again, but doesn't address that. Instead, she says, "Then the vampire and Patch run for sheriff to protect vampires from vigilantes with stakes." Her hands clench into fists, and I know she's thinking of the Devils at the front gate.

His eyebrows lift again. "A patriotic element, too. So far this story has everything a kids' movie should have to make it bearable to parents—violence, murder, romance, and politics. What happens next?"

Meg leans back in her chair. "More fun. The vampire and Patch fight the good fight, and there will be singing and dancing at their big political rally. And then Election Day comes."

Flem claps. "And we win! Yay! A vampire victory!"

She shakes her head. "No, they lose because the polls close before night comes, and vampires can't get out to vote. But she and Patch have learned something about themselves and vow to fight on."

Now Flem is shaking his head. "No. We can't have losers in a kids' movie, especially a happy horror movie."

"Well, I guess I can change that—"

He holds up a hand. "Wait! I have a genius idea!"

Meg reaches over and her fingers clench my fur. Then she hangs that pretend smile on her mouth again. "Oh, how marvelous! What, pray tell?"

"All this talk about vampires is starting to bore me. Vampires, even in a fun musical, are so yesterday."

"But we're real today."

Flem shoo-shoos her with a flap of his hands. "Reality is not a factor here. No, I think we should twist the whole thing." Now he's the one beaming. At himself. "We start out with vampires like you said, but then they're attacked by zombies and turned into ..." He chuckles. "Wait for it ..." He laughs out loud. "Vambies!"

Meg's jaw and mine drop at the same time.

"Yes!" He looks at me. "A vambie kitty-cat. And it's so Disney—it rhymes with Bambi."

Now I'm the one shuddering.

"We'll have a fresh new kind of monster. Eating brains *and* sucking blood! Rotting away but never all the way! Will they still suck blood and lumber around when they're skeletons?" He waves his questions at us. "You work out the details and come back tomorrow, same time." He chortles and claps again. "Oh, management is gonna love this!"

"Mister Flem—"

"Call me Harvey."

"Mister Flem, I'm not sure I can do that."

He smiles. Humans are such masters at facial expressions. I never knew that a smile could be evil. "You mean whore your talent?"

She doesn't say anything.

He shrugs. "Fine! It's my concept, I can assign it to a more compliant writer. And you can pay back the advance we gave you."

Meg collects her notes, puts them in her purse, picks me up, and stands. Her shoulders sag, though, and when I look up at her face, her gaze is fixed on the floor. "That won't be necessary. I'll do the treatment."

He leans forward as far as his belly will allow. "See that you do. Vambies! Dismissed."

14: Meg and Nick

Shamed by her capitulation to Flem, Meg stops in the waiting area, takes a deep breath, and lets out a single, sorrowful sob. How can it be that Flem can delight in crushing a soul?

The associate producer, Jeanine, gestures at her desk phone. "I listened in. I listen to all of Harvey's meetings—it's like on-the-job training. Oh, I could do such wonderful things with the story you started with." She shakes her head. "What're you gonna do? That's the way it is, right? But vambies?" She rolls her eyes. "Stupid."

Meg nods her thanks for the sympathy and scurries out, grateful that she has Patch to hold on to. He seems to sense her distress, because without her petting him, he starts up a heart-warming purr.

She noses her car through the cluster of Devils still clotting the entrance into Disney. When she reaches Alameda Avenue, a shout comes at her from down the street. "Hey, sweetheart!"

It's the big red-headed guy, standing beside a black pickup, his bloodhound straining at the leash beside him. The truck is one of those jacked-up rigs with monster tires and a light bar on the cab. Luckily, he's four car-lengths away, so she turns away from him. As she checks her rearview mirror, he tosses his dog into the truck bed and clambers into his truck. Then he does a U-turn and follows her.

Damn. She doesn't need this crap right now. She's edgy with the beginnings of blood hunger, and she bets Patch is too. She had been so distracted by having to face Flem again, she'd left the Death Savers at home. But it won't take long to get there, and there's no reason to stop along the way. They'll make it before the pain gets bad.

The creep is still on their tail when they turn off of the highway to head home. *Blood-blood.* The pain is rising, and they're going to need to feed soon. If Mr. Vampire Killer follows her all the way home and tries something there, she foresees a mess in her parking lot that she doesn't want to have to deal with. It'll be sure to draw cops. And that gives her an idea.

After checking to make sure that the truck is still following them, she says to Patch, "Hey, how about a little snack before we get home?"

He bares his fangs, then gives a low growl. She suspects a snack anywhere anytime soon would suit him fine. She checks her watch—it's after ten. "Great. I know just the place." The Griffith Observatory closes at ten and should be emptied out by the time they get there. Another check of the rearview mirror shows her snack still on their tail.

~

Running the plates on the pickup following Meg doesn't get Nick much more than the driver's name, Vincent Hunter. A harassment complaint a month back was dismissed, and Nick suspects the "Death to Vampires League" bumper sticker on his truck had something to do with the complaint.

Given what the Devils do, he thinks Meg is in danger. The guy is huge, and his dog is big, too. And Hunter was packing one of those wooden stakes when he got into his vehicle to follow her.

When they turn onto the road up to the Griffith Observatory, he wonders what Meg's doing. She could be safe at home with her door locked and 911 to call. Although, considering her experience with L.A. law, she's probably more afraid of them than she is of this jerk. Rightfully so.

The observatory will be closed, and it's darned deserted up there at this time of night unless there are drug deals going down. The road is a dead end, and she'll have nowhere to run.

She goes all the way up to the front of the building and parks there, Hunter right on her tail. Nick pulls over in the empty lot a hundred yards down the hill and turns off his lights. The long, wide sweep of grass lawn in front of the observatory will make it hard to sneak up and see what they're doing—in human form, that is.

Grabbing his knapsack from the back seat, he hurries into a stand of trees by the lot, strips and packs his clothes, puts the knapsack on his back in case he needs his stuff when he's up there, and *shifts*. In coyote form, it's easy to stay in shadows and lope up to the building unseen. He gets close and lurks behind a bush.

The building's exterior lights make it easy to see. Meg gets her cat out of her car and carries him up the steps. She has to know Hunter followed her, but she doesn't look back at him. He parks beside her car, gets out of his truck, collects his bloodhound, and goes after her.

What is she going to do, throw the cat at the guy if he attacks her? Come to think of it, that might not be a bad idea, considering Patch's tendency toward violence. The claw wounds on the back of Nick's hand itch when he's in his human form.

She goes up the steps to the main building, Hunter close behind her, his bloodhound on a leash. Meg stops and turns to look down at Hunter. He halts a dozen feet from her, his dog straining to get to her. Meg says, "I would leave now if I were you."

Hunter pulls his stake out of its sheath and laughs. "What're you going to do, bite me?"

She gazes down at Patch. "What do you say, Patch? Should we give him something to chew on? Rather, give *us* something to chew on?" She goes back to Hunter. "It's more like gnawing, but yes, I will bite you. Your pooch isn't safe, either. You really should go."

Nick remembers her warning him about the blood hunger. She plays fair. He admires that.

"I should go? Now that I have a real vampire ripe for puncturing?" He drops the dog's leash, aims his stake at Meg, and charges up the steps.

Nick leaps over the bush and puts himself between Meg and Hunter. He can't speak, but he sure can growl, so he does.

The guy and the dog stop. Apparently, Hunter has never dealt with a two-hundred-pound coyote. "What the hell?" He looks to his dog. "Want to chase a coyote, Fang?"

Nick growls louder, and the dog backs around behind its owner. Fang is smarter than Nick gives dogs credit for. Hunter glares at him and passes the stake from hand to hand. His paws are meaty, with thick fingers. Three fingers on his right hand have *D*, *V*, and *L* tattooed on them, and there's a ruby ring on his left hand.

Nick advances on Hunter and he retreats, pushing the dog back with his legs. Then a low moan comes from behind Nick. He twists to see Meg's face contorted as if pain wracks her.

Patch lets out a similar moan and follows it with a hiss. Meg screams, and he understands what bloodcurdling really means. She drops Patch, and he charges in Nick's direction like a sprinter out of the blocks. Meg is just as quick.

She streaks past Nick, ramming him in the side with a stiff-arm on her way. Her astonishing strength sends him tumbling ten feet away. He scrambles to his feet, his ribs blazing with pain, but she's already at her attacker. Or is it her prey?

Hunter lashes out with his stake, and its sharp tip slashes her cheek. Then her hands, tiny in comparison to Hunter's bulk, slam into his chest and she sends him flying onto his back. He's starting to push himself up when she lands on him, straddles his chest, grabs his ears, and cracks his head against the concrete. He goes limp.

The bloodhound charges Patch, and the cat leaps straight at a dog that is easily three times his size and outweighs him by a hundred pounds. Patch clamps his claws on the sides of the dog's head and twists his body. A *snap* cuts the air, and the dog collapses and twitches, his neck likely broken. Patch rips at the dog's neck with his teeth and is lapping up blood within seconds.

Nick creeps closer. Meg has her mouth to Hunter's neck and sucks at a slow flow of blood. Considering the power she and her cat have, he keeps his distance. She's not the one in danger here.

After a long minute, Meg leans back, her knees on either side of the man, revealing a small hole in Hunter's neck. The slash in her cheek is a dark red line, but no blood seeps from it. Patch leaves the lifeless bloodhound and trots over to Meg's side. He headbutts her, and she reaches out and scratches his neck, all signs of their berserk fury gone.

Hunter's neck stops bleeding. The wound seems to absorb the traces of blood around it, the blood moving to the edges of the ragged hole, and then the hole closes. In less than a minute, there's no sign of Meg's bite.

Meg stands when the man quivers, his arms and legs spasming. After he quiets, he opens his eyes, blears up at her, then touches his neck.

Meg says, "Welcome to the club."

He opens his mouth and his lips move, but no sound comes out. His eyes widen.

"You have to take a breath first."

He does, and this time he's audible. "What did you do to me?"

She shrugs. "I had the munchies. Bad timing on your part. But I warned you."

He scrambles to his feet and goes to his dog. More silent lip-flapping until he takes another breath. "You killed Fang."

"Patch gets the credit for that. A good thing, too. If he hadn't, there'd be a vampire dog running around, and that wouldn't be good for the people and animals he'd attack to survive." She pulls out her phone. "Maybe your friends will take care of you."

Hunter feels his neck where Meg bit him. "I tingle inside. What's happening?"

Meg swipes at her phone to wake it up. "What did that bumper sticker the Devils guy was selling at Disney say to do if I see a vampire?" She squints at Hunter. "Oh, yeah: Text *vamp here* to 385." She types with her thumbs.

Hunter feels his chest. "My heart's not beating."

She turns her gaze to Nick, and her brows rise. It's probably the knapsack on his back. It feels silly to do this, but he wags his tail. He wants to be on her good side right now. Then her phone dings.

"Oh, look. It says *on the way*." She picks Patch up. "Time to go, buddy."

Headlights of two cars appear in the distance, down toward the bottom of the long driveway. Meg slips into her little car and puts Patch in a seat. Nick applauds her with a good long howl, and she turns and gazes at him again. Then she guns it out of there.

He turns his attention to Hunter. Will he chase after her?

Hunter feels for a pulse in his neck and then in his wrist. He mouths words, then breathes in and says, "I'm dead."

That's not entirely true, but if he doesn't get out of here before his fellow Devils arrive, he will be. Nick races down to his car and manages to *shift* and dress before the cars reach him. Seconds later, Hunter's truck barrels down the road and into the dark, passing his fellow Devils going the other way.

She didn't kill him.

Even though he was going to kill her.

And she could have, easily.

What she did do was administer a helping of poetic justice.

He has thinking to do.

15: Nick and Meg

The next morning, Nick's ribs are sore from Meg's shove, but he gulps ibuprofen and stands under a long hot shower to relieve most of the discomfort. That doesn't, however, deal with the discomfort in his head about what happened last night. He stuffs that into a Meg compartment in his mind and closes the door. He has a feeling it's not going to stay there.

Enough with musing, time to head for the office.

The thing is, Meg didn't actually do anything illegal last night at the observatory.

Everyone has the right to defend themselves, and the guy attacked her with a lethal weapon. There's no law on the books for turning someone into a vampire, either, though maybe there should be. His sense of justice pokes at him to do something about that. He shoves that into another compartment and closes that door, too—he can't imagine a quicker way to be declared a nutjob than pushing for anti-vampire laws. He'd probably be attacked for racial profiling and discrimination, too. Not to mention that he doesn't want the scrutiny that would come with it, considering his nature.

A case file awaits him on his desk. The captain has officially assigned him to the disappearance of a cadaver from the county morgue, one female identified as Myrtle Murrow by her twin sister, Megan Murrow. It doesn't take long to add to the file what little he can admit to knowing, mainly that he checked her ID and she is who she says she is. His vampire theory is already in there, but there is no actual twin sister for Meg.

He's relieved when an email comes from the lab and he can turn to the toaster murders. The bottles of Everlast Elixir in Stella Golden's refrigerator did contain blood. And several had two sets of fingerprints on them, hers and Meg's. He takes out the file for Stella and adds the information.

It doesn't make sense. What motive would Meg have to murder an aging star? From what he's seen of Meg's life, he doubts she knew Stella. More than that, he doesn't think Meg is a killer. She sure wasn't last night, even when she had the opportunity, the means, and a strong motive.

But her prints are on those bottles ... and the ones in Flint Ascot's fridge. They have to mean she is somehow connected to the killings.

Then a little light sneaks out from under the door to the Meg compartment in his mind, the one where he stuffed his muddled feelings about her, and it shines on a new thought. No, her fingerprints on the bottles only prove that she had something to do with the *bottles*. Otherwise, there's no link between the two victims and Meg.

No, wait, there's one. The A.V.A. She knew Ascot and delivered juice to him. He used to pet her cat. Was Stella on her route too? He pulls out the route sheet from the A.V.A. Nope. Stella's place is miles from Ascot's house and not part of Meg's route.

So how did Meg's fingerprints get on bottles in the refrigerators of two movie stars who were murdered?

One more thing. He takes out Flint Ascot's folder and opens it next to Stella's. The crime scene photos show virtually the same thing. Skeletons and ashes. He writes "V?" in both files.

Then he opens the file on the masher murder in Hollywood Lake Park. More bones and ashes. He adds a "V?" to that file, too. With the captain looking so closely over his shoulder that he can feel his mental breath on his neck, he doesn't dare write the whole word. Things are bad enough around here without causing his boss's head to explode.

Behind him, the captain's voice rumbles. "My office. Now."

Nick trails him into his office and takes one of the two chairs stationed in front of his desk. This time he takes the right chair; last time it was the left. He's noticed that when he doesn't conform to a pattern, the captain darts a little frown at him that he takes for irritation. It's not much in the way of payback for his sticking Nick with desk duty for all those months, but every little bit helps. However, he doesn't smile at the captain's little frown. That would risk lighting a fuse, he suspects.

The captain levels his patented stony-eyed gaze at Nick. "Well?"

He's played this game before, messing with Nick's mind. This time Nick smiles. "I'm fine, sir, thank you for asking. And you?"

The captain blinks, grits his teeth, and a red flush appears on his lower neck. He can't badmouth Nick for being polite and asking after him. Then Nick thinks this might have been a bad move, what with the possibility of an exploding head.

The captain takes a deep breath and lets it ease out, an anger management technique Nick's glad to see him employ. "I'm, er, well, thank you. I was inquiring about the missing corpse case."

"Forensics got the report on the morgue to me this morning. Steve's fingerprints were on the refrigerated compartment door, along with smudges from, possibly, someone else, but they weren't clear enough to identify anyone. But they did find a partial on the door handle that matches the woman we booked. As weird as it seems, Steve might have been telling the truth about how he got into that refrigerated compartment."

"Could it have been the print of the other woman, the one who claims she's a twin sister?"

"Since they're identical twins, their fingerprints would correlate highly, but would not be the same. And you saw her walk out with me."

"I'm not sure I buy her story on how she got to the morgue. Manny found her in the hallway. She could have been the corpse that esca—" He shakes his head. "Except I'm not ready to believe in walking corpses. This is not a zombie apocalypse." He smooths his hair, a calming gesture. "I hope."

Nick's given up on things in this case making sense long ago, so he doesn't have a problem with nodding and saying, "Me, too."

The captain places his palms flat on his desk and leans forward. "This all started with you bringing in a suspect you said was a vampire. I'm giving you two days to find that imaginary creature. If you don't, you will bring in the twin sister for questioning."

"But—"

"You have a problem with that?"

"Nosir, of course not."

He stands to go, but the captain raises a hand to stop him. "What about these, what do you call them, broiler murders?"

"Ah, toaster murders. I'm working on a lead." He thinks the bottles with Meg's fingerprints is a lead, but he sure as hell doesn't know what it points to.

"See that you do. And I want that woman in here if you don't find our missing cadaver in two days."

It's time for Meg's evening V1 delivery route, and she's in her uniform and ready to go. But not really. She stares at her reflection in the bathroom mirror and runs a fingertip alongside the gash in her cheek. It runs straight up and down, deep, almost all the way through her cheek, and maybe two inches long. There's no blood, of course. And it will never heal.

Should she put a bandage over it before she goes in to work? There's no real need—the vees at the A.V. A. know this kind of thing happens all the time. A vampire can rack up a mess of nicks, cuts, and scrapes that stay there unless they're lucky enough to have someone like Doc Lovely to cover them up. Or, even worse, they break something that will be broken forever. She sees vees wearing all kinds of braces to deal with breaks that can't heal. Worse, they suffer a lot of pain when they feed and the blood starts up their bodily functions.

Still, she doesn't want to look like this to her delivery customers. A bandage would do, but then there would be questions. If she goes in a little early, maybe Doc can help—he works wonders with crazy glue and makeup. Even though the result usually looks like a scar, she guesses that's better than a deep gash.

What will this do to her Disney deal? They—well, Flem—wants her looking good, and scarred isn't that.

When she leaves the bathroom, she finds Patch sitting just outside as if he's been watching her. The connection between them is a lifeline right now. She squats next to him and scratches behind his ears. "Hey, buddy. Come on into the kitchen and I'll heat up some V1. I think I'll run the route by myself tonight. I'll put on that DVD of *The Aristocats* before I go if you want, and I'll be back not long after it's over."

He looks her in the eye. "Mrrrf," he says, and then trots into the kitchen. She takes that as agreement and goes to heat up their blood.

While the microwave hums, she chews on their encounter with the Devils guy and his bloodhound. She doesn't feel bad about defending herself ... but there is a little guilt about luring him into a trap. She didn't have to do that; she could have come home, run into her apartment, and called the police. He would still be a totally alive asshole.

Well, no, she wouldn't have called the police, considering. There's no shame in snacking on the guy, though. That's the nature of blood hunger—it can't be resisted. But she warned him, and she did take only a little blood. No regrets on turning him into a vampire. He deserves every bit of the horror he's going to experience. She wishes she could be a shadow in the corner when his Devil buddies catch up to him with their sharp, pointy stakes. Delicious irony. Or maybe she'll run into him down at the A.V.A. one of these nights.

Overall, she feels good about her encounter with that lunatic. One thing nags at her— a trace of memory from when the blood hunger was taking over, mind and body. What she remembers is blurry, but she could swear that a giant hunchbacked coyote jumped into the fray to keep the Devil from attacking her. She also has a clear memory of a giant coyote watching her as she left the scene. It seemed to be wearing a knapsack, which is ridiculous. Or a hallucination. And it howled at her. And wagged its tail.

The microwave beeps, and she puts a bowl of V1 on the floor for Patch and pours hers into a mug and smiles at the V1 logo on its side. "Hey, Patch, do you remember seeing a big coyote last night?"

He looks up from lapping blood, takes a breath, and gives her an angry hiss. If that means what she thinks it means, that critter wasn't a phantasm. That's just what her life needs right now, a friendly monster coyote.

Maybe she should just chalk it up to life in Los Angeles, the Land of the Weird.

When they're finished, they do their usual sit-on-the-couch thing while after-blood lassitude enervates them. There is pleasure in having her body come temporarily alive, but she hates being reduced to a puddle, even for a short time. She wouldn't want to move even if that giant coyote charged in and started gnawing on her.

When the stupor wears off and vigor returns, she gives Patch a last skritch behind the ears and moves him from her lap to the couch. "Time to get to work."

It's not yet nine o'clock when she pulls into the underground parking at the A.V.A. Because at night the staff is all members of the Night Shift who don't really need sleep, the place buzzes with activity 24/7, thanks to the blackout curtains over the windows during the day.

After getting her delivery schedule and loading crates of V1 into her van, she hurries to the clinic.

Doc Lovely is just shutting the clinic door when she runs up to him. When he turns to face her, she sees weariness in his eyes, in the dark circles beneath them. Despite that, though, he is still beautiful. She doesn't know if his looks are natural or not, but it doesn't actually matter, does it? When he sees her, he smiles. "Meg." And then he frowns, steps closer, and softly, ever so softly, runs a finger down her cheek alongside the gash.

His remarkable green eyes seem to sadden. "Oh, Meg, lovely little Meg. What happened to you?"

She's already feeling soothed by his smooth baritone. Even his voice is perfect. "One of the Devils attacked me with a stake. Can you help me?"

His shoulders slump and he sighs. "I can help, yes, but I don't think that's a good idea tonight. I'm exhausted, and I will make mistakes if I don't stop now." His gaze flits around her face. "And I don't want to make a mistake with your loveliness." He stretches his arms out wide, and he yawns. "Tomorrow night, but an hour earlier. I'll still be fresh."

She nods at his office. "Do you have any big Band-Aids in there? I have deliveries tonight, and I think I ought to cover this up—it looks pretty bad."

"Yes, of course—it is unsightly. Though there's no danger of infection, it needs to be as clean as possible for the restoration." He leads her inside the clinic and puts a bandage on her cut. He pats her good cheek and doesn't seem troubled by her cool flesh. "Be careful with that. I can make you look better, but you need to keep the wound from further harm."

She follows him to the underground parking where he gets into his red Mercedes. Giving him a little wave, she says, "Tomorrow, Doc," and leaves him for the loading dock.

Just as she climbs into her van, another driver, a big guy they call Sarge who was a former Special Forces grunt, hails her. "Hey, Meg, got a minute?"

Rolling down her window, she gives him a smile. "You bet."

He doesn't smile back, even though he's always been friendly. The guy is huge, as big as that red-headed Devil but much broader. The dog tags visible in his open jumpsuit clink when he leans down to talk through her window. "I just want to ask you to keep an eye out for Andy while you're out on your run."

Andy's a sweet guy, and he often roams the hills near her route. He's another army guy who suffers from a double dose of PTSD—the first from his service in Afghanistan, the other the PTSD that becoming a vampire often causes. She's seen traces of it in herself. Andy stays in one of the shelter rooms for homeless vees that the A.V.A. keeps there, but sometimes things get to him and he goes feral for a night, out hunting in parks for squirrels and other wild animals to feed on—no people. He's always sorry he does it afterward, but it seems to relieve pressure in him. Drugs to treat PTSD don't work on vees because they can't take pills or get shots.

"Sure. Has it been long?"

Sarge says, "A couple days. It's not like I'm his keeper, but the thing is, we were going to go see the new Marvel movie last night, and he didn't show."

It would be nice to have someone to go to movies with. "I hope he didn't run into the Devils. I, uh, saw one last night."

Sarge's gaze shifts to the bandage on her cheek. She nods. "He had a stake." She thinks of watching the Devil turn into a vampire and run for his pseudo life, and she can't help a grin. "But he's not so fond of stakes anymore."

Sarge frowns at her. "You oughta carry some Mace or something like that."

"Good idea."

He points to her bandage. "You gonna see Doc about that?"

"He's going to fix it tomorrow."

Sarge holds up a meaty forearm and points at a cluster of thin lines in his skin on the underneath side. "He did a great job on my arm. Fell into some bougainvillea and the thorns did a number on me."

She winces. Bougainvillea thorns are wicked. His wounds look like fine scars, not so bad on a big veteran like Sarge, and a whole lot better than raw slices in undead flesh. She shakes her head. "Nature's beauty can be dangerous." She starts her van. "I'll keep an eye out for Andy, but I'm sure he's fine."

16: Nick

Vampires seem to have become a major theme in Nick's life. Also having to get up before sunrise. But when the dispatcher calls, duty calls, so here he is in an alley, a mug of coffee in his hand, staring down at a corpse with a wooden stake driven into its chest at the right spot for a heart.

There's nothing striking about the victim—he looks like a hundred other homeless guys Nick has seen on the streets, under viaducts, and in alleys. Bearded, a white man, he thinks, but with skin tanned so deep a brown it's hard to be certain. Running shoes with a hole in one sole, grimy jeans, a pink T-shirt with a big red bloodstain around the entry wound. There's bleeding on his neck, too, but the shirt is bunched up too much for Nick to see a wound. It can wait until the ME gets there.

It's chilly just before dawn, and he warms his hands with his travel mug while he waits for Manny. Sipping black coffee, he tries to ignore the smell of blood. Finally, Manny's van arrives and he jogs down the alley with a coffee cup in one hand and a medical bag in the other.

Manny studies the victim. "Really? A stake in the heart?"

"Yeah. Not only that, but it has D.V.L. stamped on it. Maybe the league has scored its first vampire." Nick thinks of the mess that the masher murder was. "Or maybe its second."

Manny pulls out a flashlight, squats and examines the corpse, poking and prying, examining the fingernails. He pulls the neck of the T-shirt down to reveal bite wounds in the area of the jugular. Nick gets a few photos with his phone—sunlight is edging down the alley, so they'll soon see if this actually is a vampire.

After the photographer arrives and gets pics, Manny bags the stake. Nick searches the alley. He finds a red MVDA hat under a dumpster maybe ten feet from the victim. He bags it and joins Manny to wait for the sun.

Manny says, "The stake probably killed him, but something chewed on his neck. A rat? Feral dog? Whatever it was got an artery, and the victim would have bled out if the stake hadn't stopped his heart."

Sunlight gets to the body, creeping onto one dirty hand. Nothing happens. The corpse stays a corpse, no smoke, no ashes, no bones. Definitely not a vampire. Could be the Devils have made a nasty mistake.

Nick says, "At least this time it looks like we have a cause of death to report to the captain." He downs the dregs of his coffee. "I'll go in and start a report. I need to take a closer look at the Death to Vampires League. Their paraphernalia is becoming a little too ubiquitous for me."

"I'll walk with you, need some gloves from my van."

As they near the opening of the alley to the street, a kid about eighteen peers around the corner. When he spots them, he wheels and darts away.

Nick tosses his empty cup to Manny and pursues at a run. When he gets to the sidewalk, the kid is maybe thirty feet away. This is a murder suspect, as far as Nick is concerned, so he snatches out his gun, keeps running, and shouts, "Halt, police! Stop or I'll shoot!"

The kid skids to a stop and puts his hands up. "Don't shoot! I didn't do nothing."

When Nick reaches him, he tells him to turn around. The kid's as grubby as the dead guy, skinny and tired-looking. His expression is like an abused dog whose master is about to swing the stick again. When Nick gestures at his hands with his gun, he cringes. "You can put your hands down."

He does.

Manny joins them. "Why'd you run, boy?"

The kid sniffles and wipes his nose on his arm. Nick's thinking an opioid junkie. The kid keeps his focus on the sidewalk as he says, "Just don't want no trouble. Didn't do nothin', neither."

Nick points back to the alley. "You know anything about that dead man back there?"

His gaze darts to the left and down. He knows something. But he says, "No. Never seen him before."

"You weren't close enough to see his face, so how do you know that?"

The kid clamps his mouth shut.

"So you knew he was there. Why'd you look into the alley?"

He shrugs. His gaze stays aimed at his toes. "Just curious. All the cop cars, you know."

Nick reaches for his arm. "Let's go. Maybe you'll remember better downtown."

The kid flinches away. "Okay. I knew he was there, and I was hopin' he had some cash. He sure wasn't going to need it no more."

If the kid was the one who stabbed the victim, he'd have robbed him then. At best, he's a witness, not the killer. "What did you see? You help us, you can go on your way."

The kid checks up and down the street. It's deserted. "Maybe I saw a truck. And maybe a big guy ran out of the alley."

"More."

He wipes his nose again. "Red hair. Black truck, jacked. Light bar on top. That's it." He looks up. "Oh, he lost a red hat while he was running."

Hello, Vincent Hunter, a freshly minted vampire out hunting for blood. Nick makes a note of the kid's name and the shelter he hangs at. "You're not in trouble, but I may need to talk to you again."

He nods.

"Okay, go." The kid hurries out of sight and around a corner. Nick hopes he's still alive when they need him as a witness, and he wishes he had cause to hold him now and get some food into him.

At Manny's van, he refills their cups from a thermos and then narrows his eyes at Nick. "You're holding out on me."

Nick's gut twinges. He's right. But, since he doesn't know if what Manny is talking about is what he's not telling him about, it's easy to say, "I don't know what you're talking about. Besides, I wouldn't do that to you."

"You are."

"Never, I—"

Manny dangles the baggie containing the stake in front of him. "Vampires."

"Oh, I know my theory is a reach, but—"

"A body is mysteriously missing from the morgue. One that you said was a vampire."

"Maybe I've been reading too much fiction about—"

"How about we call it fact? Last night I Googled Meg Murrow and vampires."

Oh. He says, "Oh."

"She's the vampire you arrested."

Busted. "No, that was—"

"Her identical twin sister, Myrtle. Sure it was. Unfortunately, nothing on the internet about Meg Murrow mentions a twin sister."

It pisses Nick off to be caught in a lie. Unfortunately, he doesn't usually get pissed at himself for lying, he gets surly and lashes out at the one shining a light on him. "Well, listen to mister amateur detective. Who do we have here, Agatha Christie? You forget that I'm the detective?" He turns away, but Manny stops him.

"Wait. There's a way out. For you and for her."

Nick turns back. Manny scowls, and Nick doesn't think it's at him. He feels bad about his outburst. Not enough to apologize, though; he's still too ... what? Afraid? "Yeah?"

Manny says, "You know I should report this to the captain."

Nick's anger evaporates, and fear surfaces. He starts out being afraid of losing his job, but then the terrible trouble barreling down on Meg swamps that. A way out? Great—but there's a *but* implied in what Manny said. "But ... ?"

Many opens his mouth a couple of times but nothing comes out.

Ah, he gets it. "You really, really want to examine a vampire."

Manny lets out a long breath. "In a way, I already have, there in the cell, I just didn't know at the time. And she was technically dead, which I put in my report. But ..."

"But you want more."

"You know where she is, right?"

"What would she get in return?"

Manny's gaze drops to the ground. "I was thinking a report gets filed on Myrtle Murrow's cadaver being found and autopsied. I'll make sure the captain gets it."

Nick doesn't think Manny likes breaking the rules any better than he does. But a report like that would get the captain off his case and he could concentrate on solving these weird murders. And it would get Meg out from under the danger he's created for her. "You're not afraid of being with a vampire?"

He shrugs. "I already have been. Nothing happened. And she was perfectly civilized at the morgue. It doesn't seem all that dangerous to me."

Nick flashes on Meg toppling that huge Devil to the ground and then feeding on him. "You have no idea." But she might go for this. "I'll ask her."

Manny lifts his gaze, his eyes bright. "Tell her I won't hurt her or anything. No cutting. I only want to see what she's like. It'll be like a routine physical exam."

"So you're saying you believe in vampires."

"What's not to believe? A woman has no pulse, doesn't breathe, her body is room temperature—and she walks out of the morgue after apparently overwhelming the morgue assistant and escaping."

"Well, that is an indication."

Manny sticks out his hand for a shake. "Still friends?"

He accepts the handshake. "Still friends."

Manny studies the body waiting for him in the alley and sighs. "Back to work."

Nick calls in an all-points bulletin for Vincent Hunter and his truck. Since it's daylight, he doesn't expect any results until after dark and Vincent emerges from hiding to hunt. Then it occurs to him that Meg is probably still up.

He discovers that he really likes the sound of her voice when she answers—throaty, soft, intimate. "Hello?"

"It's Nick."

"I don't want to talk to you. Or listen to you. Or anything to you."

"I may have a way to get the captain off your trail."

"I guess I can talk to you about that."

So he tells her about Manny wanting to examine her and then file a false report on the missing Myrtle. Guilt pokes at him when he tells her that part, but he pushes it aside.

She says, "The guy who wanted to cut me up? Are you crazy?"

"No, no, he doesn't want to do that, just an exam. Actually, maybe he would like to do that, but this will be like going to the doctor. He is a doctor, after all. You know, stethoscopes and blood pressure and stuff like that."

He takes a couple of swallows of coffee before she answers. Her voice comes back on. "Give him my number and I'll see."

"Great."

"Don't get the idea that this makes up for what you did to me and Patch."

The line goes dead. He texts Manny her number and lets him know that she's up. Maybe now he can focus on being a detective. Meg will be all right, and he has murders to solve.

17: Patch

I'm happily curled up in my regular spot on the couch when Meg settles in at the kitchen table to work on her new movie treatment for our next Disney meeting. Her phone rings. "Yes?"

She listens, then says, "Yes, Doctor Chesterfield. Nick told me about your interest. He said you might be able to make this problem with the police go away?"

She nods at something. "Okay. Now?" She closes her computer. "Listen, since the sun is up, I can't open the door to let you in. So I'll leave it unlocked and you call me when you're outside. We'll get into the bedroom and close the door. I'll text you when it's safe for you to come in."

Meg busies herself tidying the apartment—she's always been a bit of a neat freak—and then her phone rings. Apparently it's the guy, because she picks me up and we go into the bedroom and shut the door. She texts him, and a moment later the front door opens and closes. Our visitor's voice sounds tight but friendly. "Ms. Murrow?"

She leaves the bedroom and greets the newest threat to my continued existence, a pudgy guy carrying a black bag. Meg is her usual polite self. "Doctor Chesterfield."

He waves a hand. "Please call me Manny, everyone else does." He seems nice enough. Dressed in jeans and a polo shirt, his vibe is that of a regular guy.

I don't trust him. I jump up on the couch to be in a better attack position.

Meg lifts her chin, something she does when she encounters a headwind. "I am not happy about this."

"I'm trying to help you."

She frowns at that. "You just want to play with my body."

He shakes his head. "If that's all it was, I could report you and examine you in jail."

"Oh. Yeah."

He gazes at her. "I believe you're innocent."

Score one for Manny. "You're Nick's friend?"

"Yeah. He is sorry."

"Yeah. He is."

Manny lifts his black bag. "Where would be a good place to do this?"

She takes a breath and sighs, then gestures at the couch. "Here?"

"Fine." He puts the bag on the coffee table and squeezes into the small space I've left at one end of the couch. I'm not moving over for a breather who is a pal of that jerk detective.

Meg lifts me, deposits me at the other end of the couch, and sits next to Manny. She could've asked me to scoot over. What am I, chopped liver?

He folds his hands. "I don't know anything but what fiction tells us about vampires. How did this happen to you?"

"I was bitten by a vampire." I can't help but think about when she rose from a shallow grave and grabbed me. Thanks for the downer, Manny.

He waits a beat, then says, "And ... ?"

Meg glances at me. "I'm sorry, that brings back bad memories." She sighs. "According to the American Vampire Association, centuries ago, in Transylvania, the rabies virus mutated into a microparasite. That's what infects us and turns us into vampires."

"So it feeds off of blood you take in. Bizarre." He removes a stethoscope from his bag.

She says to the doctor, "I'm nervous about this."

His gaze seems kindly. "Me, too. I don't usually work with people who aren't dead."

Her grin has a bitter, down-turned tinge to it. "I'm not sure I'm an exception."

Manny has the grace to chuckle at that. "You've been examined by a physician before, haven't you?"

"Sure, but not when I was, to be straightforward about this, undead."

"Ah, yes. Undead. Well, we'll see about that." He puts the stethoscope on and presses the little round end on her chest. He listens. And watches her chest. And listens.

He glances up at her. "No heartbeat. No breathing, either."

She takes a breath to say, "I have a pulse after I feed. And I can breathe when I want to, it's just not autonomic, the same way my heart isn't anymore. Luckily, breathing can be voluntary, otherwise we couldn't speak."

Still with the stethoscope on her chest, he says, "Breathe deeply." She does. He moves the round thing to the other side of her chest. "Breathe." She does, and he takes the stethoscope away. "Lungs are clear." He gestures at her chest. "I had noted that you do breathe before talking. Of course you do to get air going through your vocal cords, but is that characteristic of all vampires?"

She lifts one shoulder in a mini-shrug. "As far as I know."

"Uh, would a blood sample be possible?"

"No." She pulls off the bandage on her cheek. "We don't bleed, and we don't heal."

Manny leans close and peers at the open wound. She can't wait to see Doc Lovely so he can work his magic.

He says, "How old is this wound?"

"A couple days."

"I don't see any signs of—"

"Healing. Right."

I hate that Devil guy for what he did to my associate. I wish she had finished him off like I did the bloodhound. But she has this moral streak in her. Me, like all cats, I'm a proponent of situation ethics. Especially when dogs are involved.

He lifts a blood-pressure cuff from the bag, but sets it back down. "No point in this." He peers at her. "You say you can have a pulse?"

"For a time. After feeding."

"Is it possible for you to demonstrate that?" Then he puts his hand to his throat. "Oops. Never mind."

Meg smiles at the doctor. "We don't feed off of people." She shoots me a quick look at her little lie. "It'll take just a minute."

Enough about her, what about me? "Mrow," I say.

Manny turns and reaches toward me, smiling. "So you're a vampire kitty-cat. A very handsome one, I must say." He stretches his hand closer and gives me a little skritch on top of my handsome head. Even though my skin is currently numb, his touch causes the reaction I always have—I want more, of course, and give his hand a little headbutt.

While Meg goes into the kitchen, I stand guard—I sit guard—I wallow-in-pleasure guard as Manny's scratching goes on. The refrigerator opens and closes, the microwave hums and then beeps, and Meg returns with a mug in one hand and my bowl in the other. She sets my bowl on the coffee table, and I'm on it in a flash, lapping up blood while keeping an eye on the breather.

He wrinkles his nose and shies back from her when she sits next to him, her mug of warm blood in her hand. "And this is ..."

"Bovine blood." She takes a long sip.

"How ... civilized. So what I read and hear about vampires isn't true? You're not out there in the dark ripping throats open?"

She takes another swig. "There'll be a pulse soon. And, no, we aren't out there ripping." Meg glances at me again. "On a regular basis, anyway. There are feral vampires, though, and they do what you say."

She points at his stethoscope, hanging around his neck. He puts it on and listens to her chest. "Amazing. It's faint, but there. How long does it last?"

She finishes her blood as I lap up the last of mine. The tingle spreads through my body. Meg says, "Depends on how much you drink."

He reaches for her forearm, then hesitates before he touches it. "May I?"

She nods.

He touches her arm. "Still cool, but maybe a little warmer."

"We seldom warm all the way up; that takes a lot of blood, and it isn't cheap."

He slides his fingers down to the underside of her wrist. "Yes, a pulse." He puts his stethoscope back into his bag. "I would love to talk with you for hours, but I see that your eyelids are drooping."

"Yeah, it's a slump that hits shortly after a good helping of blood. It lasts for a few minutes, and then we have fresh energy. We can feel things better, too."

I take that as my cue and totter into her lap. She scratches behind my ears. "Well, this wasn't as awful as I thought it would be."

She graces him with a smile. "Thank you for helping me. You're a nice man."

"Just a curious one. Are there more vampires in Los Angeles?"

Meg nods.

"A lot more?"

She shrugs.

"Do you know each other?"

She shakes her head. "I don't know you, Manny, and you're a friend of Nick's. I don't want my friends harassed."

Manny raises a palm as if surrendering. "I get it. Sorry." He fishes a business card from his shirt pocket and hands it to her. "My cell is on there too. Maybe we can talk more sometime? I'm fascinated. And I'm on your side. Please call me anytime I can be of help."

Meg nods. "Are you going to write that report?"

His mouth turns down. "Yes. I don't like it, but Nick—and you—need help getting out of the mess he's created. It's worth a little guilt to make things right for an innocent person." He smiles. "And I got to examine a real vampire!" His smile vanishes. "But who can I tell about it?"

Manny stands and goes to the door. "Don't get up."

Meg's smile is sleepy. "I can't."

I'm on the drowsy side, too.

Manny grips the doorknob and Meg says, "Don't! The daylight."

"So that part is true?"

She nods. "Please wait until Patch and I go to the bedroom."

He says he's sorry and sits back down on the couch. It doesn't take long for us to liven up enough so we can retreat. The door clicks behind him, and we're alone again.

Good.

18: Nick and Meg

Nick goes for a leisurely breakfast at the Pancake Parlor and gets to the office at nine. It's not five minutes after he sits at his desk and boots up his computer when the captain calls him in. He prints out his phone photos of the newest body and enters the captain's office.

Hoping that it's good to be preemptive, he places the pictures on the captain's desk. "There's been another murder—a wooden stake to the heart, his throat torn open. It looks to me like it was staged to look as if the victim was a vampire. He wasn't one, though."

The frown on the captain's face widens out into puzzlement. "Vampires again?"

"Not this time. The stake in the heart looks like the work of the Death to Vampires League. But there were wounds on the victim's neck consistent with someone, or something, biting as if going for blood."

He squints at me. "When was the last time you were checked out by the psychologist?"

"I haven't been."

"You're way overdue." He pushes the photos at Nick. "Do you have any evidence that any of these so-called vampires were actually murdered? Causes of death?"

"I do for this one, but not the others. But surely—"

"Surely? I deal in facts, boy, facts. Speaking of facts, where is that fact of a corpse that someone stole from the morgue? You do understand that's a priority, don't you?"

Sometimes it helps defuse the captain if Nick hangs his head, so he does that and looks down. "Yessir, I do. I'm on it."

"Actually, you're not on it. I'm sending a team to pick her sister up this morning. Give me her location."

"You gave me until tomorrow!"

"And you're dragging your feet. You have some reason for hiding this woman?"

Yes, he does. "No, I don't."

The captain picks up a pen and poises to write on a pad. "Her address."

"You don't understand. It's daytime. If they pick her up now—"

"So she's a vampire too?"

"I ... can't say. But she could be." Man, does he sound lame. But he can't reveal Meg's true nature to the captain or she's done for sure.

"Well, that's her problem. Now is when I want that information." He juts his jaw out. "You are going to do your duty."

His duty. Yes. He swore an oath to uphold the law, to "well and faithfully" discharge his duties. This is his sworn duty. He gives up Meg's address.

The captain picks up his office phone, then glares at him. "I don't know what you have going on with this subject of interest in a murder and a missing dead body, but you are not going to be communicating with her. Correct?"

It's an act of will and surrender for him to say, "Correct."

The captain punches a button on his phone. "Get me Johnson and Murphy, tell 'em I have a mission for them." He picks up the slip of paper with Meg's address as he listens.

"Not back until ten? Okay, as soon as they get here, send them to this address." After he reads it off, he adds, "They are to arrest the woman known as Megan Murrow at that apartment and bring her in."

He hangs up and gazes at Nick, his expression snake-like. He taps the photos Nick had put on his desk. "You have murders to solve. Dismissed."

Trying to avoid the clock on his computer screen, Nick focuses on a new lead in the masher murder. The dog-tag victim was rousted for suspicion of vagrancy and gave an address where he claimed to live. It's the address listed for the American Veggie Association. Which fits. Of course a vampire would have been staying at the American Vampire Association.

But a quick call doesn't give him much more information than the fact that Andrew Markham has been missing for a few days. He'll go by later and look at his room, but he doesn't have much hope for learning—

He can't stand this. The clock at the bottom of his monitor now reads 9:46. Meg will soon be doomed. He's hot inside, and his hands curl into fists that want to pound the captain. But that's wrong. He's just doing his job.

And Nick is just doing his.

He picks up his phone.

Sets it back down.

Doing his duty. Obeying orders.

Dammit!

Manny appears in his doorway, papers in his hand. He drops them on Nick's desk. "Here's the report. Myrtle Murrow, found misplaced under a wrong name, death by natural causes."

Hope surges in him. "Does the captain have it?"

"Nope, I just finished and thought you'd want to know. It won't be official until I get it uploaded and sent out." He picks up the papers. "You don't look all that delighted." He sighs. "But I guess I know what you're feeling. I hate the thought of cheating too, but this time it feels like the right thing to do."

Nick grits his teeth and moans. "It's too late. In a few minutes, the captain will have a team on the way to bring Meg in."

Manny's eyes widen. "In the middle of the morning? You saw what happened when the sun hit what was left of those vampire remains."

Why'd he have to remind Nick of that? He tries to force the images from his mind, but he doesn't have much luck. That's what he's brought down on Meg.

Realization shows on Manny's face. "You haven't warned her."

It's hard to say the words. "It was an order."

Manny's voice crackles with sarcasm. "Aren't you the good soldier?" He pulls out his phone and keys in a number. "Meg?" He fires a glare at Nick. "This is Manny. There are cops on the way to bring you in."

Relief runs through Nick. She's still free, she has a chance.

Manny says to Meg, "Nick."

He can't make out her words, but he hears her anger even from across the desk.

"You've got to run. Do you have anyplace you can go? I could come get you, but how can you get out? It's daytime."

After he listens, he says, "Good." He ends the call and turns to go. Nick calls after him, "Well?"

He turns back, his expression dripping with loathing. He drops the fake report in a wastebasket and leaves.

What did he mean by "good"? What is she going to do? That was cruel, to leave him hanging.

No, it wasn't. He deserves it.

How can it be right to be true to your duty and wrong at the same time?

~

After Manny's warning call, Meg calls the A.V.A. Rescue Squad. She gathers all their V1, the cow kind, in a shopping bag, and tosses in all their Death Savers. Then she packs her duffel with changes of clothing, bathroom stuff, her notes on the movie, her purse, and her laptop.

Then it's hurry up and wait. She can't even peek out the window to see when they arrive, not unless she wants her face burned off. She doesn't know how long she has until the cops get here. *Oh, hurry, hurry!*

A knock comes at the door and she rushes to it. "Yes?"

"A.V.A."

A lake of tension drains from her, making her knees want to give way. "I'm heading for the bedroom. Give me a count of ten." She grabs Patch, hurries into the bedroom, closes the door, and listens for the front door to open.

After they're in, she and Patch emerge. Two of the A.V.A.'s daytime breather employees, a guy and a woman in A.V.A. jumpsuits, stand ready beside a gurney. The A.V.A. lost a lot of vees to sunlight until they created the rescue squad.

She tells the guy, "We may only have a few minutes. There are police on the way."

The man—the name on the uniform is Sayed—raises his eyebrows.

"Don't worry, I haven't done anything illegal."

"No problem." He hauls a black body bag from under the gurney and unzips it. He smiles. "Got your size right here."

Note to self: This affinity for body bags is a habit she needs to break, real soon.

She points out the groceries and her duffel bag, and the woman fetches them while Sayed helps her and Patch into the body bag. When Sayed zips it up, Patch tenses against her. Stroking his head, she whispers, "It's okay, Patch, we'll be okay."

She hopes.

~

A very long hour after Manny leaves, Nick's office phone rings. The captain tells him to report to his office immediately.

Waiting for Nick is not only the captain but Johnson and Murphy, the detectives the captain sent to arrest Meg. Hope flares in him. If they're here, maybe she got away.

The captain confirms it. "The perp was not there. There was no sign of her."

He wants to argue that she's a suspect, not a perp of anything, but stays quiet.

Johnson says, "No food in the refrigerator except for some beet juice, no purse, a few items of clothing."

The captain looks to Nick. "You warned her."

"I did not."

"The investigators can settle that. Hand over your phone."

Johnson steps to one side of him, Murphy the other.

He sets his phone on the captain's desk. "Investigators?"

The captain says, "Nick Silver, you are under arrest for theft and abuse of a dead human body and the unauthorized removal of human remains. Murphy, read him his rights." He taps the desk. "Your badge and your gun."

Nick looks to Murphy, who's been sort of a friend. "Human remains? Does that sound crazy to you? She walks, she talks. She's not a dead body."

Murphy shrugs. "I wouldn't know. That's not what the captain told us."

Captain Numm reads from a printout. "According to this, our own Doctor Manfred Chesterfield, medical examiner, checked the woman right here in this station and reported that she was dead. She was last seen in your custody. Tell me where she is and we can forget this."

He doesn't know where she is, though he thinks he knows where she could've gone. But he's pleased to be able to honestly say, "I don't know."

Captain Numm reddens. "Johnson, I want an all-points bulletin out on Megan Murrow asap." He looks to Nick. "Does she have a car?"

An APB? And he can't even warn her to keep out of sight. "Yes, but I don't know the plate."

"What make is it?"

How can he not answer? He knows. "Older Miata. British racing green."

Murphy says, "There was a green Miata in the suspect's parking lot. She must be on foot."

"Johnson, do a search with the DMV." He taps on the desk again. "Your badge and your gun." After Nick surrenders them, the captain gestures to the two cops, and they continue with the arrest. As Nick's rights are read to him, Johnson completes his humiliation by cuffing his hands behind his back.

Talk about a bad day at the office.

The dim interior hallways of the A.V.A. are soothing to Meg's weary eyes. At what breathers think of normal levels, even ordinary indoor lighting can become irritating. On the first floor, just off the elevator from the underground parking, are twenty offices that have been converted into bedrooms, some for two people, some singles—she's lucky there is a single open today, so she settles herself and Patch in a spare but comfortable room. It even has a little refrigerator she can put their V1 juice in. Luckily, Patch has no need for a litter box.

The rooms are for vees who have lost their source of income after being changed and are homeless. The A.V.A. has a job placement service that works on getting them night jobs, and they can stay there until they land something. Some men and women, so damaged by PTSD from becoming a vampire that they can't function well in the "real" world, are semi-permanent residents like Andy.

She doesn't blame them; it all seemed so hopeless when it happened to her. Then she worked her way out of it and came to California to pursue a new career. But now it seems hopeless again. She feels too puny to fight the combined forces of millions of breathers and sunlight.

And movie producers who grope you.

And police officers who betray you.

Even though her door is open, a soft knock comes. She stuffs the last of her shirts into a dresser drawer and turns to find Sarge filling the doorway. "Hey," he says. "If there's anything I can do to help, just say it."

There is one thing. "How about when you do your delivery run tonight, you take me by my place so I can get my car?"

He nods. "You got it."

Sarge seems down to her. His big wide shoulders slump, and his face shows no emotion in a way that says a lot is being held in. "What is it, Sarge?"

"Andy gave the A.V.A. as his address the last time cops questioned him when he was out roaming. A detective called this morning and asked about him. Said it was a homicide investigation."

Homicide? Oh, poor Andy.

She looks at Patch, listening quietly on the bed.

Poor us.

19: Nick and Meg

Now that Nick's out on bond after the arraignment, he goes to the station and cleans out his desk. Of course, he's on suspension until the trial is over, but Captain Numm has demoted him to patrolman. He'll have a spot in the squad room if he survives his trial, but no more cubicle. Luckily, his patrol uniform still fits. He thinks running the hills as a coyote keeps him in shape, because he never has time for the gym.

Manny appears in the doorway. "I heard. Pretty serious charges."

All he can do is shrug. "It gets better. The DA added obstruction of justice."

"What level?"

"Felony."

"Must be because there's a body involved."

"Ha." He has a favor he hopes Manny'll do if he's not still angry with Nick for not warning Meg. "You still pissed because I didn't call Meg?"

"I am. It was a shitty thing not to do that. She could have been killed."

Okay, now he feels a lot worse than he did. His little pity party is a touch overshadowed by her close encounter with doom. Still, he was in the right. He was. Really. "I *couldn't* call her. I was under—"

"Orders. I know." Manny's body language is not that of the relaxed, friendly guy he's been for more than a year. "I got your voicemail. What do you want?"

"There's a preliminary hearing tomorrow at the courthouse, and I hope you'll come and testify. Maybe my lawyer can get the case dismissed. After all, I'm not guilty. I didn't do anything wrong."

"Testify as to what?"

Nick had fished Manny's fake report out of the wastebasket. He holds it up and says, "Well, if you could enter this into the record and discuss your findings, then—"

Manny shakes his head vehemently. "I will not commit perjury under any circumstances."

"But this is wrong! I'm innocent! Meg is not dead. You've seen her, talked to her. I didn't remove a corpse, because she isn't one."

Manny shrugs. "That's a judgment call, at best. As to whether this is wrong, as I remember, Meg is innocent, too. Yet somehow, I first encountered her in a jail cell. Put there by you."

"I was following the law."

"The captain claims you've broken it."

He would hit Manny with "innocent until proven guilty," but he remembers how he brushed that aside when Meg called him out on arresting her.

"This isn't right! Don't you understand?!"

"I do." Manny's gaze is level and calculating. "Do you?"

Doc Lovely answers Meg's knock on the clinic door at the A.V.A. She hopes he can fix her face before she goes to her meeting with Flem at Disney. "Hi, Doc. I was hoping you could help me with this." She points to her cheek.

He smiles, as warm and friendly as can be. She thinks if she were a breather surrounded by vampires, she'd be a little tense, but not Doc. "Please come in, Meg."

He sits her up on an examining table and shines a bright light on her cheek while he looks at the gash through a magnifying glass. The light is uncomfortable, but she's on the numb side right now, so it's bearable. He says, "We're in luck. The edges are clean and straight, not jagged at all."

He turns the light off and leans back. The look on his face is sympathetic, and he runs his hand down the uninjured side of her face in a kind of caress. "So beautiful. So perfect." He studies the cheek with the cut and shakes his head.

That scares her. "Can't you do something?"

He must hear the worry in her voice, because he smiles again. "Oh, yes. I was just regretting the damage to such a lovely face."

She doesn't think she's all that lovely, but it's nice to hear. "So you can?"

"I can. But not tonight."

"But I thought—"

He holds up a hand. "I know what I said, and I can do it tonight if you insist. But I was thinking of ways to restore you as perfectly as possible, and I've ordered a new surgical epoxy glue that is excellent on flesh. With that and makeup, I believe I can make that ugliness almost vanish."

Since she'll be scarred no matter what, she'd be happy to get it over with now. But he's the expert, the surgeon to the stars. Who is she to say no to anything he wants to do?

She nods. "Okay." He puts his equipment away and she hops off the table. "Tomorrow?"

There's his smile again. "Yes." He pulls out his phone, swipes to a calendar. "Oh, tomorrow won't work. I'm the lead speaker at a charity event to raise funds for plastic surgery for orphans. The next night?"

She pulls out her phone and checks her schedule. "I'll be delivering to your house that night."

He brightens. "Excellent. You've seen my clinical setup there." He checks his phone again. "I have a consultation with an actress at nine that night, but it won't take long. After you fill my order in the clinic, come into the house and find me. I had the glue shipped overnight, so we'll be ready." He nods, puts away his phone. "Good thinking. We'll be much more comfortable there."

Just as she reaches the door, he says, "Hold on."

He comes to her with a darkish pink bandage in his hand. "I want to keep that wound protected." As he puts it on her cheek, he chuckles. "They call this flesh-colored, but I've never seen skin this color."

She's glad he thought of this. She should be able to get through her Disney meeting.

"Doctor, I can't thank you enough."

He nods. "I appreciate that, but this is really more about me—I hate ugliness and want to make the world as beautiful as it can be. Especially the people in it."

Back in her room, she's filled with hope as she picks out clothes for Disney—the Black Sabbath T-shirt with the horned skull matches her mood, and she goes with her black jeans to complete the picture.

She's about to head for the breakroom to heat up a bottle of V1 when Manny calls and asks if he can drop by. She owes the guy a lot, and she's happy to say yes. "But you do know you are walking into a big-time vampire den, right?"

He chuckles. "That's part of the appeal. Got a minute?"

She does, and ten minutes later there he is, coming through the breakroom door at the A.V.A. A couple of vees on the way out slow as they pass him and inhale deeply. She doesn't think he notices them, but his fresh-blood scent permeates the room. If only her mouth could water ...

She goes to greet him. He holds his hand out for a shake. She hesitates, but what the heck, he already knows. He doesn't react in a negative way when he grips her hand. He says, "Cool."

She doesn't know whether that's an accolade or a gauge of her body temperature. But so what? "Would you care for a bottle of V1?"

Now he reacts. His eyebrows head for his hairline, which makes her laugh. "The veggie kind, although I will join you."

He relaxes and says sure. After she's warmed her bottle of blood and given him a chilled bottle of beet V1 from the fridge, they sit at a table.

Manny says, "I actually have two reasons for wanting to see you. The first is to find out how you are doing."

"Okay. I wish I could go home, but I'm afraid of being hauled into jail. Patch and I have a room here, and I still have my job. Plus I have a script meeting with Disney tonight." She's a little surprised when he doesn't whip out a pitch for a screenplay—he could be one of the three people in Hollywood who isn't writing one.

A swig of V1 starts a trickle of energy in her middle. "What can I do for you? You sure helped me a ton."

His expression saddens. "I tried, but then Nick was arrested and my plan sank."

She gives him a heartfelt smile. "In this case, it really is the thought that counts."

He takes a hesitant sip of veggie V1, then grins and takes a big gulp. After a satisfied sigh, he says, "This stuff is great."

"Number one with vampires, you know."

He chuckles. "Vampires is what you can do for me. I'd like to study more vampires, basically like I did with you, maybe run some other tests, EKGs, you know. If there's a spare room, I could set up a little clinic. I don't know what I can do to actually help vampires, but maybe something will turn up."

"Wow. That would be great. We'd have two doctors here. That can't hurt."

"Two?"

"You know Doc Lovely?"

He nods. "Well, I know *of* him. Fantastic surgeon."

She tells him about what Doc does for them. She points to the bandage on her cheek. "He can close this and, with makeup, it will just look like a thin scar."

"I'd love to assist him."

"When you're set up, I'll introduce you." Things go quiet while they drink. Because she knows he's friends with Nick, she can satisfy her curiosity. Nick did, after all, save her. After nearly doing her in, yes, but still. "Nick is sorry, right?"

"He says he is."

"Truly?"

Manny gazes at the floor long enough that she doesn't think he's going to answer, then looks up at her. "Yes. But I don't think he gets it that a mechanistic interpretation of 'the law' can betray the interests of justice. And you."

Jeez, what are vees going to do if a straight arrow like Nick can't "get it"? Her heart hardens ... and then she thinks of Nick offering her his hand in the coroner's office right before he led her out to freedom, short-lived though it was. It was a gentle gesture. That was when he was doing the right thing. "How is Nick faring?"

Manny sighs. "Holding up. The captain busted him back to patrolman, arrested him, and he's been suspended." He runs down the charges against Nick.

Nick loves being a detective, Manny tells her. It's his life. "Well, I hope he beats those ridiculous charges," Meg says.

Manny shakes his head. "I don't think that's likely as long as he can't produce the corpse he allegedly stole from the coroner. They also charged him with obstruction of justice because they believe he's refusing to tell them where the cadaver is."

That would be her. Ewww. But that's a plus for Nick. "Is there anything you can do?"

"I don't see what. I'm not going to lie for him, and I'm sure not going to tell anybody where you are. He's got a preliminary hearing tomorrow. Technically, it's possible the charges can be dropped then, but the district attorney holds all the cards."

She imagines Nick in that jail cell she was once in, sitting on a bunk, hunkered over, elbows on his knees, those pretty blue eyes sad and downcast. He's going to have his life taken away from him.

The injustice of having your life taken away from you is something that she can testify hurts with an ache that never stops.

She asks Manny, "Will you be there?"

"I've been subpoenaed, probably to verify my initial report on you and witnessing that your body wasn't at the morgue."

"But it— I *was* at the morgue."

He shrugs. "Not in a totally deceased form."

There's nothing she can do. "Hey, I've got to get going to my Disney meeting. I'll take you by the director's office on my way out."

When she leaves him there, she says, "Tell Nick ..." What does she want to say? No matter what he did to her, he's still the guy who warmed her when they first met. And he did do right by her in the end. "I wish him luck."

Manny adopts a sardonic expression, one eyebrow cocked up, mouth turned down on one side. "Which kind?"

She laughs. "Oh, let's make it the good kind."

Nick's going to need it.

Manny sticks his hand out for a shake. He's amazing, the way he ignores her creepy side. "Luck to you in your meeting."

She sighs. "Thank you. I desperately need this gig, but it keeps getting tougher."

"You want me to let you know how the hearing goes?"

"Sure. I'm interested in seeing if the truth will set one of the law's biggest fans free."

Manny shakes his head. "Don't hold your breath." His face falls. "Oh. I didn't mean—"

She can't help but laugh, and he smiles.

20: Meg

Meg rolls up her car windows and puts up the top before going to Disney in case the Devils are still fouling the planet with their protest. She's glad to see that they aren't there when she turns onto Buena Vista Street. Patch stares ahead from his car seat.

"Hey, Patch, looks like no hassle tonight." She wonders if one of the Devils becoming a vee confused them and they don't know what to do. Did they stake that guy? It's sort of an "the enemy is us" moment for them.

Patch ignores her. Actually, "ignores" sounds as if it's an intentional snub. She thinks he's just always in the moment and totally focused on that. She reaches out and adds a scratch behind his ears to his moment. He utters a faint "mew" and bends his neck down for more.

But they're at the gate and she goes back to driving. Once again, the name of Harvey Flem gets her right in. Her stomach tries to knot up. She has done the best she can to build a decent story around his idea of "vambies," gagging all the way. It was a struggle, and not one that she won. To begin with, the idea of a vambie is inherently inconsistent. Vampires are undead—their flesh stays the same, they don't change or age. Zombies rot. So how can a vambie's flesh both rot and remain unchanging at the same time?

Zombies eat brains. Vampires drink blood and can't eat anything else because it won't digest and rots in their stomachs. So, logically, a vambie would eat brains and then said brains would rot in the vambie's stomach. Which would generate a gas buildup that would lead to either bellies exploding or truly horrendous flatulence. To her way of thinking, neither one is a desirable outcome for a children's "happy horror" movie. She can, however, imagine Flem going for that.

She lets out a sad chuckle. How about a story about a heroic space vambie that propels itself around the universe using hyperfart thrust?

Basically, she's got nothin'. She's going to have to tell Flem that and beg him to let her write a straight vampire musical.

Jeanine is at her station, her shoulders looking particularly wide in a pale blue sundress. Patch snug in Meg's arms, she goes to the desk. "Hi."

Jeanine's smile is sweet and her voice melodic. "Oh, Meg and Patch. I'm so glad to see you." A frown creases her brow and she touches a finger to her cheek. "What happened?"

Meg presses on the bandage to make sure it's in place. "Oh, just a blemish. It'll be gone soon."

Jeanine glances at the producer's closed door. "Any luck with 'vambies'?" Then she mimes sticking her finger down her throat at the retch-worthy idea.

Meg's glad Jeanine gets it. "No. I know I'm creative and imaginative, but I can't come up with a way to make vambies work. I can figure out what would happen if you cross a dog with a cat—it would keep chasing itself up a tree—but cross a vampire and a zombie? No."

Jeanine presses a button on her phone. "Ms. Murrow is here to see you."

Flem's voice comes. "Send her in. Is that damn cat with her?"

"Yes, Mister Flem."

"Damn."

Jeanine doesn't seem to notice Patch's *sotto voce* hiss as she gestures toward Flem's door with a long, muscular arm. Her fingernails are a blue that matches her dress. Meg could use some dress-up tips from her. Jeanine whispers, "Good luck" and then points at her phone. "I'll be a little fly on the wall."

Flem's first words when she enters his office are "What's with the bandage? Your contract requires you to look good, and that ain't it."

"Oh, just a little plastic surgery to take care of a tiny blemish." That should satisfy him, here in the world capital of plastic surgery. "The doctor assured me that it will go away and soon be invisible."

He claps his hands and beams at her. "So hit me with my vambie movie. It's gonna be a monster hit." He chuckles at his "wit."

Placing Patch on the chair beside her, she opens her folder to her notes. She takes Flem through all the reasons why the concept of vambies can't work, and can she please just write a vampire musical? But then she makes the mistake of joking about a space vambie and hyperfarts.

He laughs and gives her a thumbs-up. "You had me worried at first, with your talk about how it can't work, but that was all setup, wasn't it?" He giggles and rubs his hands together. "A space vambie eating alien brains and zooming around with hyperfart thrust. Genius!" His face grows still and serious. "One technical question, though. Does the power of hyperfart thrust depend on the IQ of the brain he eats?"

She refuses to go there. "Mister Flem, that was a joke. I can't do a vambie movie. I'll pay back the advance, but it'll have to be in installments."

He drops one hand into his lap and stares at her. Or, rather, at her chest. Her T-shirt is a little snug—since she can't gain weight, it must have shrunk—but she avoids thinking about what she thinks he's thinking about. But it probably includes "perky."

Then he gives her a grin normally seen only on sentient pond scum. With his other hand, he gestures for her to come to one side of the desk. "I believe we can work something out. Let me show you how good it will be to partner with me."

Keeping her gaze focused between his tiny, cold eyes, she does as he wishes. When she reaches the side of the desk, however, her peripheral vision can't help but see that his hand is rubbing his crotch.

Oh, God, his other hand joins the busy one and together they unzip his slacks. The pond-scum grin widens. "Help yourself. All the ladies love it."

She widens her eyes and makes an O with her mouth, then covers her mouth and titters. "Oh, Mister Flem, you shouldn't have."

"Well, I'm a generous kind of guy." His gaze drops to the bulge making its way through the open fly. "Oh, look, Little Harvey is glad to see you."

If she could blush, she'd be crimson right now. Instead, she takes out her phone and turns the camera lens his way. "Oh, I just can't tell you how that makes me feel. Mind if I take a photo for a keepsake?"

She glances at Patch. His eyes widen, and he cocks his head at her. She winks at him. Patch hops onto the desk and sits where he can see the action. Her cat's built-in smile seems a little bigger than usual.

Flem spreads his legs and gestures toward his happy pants. "What a sweet idea. Of course."

She gets a wide shot that includes his face, and then zooms in on the lump in his tighty whities. After she takes the shot, she switches to video mode, starts recording, and then puts on an unhappy face. "Awww. It looks to me like Little Harvey is terribly cramped in there. Aren't you going to let him come out and play?"

It's sick, how big a smile that puts on his face. And he actually licks his lips. She manages to keep her expression cool while he fishes out a mostly flaccid imitation of a giant, limp albino slug. She says, "Smile!"

The idiot does. Keeping her phone aimed his way, she says, "Talk to me about"—*giggle*—"our working relationship, Mister Flem."

He smiles at the phone. "Really, considering the intimate nature of how we'll work together, don't you think you should call me Harvey?"

"How intimate will it be ... Harvey?"

He gestures to his exposed junk. "Little Harvey is all yours, anytime you want." He looks like he's about to drool. "I insist."

She zooms in for a close-up and then back to a wide shot. "This is perfect."

Then she turns off her phone camera, goes back to the other side of the desk, and puts her papers in the folder. Patch's cat smile now seems to be beaming at her. She beams back at him.

Flem sits forward, his face twisted into puzzlement. "What are you doing?"

"Leaving." She holds her phone up. "I delivered what I promised for the advance, a treatment for a film about me and my vampire cat. I even reshaped it into a stupid musical for you. So, I believe I have fulfilled my part of the contract and"—she waggles the phone—"I don't expect to hear anything from you about paying it back, if you get my drift."

His mouth gapes open and she slips her phone into her pocket and pats it.

Flem fumbles his way to putting Little Harvey in its place and zipping up, then leans forward. "You'll never work in this town again!"

Patch walks across the desk until he's in Flem's face, then bares his fangs and hisses.

Flem shoves with his feet and zooms backward until his chair bangs into the wall behind him. A framed poster of *The Cat from Outer Space* falls on his head.

Chuckling as she gathers Patch, Meg wheels and leaves his office. She's tempted to slam the door, but then she thinks it will burn even hotter if she smiles and closes it gently. So, with a saccharin "Ta-ta," that's what she does.

Outside, in the reception area, Jeanine smiles at her and puts her palms together in silent clapping. She adopts a businesslike tone when she picks up a pen. "Do we need to schedule another appointment, Ms. Murrow?"

The twinkle in her eyes makes Meg smile. Jeanine writes something on a slip of paper while Meg says, "I don't think that will be necessary."

She hands Meg the paper. "Have a nice day, then." She leans close and whispers, "You just made mine."

Meg reads the note: "Email me those pictures?" followed by an email address. Jeanine raises her eyebrows when Meg looks up at her. Meg flashes the OK sign and tucks the note into her pocket. Jeanine gives her another round of silent applause.

When Meg drives them home, it hits her that she's managed to blow her connection with a major motion picture studio. She's sure Flem will soon have her name blacklisted all over Hollywood, so she figures she no longer has a screenwriting career ahead of her.

But, considering the fetid swamp she just left, maybe that's not a bad thing.

She strokes Patch's soft fur. "Hey, buddy, want to come with me on tonight's delivery run?"

"Mrrowf."

She drives on, a smile on her face. It may have been a defeat, but it sure feels like a victory.

21: Nick

Nick has never been on the wrong side of the law, yet here he is, sitting at the defense table for a preliminary hearing because he's accused of being on the wrong side of the law. Faith Vasquez, the union lawyer provided by the Los Angeles Police Protective League, busies herself next to him, making notes on a yellow legal pad. He guesses she's about his age, so she isn't long out of law school. She looks sharp in a black suit coat and skirt, but he hopes she isn't dressed for a funeral. She has assured him that although he has a totally loser case, she'll do her best for him anyway.

The district attorney, Reginald Smith-Arrow, lean and sharklike in a black pinstripe suit, stands by the prosecution table while he awaits the swearing in of his first witness. There's a touch of gray at the temples of his swept-back hair, but honestly, it looks a little too perfect to be natural. Although it does add a hint of gravitas.

Faith had told Nick that in prelims the prosecution often calls only one witness—the one they are sure will nail the case closed when the trial comes. That's usually all it takes to send a case to trial. He doesn't have to prove that Nick is guilty, just that there is probable cause to go forward.

The witness being sworn is one Manfred Chesterfield, medical examiner, former friend.

Judge Isaiah Washington is a kindly-looking man with short, curly, white hair and skin the color of a latte, but he had given Nick a major glare when the reading of the indictment came to desecration of a corpse. And it got even more hostile when the obstruction of justice part came along.

When the swearing in is done, Reginald approaches Manny, holding a sheet of paper. "Doctor Chesterfield, what is your relationship with the Los Angeles Police Department?"

"I'm a medical examiner. Going on seven years now."

"Excellent. Were you called to the Hollywood Community Police Station on May nineteenth of this year?"

"Yes, I was." Manny looks sharp in a suit, and his manner is serious and authoritative.

"What was the reason you were called to the station?"

"A female prisoner was reported to have died in her cell."

Reginald points at Nick. "Is that the officer who arrested the woman, Detective Nicholai Silver?"

"Yes."

"Was the female prisoner he incarcerated named Megan Murrow?"

"As far as I know. That was the name in the logbook. I did not see identification."

Manny sticks to the truth and stays away from shades of gray. If it isn't a fact, he won't testify to it. That's probably not good for Nick's case, but he's in favor of Manny's honesty.

Nick glances at his attorney. Faith is focused on the testimony, but to his amateur ear, there's been nothing to object to.

The prosecutor says, "I see. Can you describe the deceased woman?"

"I no longer believe that she can be described as deceased."

Nick's eyebrows shoot up, and so do those of his lawyer and the prosecutor. The judge scowls. Reginald recovers quickly and doesn't go down that rabbit hole. "Please describe the woman in the cell."

Manny raises a hand. "But—"

"Describe her, please."

Manny sighs and then delivers a precise description of Meg as she was that night—blond, Caucasian, twenties, petite, attractive, dressed in gray sweatpants and a blue tank top. And lying on the cell floor.

Reginald lifts the sheet of paper in his hand. "Your Honor, may I enter Exhibit One into the record, a report made by Mister Chesterfield regarding the prisoner in question?"

The judge asks Faith, "Any objections?"

"No, Your Honor."

"Exhibit One is admitted."

The prosecutor hands the paper to Manny. "Is this a true copy of your report filed on May nineteenth regarding your examination of the woman found in the cell at the Hollywood Community Station?"

Manny examines it. "Yes."

"That is your signature at the bottom?"

"Yes."

"And does this report state that the female was deceased and that you ordered an autopsy?"

Manny glances at Nick and then says, "This is not the complete—"

"A yes or no answer, please. If I want to know more, I'll ask you."

"But—"

"Although *but* is a one-syllable word, as are *yes* and *no*, it is neither of those words. Yes or no, please."

Manny looks to Nick and then to his attorney. He peers at her, then raises his eyebrows. He points at himself. When Nick looks to Faith, she's frowning at Manny. Nick says, "I think he wants you to ask him something."

She shakes her head.

The prosecutor sounds irritated. "Your answer?"

Manny returns to the prosecutor. "Yes. But—"

"No more questions." Reginald turns to Faith. "Your witness."

She shakes her head again. "No questions."

Manny's mouth drops open, and then he squints at her as if he's trying to beam thoughts into her mind.

The judge says, "The witness is excused."

Manny strides from the witness chair to the defense table. His voice low, a scowl on his face, he asks Faith, "Why didn't you question me?"

She gives him as good as she gets. "I don't ask questions I don't know the answer to."

Manny glances at the D.A. and lowers his voice even more. "There's a witness who can prove Nick is innocent."

That gets her attention. Her gaze sharpens, and she opens her mouth to speak.

The judge calls from the bench, "Excuse me, but we have a hearing in process here."

Faith stands. "My apologies, Your Honor, but I've just been informed of a possible rebuttal witness."

"A rebuttal of what?"

Manny leans close and whispers in her ear. She addresses the judge. "The report stating that the alleged deceased woman was—and is—in fact deceased."

Reginald moves like a shark, easing closer to them with fluid steps. "I object, Your Honor. This is nonsense. There was a cadaver, and it was taken to the morgue for an autopsy. We have a witness who will confirm that."

Nick's not sure the old groper, Steve, will make a good witness. But still, he's another stone tied around his neck.

The judge says, "I'll decide what is nonsense and what is not." He gazes at Faith. "Am I correct in assuming that you need time to produce this witness?"

"Yes, Your Honor."

"I'll give you until tomorrow morning at ten a.m." He raps his gavel on the bench. "Adjourned."

In the morning? If Manny is talking about bringing Meg in, that's an execution. It has to be someone else. "Who are you talking about?"

Manny looks to him. "I think I can get her to come in and testify."

Faith says, "Who?"

This is so wrong. Nick says, "Tell me it's not Meg."

Manny shakes his head. Faith snorts. "Megan Murrow? That's crazy. Dead people can't testify."

Manny lifts his shoulders, lets them drop. "That's your opinion. But I am also a certified medical examiner who knows his business. She can clear your client. In person."

The lawyer's mouth gapes. "You put my career on the line asking the judge for a delay to bring in a *corpse* to ... to do what?"

"Testify."

The door to the judge's chambers closes behind him just as Faith whirls and calls out, "Judge Washington!"

He doesn't return. Faith puts her hands on her hips and scowls at Manny.

Can Manny make this happen? "Do you think she'll do it? Where is she?"

Faith gathers up her pad and pen, stuffs them in an attaché case. She hits Nick with a .45 caliber glare. "You seem generally rational, but if you are trying to get me to present a corpse to testify, then I'm going to file a petition stating that you lack the mental competence to stand trial."

"She's not dead. Fully, that is."

She levels her gaze at him. "Your captain indicated in your file that you were long overdue for a psychological exam. You ask me, what you're long overdue for is commitment."

She starts away, but he catches her elbow. "Please. She's done nothing."

"Of course. She's dead." She snorts. "Or is she a zombie?"

Manny laughs. "That's silly. Zombies aren't real. She's a vampire."

Faith rips her arm out of Nick's grasp and stalks toward the exit. Nick calls after her, "I can prove that she is. I have news reports from CNN. Witnesses."

She keeps marching.

Manny calls after her. "According to one definition of death in California law, Meg Murrow is most definitely *not* dead."

That's a surprise to Nick, but a hopeful one. Manny knows his business.

Faith slows. She stops. She turns around. "In the law?"

Manny nods. She says, "You guys sound very convincing."

Nick takes a step toward her. "We're not nearly as convincing as the evidence is."

She sighs. "I have a feeling I'm the one who's overdue for a shrink. But, okay, you have an hour. Let's go to my office."

In Faith's office, Nick gives her the rundown on Meg's history back in Illinois. They call up the CNN article on her computer. Manny explains the relevant statutory definition of death to her and then tells her she needs to have a physician and a fingerprinter there in the morning. He stresses that special arrangements have to be made to put drapes over the courtroom windows.

Faith gives him a you're-kidding look. She drips sarcasm when she says, "Yeah, that's cool. I simply request drapes over the windows because she's a vampire."

Manny says, "No. You request them because your witness suffers from extreme polymorphic light eruption and photophobia."

That gets a little grin from Faith. "I'm impressed. I hope the judge will be as well." She sobers. "One thing, though. We are *not* going to be talking about vampires. I do not want either of you to include that in your testimony. We'll all be held in contempt of court."

As they get up to leave, she mutters, "And in contempt of sanity."

22: Patch

I think Meg gets a lot from the symbiotic relationship we cats have with people, but to be honest, so do I. Such as right now, curled up in her lap while she reads a mystery novel in the A.V.A. lounge, herself curled up on a recliner. It's a wonder to me that humans are entertained by stories about murder. Cats focus on one simple thing, all the time—living as well as we can. Although *living* is an iffy description of what I'm currently doing.

But we've had a round of V1 juice, and we're on the other side of the pleasure puddle that follows a good hit of blood and into the feels-good part. Meg's free hand drifts her fingers over and through my fur in a random scratch/caress, and it's yummy. I bring up a soft purr to let her know how well my symbiosis is going.

She lowers her book—I don't know why it's called a book, it's a little flat computer thing with a screen—and says, "Hey, Patch, what are you thinking about?"

Nothing. Absolutely nothing. And I have no urge to start up any thinking. *Go back to your reading. Keep scratching.*

"This book is about a handsome detective who reminds me of Nick." Her voice softens. "It was so nice at the beginning, when I met him. It made me think about the possibility of a relationship."

She can stop that thinking right now. A breather can never be completely safe around a vampire—a relationship could come to a messy end with an attack of blood hunger when the only available source of blood is holding your hand. A smart breather would carry a stake at all times, if not wear a suit of armor, and seems to me that would be a damper on a relationship.

Her musing does warrant a comment, though. So I take a breath, look up and make eye contact, bare my fangs, and hiss.

She laughs. "Somehow I knew you'd say that. Yeah, I know it's impossible. Anyway, not only is Nick a traitor, but he'll soon be locked up. I'm much better off with fictional detectives."

She pulls out her phone. "Speaking of relationships, do you want to see the pics and the video I took of our friend Harvey Flem and Little Harvey?"

I hiss again. I saw the real thing. Disgusting.

She scrooches her hand into the pocket under me and pulls out a slip of paper. I could resent being disturbed, but one must make allowances for one's associate. She says, "I almost forgot to send them to Jeanine."

I return to nothingness as she types on her phone for a bit and then says, "There. She'll no doubt get a kick out of those."

As she slides her phone back into her pocket, it rings. Her ringtone is the Grateful Dead's "Don't Murder Me," a sentiment I hold dear. She checks the screen and then answers with, "Hey, Manny."

She listens, then says, "Sure, we can talk. Patch and I are in the lounge on the third floor. Grab a veggie V1 from the break room on your way."

I have continued peace and quiet for another ten minutes or so, and then Manny comes in and takes the chair next to us, a bottle of V1 in one hand. Meg says, "You look relaxed for a guy whose friend is on trial. How's that going?"

I tune partway out, choosing to sink into a shallow catnap, the kind where we doze but keep track of things going on around us, our eyes closed but our ears swiveling like little sonar installations. He says, "It's tough. The prosecution won't let me testify as to the true nature of your, er, ailment and condition."

"Can't Nick's lawyer ask you about that?"

"Yeah, but she's reluctant to do that because I'm a friend of Nick's. She's not sure my testimony would be credible after the prosecutor attacks it."

Meg sighs. "I don't know why I say this, but I do hope Nick will be okay."

Manny gazes at Meg. "There is one witness who would be credible."

"Then call him."

"Her."

She holds up a hand. "Oh, no—"

"You could shatter their case in one minute."

I come out of my drowse and utter a low growl.

Meg's fingers start stroking me again, and it almost causes me to lose track of what we're talking about. "Nope. A, he betrayed me; b, I'm on the run; and c, the exposure could literally kill what's left of me. And he betrayed me."

"But you could save Nick."

"Who's going to save me? And then, when word gets out about me being a vampire, I'll be traced to the A.V.A. They don't tolerate any publicity, and I'll lose my job."

"I'm sure I can help you find another night job. And you've got your deal with Disney."

Her chuckle is sour. "No, I blew that one up last night."

"I'm sure I can get Faith—she's Nick's lawyer—to avoid talking about vampires. In fact, I know she absolutely doesn't want that to come out."

"But what if it does?"

He studies Meg for a long moment. "What's the matter with you? You weren't afraid when you ran for sheriff in Bloomsburg."

Ah, those were the days, campaigning for vampire protection with Meg, appearing on television, starring in commercials ...

Manny puts a hand on her knee. I'm tempted to bury a few claws in it. He says, "Please. Maybe we can set up witness protection for you."

I've seen that in movies, and the bad guys always find out and then kill the witness. In our case, witnesses. I sit up in Meg's lap and glare at Manny.

Meg's voice is sad but firm. "No. You know the bad guys always find out and then kill the witness." She strokes me and adds, "Witnesses."

What I said.

"Besides, the hearing is in the daytime, right?"

"You managed that before, when the captain sent his men after you."

"Sure, in a life-or-death emergency."

"Maybe I could rig my car—"

"Stop right there." Meg sets the book aside and holds me while she uncurls her legs and returns the recliner to upright. I settle back down on the new lap configuration and she says, "What is there about 'no' you don't understand, Manny? Do I want to expose myself to society? No. Do I want to wave a blood-red flag and invite a horde of Devils to my place? No. Do I want to go back to jail where I will die? No. Do I want to lose my job? No. Do I want to go up in smoke? Negatory on that, too."

"You won't go to jail. We can probably get you immunity."

"Probably? Can you *guarantee* I won't be accused of some bloody murder just because I'm a vampire? Perhaps you remember that I already have been. They could throw me back in jail for that charge. It's still on the books."

Since he clearly can't promise anything, he changes tactics. "You know Nick's not guilty. What about justice?"

"You saw what happened to me, and now I'm hiding out—I can't even go to my own home. When I see some actual justice for me, maybe. But, like you said the other day, I'm not going to hold my breath." She stands, lifting me with her. "You helped me, Manny. Your warning was the difference between being here now and being a pile of ashes and bones tossed into a dumpster. I'd do it to save you, but Detective Benedict Arnold?" She shakes her head.

Manny sighs, then stands and faces her. His eyes are moist the way humans get when they become emotional. "I'm afraid he'll lose hope."

Meg laughs, but her words are bitter. "Hope? That's not in my lexicon, and I know a lot of words."

23: Nick

Even though Nick is out on bond and spent the night at home, he didn't sleep well, so he's slumping in his chair at the defense table, waiting for things to get going. But then his adrenaline surges when the prosecutor coasts up to his table and gives him a sharky grin. He doesn't see Manny or Meg, but they're probably waiting in the witness room. The courtroom feels cozier with the heavy black drapes Faith arranged to have over the windows.

Faith arrives and sets a cup of black coffee before him. That ought to get him totally up to speed. He leans close to her as she takes papers and a pen out of her attaché case. "What do you think?"

She gazes at him for a long moment, then shakes her head. "Not good."

"But Meg—"

"I just saw Manny. There will be no Meg. She turned him down, and I've wasted the time of the doctor and the fingerprinter I rounded up. We're going to have to try to do it with only your testimony and Manny's."

He's taken her through everything he knows, which is why she thinks his case is hopeless. He'd hoped ... there'd been a little bit of connection with Meg ... but then he'd pretty much blown it when he betrayed her, hadn't he? He had no right to expect that she'd come to his rescue. He can't think of any reason why she should.

There are downsides to being a righteous ass.

The bailiff calls out, "All rise." Judge Washington enters from his chambers and takes his seat behind the bench. The bailiff calls the court into session and reminds them of what they're there for, and the judge turns to Faith. "Ms. Vasquez, do you have your witness?"

She stands. "Unfortunately, Your Honor, circumstances have prevented her appearance this morning. The defense requests this hearing be postponed for one day in order to subpoena—"

He holds up his hand. "There will be no subpoena for an alleged witness. This court is not going to do your job for you, Ms. Vasquez, and you have wasted enough time. This is, after all, a preliminary hearing. You can round up your witness for the trial."

Uh-oh. Sounds like the judge has already made up his mind.

He signals to the bailiff, who comes closer. "Why's it so dark in here?" The judge points to the drapes over the windows. "Who did that?"

The bailiff gestures at Faith. "A request from the defense, sir. Something to do with a medical condition of their witness."

"The one who's not here?"

Faith sighs. "Yes, Your Honor."

The judge taps his gavel. "Open them up." As the bailiff hurries to pull back the drapes, the judge turns to Reginald. "Does the prosecution rest its case?"

Reginald rises. "No, Your Honor. In preparation for the assumed new rebuttal witness, we have brought in an additional witness. I would like to go ahead and have you hear his evidence."

The judge says, "Very well."

The prosecutor signals to the bailiff. "Please call Captain Numm to the stand."

The bailiff goes to a door, steps into an adjacent room, and emerges to guide Captain Numm to the witness chair.

The captain looks sharp and professional in a black suit, and he almost marches into the room, shoulders squared, chest out. After he swears to tell the truth and sits in the witness chair, he sends Nick his patented death-gaze. Nick gives back a smile and a wiggly-finger wave in return, and the captain's neck turns red just above his collar.

The prosecutor elicits the captain's name, rank, and duties. Funny, he doesn't include harassing a junior detective in the list of things he does.

"Captain Numm," says Reginald. "Did Detective Nick Silver arrest the woman known as Megan Murrow for the murder of Flint Ascot?"

"He did."

"Did he lodge her in the Hollywood Community Police Station?"

"According to our records, yes."

"Did you see Ms. Murrow there?"

"No."

"Where did you see her?"

"Later, in the coroner's office."

"And then what happened?"

"Detective Silver took her away."

Faith scribbles on her yellow legal pad.

Reginald eyes Nick with a squint. "Did you subsequently request her location from Detective Silver?"

"I did."

"Did you learn it?

"He gave me an address, but she was not there. I believe Silver had something to do with that. Specifically, a warning that we were coming."

"To be clear, you believe the detective obstructed justice, namely the retrieval of a corpse that was missing from the morgue."

"Yes. And that his removal of the cadaver also violated California laws regarding the care of and disposal of a dead body."

Reginald's grin is smug. "So, to summarize, Detective Nick Silver arrested a woman who subsequently died in her cell, removed her remains from the morgue, then refused to disclose their whereabouts. Is that correct?"

"Yes. And there was the vampire part."

An almost inaudible groan emerges from Faith.

The prosecutor seems surprised and blurts, "Vampire?"

The captain gives Nick a twisted smile in his version of mirth. It's an ugly thing to see. He actually chuckles. "He told me the woman he arrested, the one who died in her cell, was a vampire."

Faith's face has grown grim. She really didn't want the subject to come up.

The captain holds up a hand. "You want to hear what's really nuts? He claimed the murder victims he was investigating, two of our most beloved movie stars, were"—he glances at the judge as if inviting him in on the joke—"also vampires. Ha!"

At this the judge raises his eyebrows and Reginald chuckles, shaking his head in an isn't-that-sad way.

Reginald says, "I believe that about sums it up. No more questions."

Nick has always thought the captain was a straight shooter, dedicated to the law and the truth despite his differences with Nick's approach. Although the captain hasn't directly lied today, his omissions add up to a completely false picture. He has managed to tell a lie while telling the truth.

A glance at his attorney shows Nick the fight he wants to see—she grits her teeth and scowls at the captain. She rises and approaches him.

"Captain Numm, you said that Detective Silver 'took her away.' Correct?"

"Yes."

"How? Did he carry her?"

"No."

"Put her body on a gurney?"

"No."

"Then tell us how he took away the corpse of an approximately hundred-pound woman?"

The flush at the bottom of the captain's neck rises a bit.

"Uh, she appeared to walk."

Faith smirks. "*Appeared* to walk? Do you believe it was an optical illusion?"

"Uh, no."

"Did she also *appear* to be dead?"

"No, I can't say that she did."

"But you say she was deceased, is that correct?"

His voice rises, and there's a plaintive tone in it when he says, "The medical examiner's report states that, and I do not have the expertise to gainsay his professional medical opinion."

"Did you speak with her?"

"I did."

"Did this dead person respond?"

He pinches his mouth shut, then nods.

"Would you please verbalize your response?"

The captain says, "She did."

"Was her speech slurred or incoherent?"

"No. It seemed normal."

"Wouldn't you expect that a dead body would have some debility in speaking?"

Reginald calls out, "Objection! Calls for speculation."

"Sustained."

Faith says, "Okay, we'll stick with the facts." She takes a step closer to Numm. "So you talked with a dead woman and watched her walk away?" Faith's smile is anything but friendly. "What is she, a zombie?"

The captain laughs. "That's silly. There's no such thing."

"Then how can you account for this walking, talking dead woman?"

"I can't. But a report is a report, and the law is the law. I follow the rules religiously."

The judge leans forward. "Captain Numm, are you sure about this ... this walking, talking cadaver?"

"I've sworn to tell the truth, Your Honor."

Faith says, "I have one more question." Her smile is sharp enough to cut the captain's throat. "Has anyone recently questioned your sanity?"

"Objection."

"No more questions for the lunati— witness, Your Honor."

Nick doesn't know about the judge, but if he were him, he'd be thinking that the captain is about a quart short of a bucketful. That can't be good for the captain's credibility. His allegations sound like the ravings of a, well, Faith nearly said it best—a lunatic.

Judge Washington addresses Reginald. "Redirect, counselor?"

In contrast to the captain's increasingly red features, Reginald has gone a bit pale. "No, Your Honor. The prosecution rests."

"Ms. Vasquez? Do you wish to proceed, or does the defense rest?"

She looks at me. Without Meg, we both know my case is still in the toilet. She lifts her chin in just the way Meg does when she's going into a fight and turns to the judge.

"I call to the stand Manfred Chesterfield."

The bailiff fetches Manny from the witness room. When Manny takes his seat, the judge says, "Remember, Mister Chesterfield, you are still under oath."

"Yessir."

Faith says, "Did your initial report on Ms. Murrow state that she was dead?"

"Yes, it did."

"After examining her in her cell and deciding that she was deceased, did you later see her at the county morgue?"

"I did."

"Did you talk with her?"

"I did."

"This seems contradictory to me. Do you continue to say that Ms. Murrow was dead?"

Manny smiles. "Yes. And no."

Faith raises her eyebrows in what looks to Nick like fake surprise. Here it comes ...

"How can that be, Doctor Chesterfield? Dead and alive at the same time?"

"It depends on which definition of death you use."

Faith steps to the defense table and picks up a sheet of paper and then approaches the bench with it. "I offer defense

Exhibit C, a copy of the California statute defining death." She hands it to the judge. "Permission to share it with the witness?"

The judge peers at it and nods. "Granted."

She hands it to Manny. "Would you read the highlighted text, please?"

Manny takes it and reads, "'Section 7180. An individual who has sustained *either* (1) irreversible cessation of circulatory and respiratory functions, *or* (2) irreversible cessation of all functions of the entire brain, including the brain stem, is dead.'"

Faith nods. "So there are two definitions of death. And you say that Ms. Murrow's condition does not satisfy both?"

"According to my initial examination, she had sustained an irreversible cessation of her circulatory and respiratory functions. She did not breathe, nor did she have a heartbeat. For a human to continue living, those functions have to be autonomic. In her, they were not."

"That meets part one of the definition, then? The dead part?"

"There aren't two *parts* to one definition, there are two distinct definitions. In the statute, it's an either-or situation. In this case, since Ms. Murrow was walking and talking, it is clear that by definition she exhibited full function of her brain and, for that matter, the rest of her body."

"So, by California law, she is both dead and not dead."

"Technically. However, I can't imagine putting a person who walks and talks into a coffin and burying her. Furthermore, to all appearances other than certain autonomic body functions and her body temperature, she appears to be quite alive."

"No further questions. Thank you, Doctor."

Clutching a sheet of paper, Reginald almost storms over to Manny. "Your testimony is contradictory, is it not?"

"Not at all. It's the law that is contradictory—in this case."

"According to one of the definitions of death, Ms. Murrow could be classified as 'human remains,' could she not?"

"Yes, if you want to ignore—"

Reginald holds up a hand. "Thank you." He refers to his sheet of paper. "According to the California Health and Safety Code, and I quote, 'Every person who knowingly mutilates or disinters, wantonly disturbs, or willfully *removes* any human remains in or from any location other than a dedicated cemetery without the authority of law is guilty of a misdemeanor.' Did you see the accused remove the body of Megan Murrow?"

"I wouldn't call it removing."

Reginald sighs. "What would you call it?"

Manny shrugs. "Ah, escorting?"

"Did the accused have an active role in the ... taking away of the body of Megan Murrow?"

"Yes."

"No further questions."

Faith whips a sheet of paper from one of her folders and stands. "Your Honor, I have here the California code regarding the disposition of human remains."

She hands the judge the sheet of paper, and he reads it. When he looks up to her, he says, "Thank you, Ms. Vasquez."

She takes it back and turns to Manny. "Since you were present at the time, Mister Chesterfield, was the alleged corpse ever asked by Captain Numm or the coroner about her wishes regarding the disposal of her remains?"

"Not within my hearing, Your Honor."

She glances at the paper. "According to the law, the preference of the deceased concerning the disposition of his or her body is a right that is strictly enforced."

She gazes at the prosecutor. "If, then, Ms. Murrow is dead as Mister Smith-Arrow says she is, then she has a say in what happens to her body."

Reginald frowns. Then he shrugs as if to agree.

Faith turns to Manny. "Doctor Chesterfield, did the alleged dead person volunteer her intentions for her remains?"

Manny says, "No, not directly."

"What do you mean by 'not directly'?"

"Seems to me that walking herself out of the morgue to go to her home was a clear expression of her wishes as to what she wanted to happen to her body."

Faith addresses the judge. "Your Honor, I believe that her, well, body language clearly indicated her desire."

The judge chuckles. "I can't disagree, and I'm sure that if Ms. Murrow were here to express her wishes, she would be quite direct about her disposal. But she is not, and we are not allowed to speculate." Judge Washington shakes his head. "There are times when the letter of the law seems to have lost its meaning, and this is one of them. It's too bad no one asked the alleged body her views on what to do with her remains."

"No further questions, Your Honor."

The judge tells Manny that he is excused. "Ms. Vasquez, do you have more witnesses?"

"I do, Your Honor. I call Nicholai Silver to the stand."

24: Meg

For Meg, morning at the A.V.A. comes after a restless night with no writing to do since her screenwriting career turned to crap. She and Patch are safe in her little A.V.A. hideout, so she decides to start working on what else she can do besides drive a delivery van.

Sitting in the one chair in the room, she says to Patch, who occupies the bed, "Okay, Patch, let's tally our assets." He looks at her, and then returns to licking his nether region. "To start with, I have one remarkable cat for a friend, and I have to admit that he's movie-star good-looking."

He stops licking and gazes at her. Does she know her kitty, or what? "We have a car. A job. A place to stay."

Patch has nothing to say to that. Probably thinking of the disadvantages they have to deal with. Let's see: Blacklisted in Hollywood. Hiding out. Cops after her. Undead.

Her cell phone buzzes. "Meg here."

"This is Marvin."

The director of the L.A.A.V.A.? "Yessir. What can I do for you?"

"I think it would be best if you came up to my office."

Why is it that she doesn't think this is going to be good news? She brushes her hair, puts on a clean T-shirt, scoops Patch up, and heads for the fourth floor

Marvin looks like he's in his twenties, but he's been a vampire for fifty years. Glued wounds scar his face and hands, and he limps—a brace on one leg mostly compensates for a fractured knee. But he's one of the good guys. His office is functional, not grand at all, steel desk, ordinary side chairs, just one dim lamp on with the windows covered by black curtains.

She likes his voice, deep and rumbly. "Hello, Meg. I've been saddened by your trouble with the Devils." He indicates a chair.

She sits and settles Patch on her lap. They gaze at Marvin. She touches the bandage over her cut. "Doc Lovely is going to help me with the cut."

"Will he do that soon?"

"Day after tomorrow."

He shakes his head. "I hoped it would be sooner."

"Sir?"

"Did you know that we monitor police radio channels? We're always on the lookout for any mention of vampires who might need help."

Oh, shit. "Nosir. I didn't."

"We have just learned that the police have an APB out for you. For murder?"

Oh God. She's toast. "I'm falsely accused, sir. I've done nothing." Patch squirms, and she realizes she's twisted the loose skin on his back into a knot. Letting go, she strokes him. He relaxes, but she doesn't.

Marvin folds his hands and gazes at her. "I believe you. The problem is, innocent or not, you can do us great harm. You know our policy. Zero exposure."

Yeah, she knows. "I do my best, sir."

"Can you imagine what the Devils would do if they learned our location after you're captured and they trace you to the A.V.A.?"

They'd line up to stab them with stakes as they come and go.

"We cannot let them connect you to us." He sighs. "There's no easy way to say this. You must leave here. Today. Now. If they come for you, you can't be here."

"But I'm a member of the A.V.A. I have a right to shelt—"

"Your membership in the A.V.A. is revoked and all record of it expunged. As far as the A.V.A. is concerned, you don't exist. And never have."

If she had tears, they'd be streaming. "This isn't right."

His face saddens. "It isn't. But it is survival."

He stands, picks up an envelope from his desk, and comes around to her. "Here's five hundred dollars. I've arranged to have the Rescue Squad take you anywhere you want to go. They will bring your car to you after dark once you're back home."

"Home? With the police prowling around?"

He spreads his hands in helplessness. "Wherever you want to go. They're at your disposal. It's the best I can do. But you have to leave. They'll meet you in the garage in five minutes."

Even though she once told Nick that she had no place to go, that wasn't entirely true. There is a place of last resort, even though it's a long way away. Back in her room, she calls Mom. "Hey, Mom. It's me."

"Oh, sweetie, it's so good to hear from you. Your dad and I were talking about you just the other day, wondering if you've met a nice vampire boy out there."

"No, Mom, no nice vampire boy." Maybe one day she'll tell her about the almost-nice breather boy who is about to become a convict. "Listen, uh, would it be okay if I came back home for a little while?" It will take only a few nights of driving, and the cash Marvin gave her should get her there. Patch looks up at her. He's never liked her dad.

Mom says, "What's wrong, dear?"

"Oh, just a change in plans. Turns out this place isn't for me."

"Well, of course you can come back. I should tell you, though, that we've turned your room into a gym and TV room."

"You and Dad are working out? That's great."

"Well, I work out. Dad watches. Sometimes me, most of the time the TV. But we can put in a cot if it won't be for too long."

Meg starts to resent losing her room, but stifles that. It isn't "her" room, it's theirs. And she's glad Mom is taking care of herself. "It'll just be until I can figure out what to do next."

"Um, I do an hour workout every morning."

Got it. "I'll be up and out of your way, Mom, no problem."

"You are such a sweetheart. Let us know when you'll get here and we'll be all ready."

"Just one thing. I'll have to have heavy curtains on the window. Preferably black to block the light."

"Oh, good! I love shopping for fabric. Maybe something with tiny pink flowers?"

She has to laugh. That's so her. "Just as long as it blocks light. Love you, Mom."

After she ends the call, she packs up what little they have there. She shares a bottle of V1 with Patch while she works on what to do and where to go. Her place? They could have it staked out. A motel, maybe, until nightfall and they'll bring her car?

A knock on the doorframe. There's Sayed, her Rescue Squad buddy, and his partner Gloria, dressed in their crimson A.V.A. coveralls. "Where to, Meg?"

Gloria adds, "We're so sorry to hear what's happened to you. We'll do our best to keep you safe."

Keep her safe. Sure, with all the forces of good and evil after her, keeping her safe should be easy peasy. At daytime.

"Patch, you know in the movies when they say, 'We're doomed'? I now know what they meant."

This just isn't *right*.

She hates that.

Hmm.

25: Nick

Although Nick thinks Faith's cross-examination of Manny did the best job possible of poking holes in the prosecution's story, he doesn't feel like she was able to prove their charges were wrong. And it's demonstrably clear that Nick at least helped, if not "took," Meg from the coroner's office, even though she walked out.

So there still seems to be enough "evidence" to take him to trial, and who knows what will happen then. And he's not confident that he'll be able to help his situation by testifying. He has to tell the truth, and on the face of it, there is a case to be made that Meg is a corpse and he helped her escape. It's all circumstantial, but he doesn't have any alternative circumstances that oppose their theory.

As he's sworn in, he's not really nervous. On edge, though, for sure. Faith has proved to be quite astute thus far, so he's hoping he can convince the judge of his innocence.

He wonders what Meg is doing right now. Maybe sleeping, since it's daytime. Or working on her screenplay. He should be taking notes on this trial—he might be able to use it in his own script. In his cell.

Faith approaches him. She looks relaxed and confident, two things he wishes he were. She takes him through his bona fides as a detective—the police academy, the three years as a patrolman, and eventually his promotion to detective. When she gets to that part, she asks, "Have you ever solved a murder case?"

Nick's glad the captain isn't there to go from his usual simmer to a boil. "I was able to solve the case of Vernon Memmer, the Napkin Killer."

"Is it true that you did so after Captain Numm told the press that Memmer was not a suspect?"

"Yes."

"How did the captain feel about that?"

Reginald raises his hand. "Objection. This calls for speculation."

The judge sustains the objection.

"Were you rewarded for solving the case?"

"I wouldn't call it a reward."

"And why is that?"

"I was sentenced ... that is, assigned to desk duty for six months."

"You did not see that as a reward?"

"I hated desk duty, and I told the captain that."

"And his response was?"

"He laughed and said that if I kept yakking about it, he would tack on another three months for insubordination."

"It sounds as if your relationship with the captain is not easy."

"It never has been."

"So, do you think that could have something to do with him bringing these charges against you?"

"Objection. Calls for speculation."

"Sustained."

He didn't need to answer; Faith had made her point about the captain's bias toward him. But what did that prove?

"Why didn't you leave, get another assignment?"

"All requests for transfer have to be approved by the captain. I filed ten applications for transfer during those six months. He would crumple the paperwork into a ball, come to my cubicle, toss it into my wastebasket, and shout, 'Two points!'"

She frowns and shakes her head. Out of the corner of my eye, he sees the judge do the same. Faith asks, "Then why not quit?"

Just the mention of quitting tightens him up, but he tries to keep cool. "I love being a detective, getting crooks off the street, protecting people. Doing my duty. It's my life."

"Is that what you were doing with Ms. Murrow—protecting her?"

"Of course."

"The captain has stated a belief that you warned her before officers were sent to bring her in. How is it possible to warn a dead person?"

He can't help but smile at the way she phrases her question. "I don't see how it would be."

"Did you warn the deceased?"

"I did not."

"Please describe your relationship with Ms. Murrow, alive or dead."

Relationship? First he was her arresting officer. Then he was her rescuer. Then he was her betrayer. Then she told him to get lost. There were things—a number of things: looks, voice, wit, toughness—that he liked about her and found appealing. But a relationship? No chance. He answers, "There was none, there is none."

"So your sole motive in taking Ms. Murrow from the morgue was your duty to protect."

"That, and the fact that the captain ordered me to."

Both the judge and Reginald perk up and lean forward. Faith feigns shock. "But wait. I thought the captain said you took the body, implying that you stole it, and now you're telling me he ordered you to take her away?"

"Yes. To the best of my memory, he said, 'Take her home, take good care of her.' I thought at the time that was a very considerate thing for him to do."

"Can you confirm this?"

"Doctor Chesterfield, the medical examiner, and the office supervisor were present. And I'm sure the captain would testify to his order."

"No further questions, Your Honor."

Wow. She managed to puncture all of the captain's allegations against Nick. Maybe there's hope after all. But here comes Reginald.

"You did not warn the corpse about the captain's orders to bring her in?"

"I did not warn Ms. Murrow."

"Did you tell anyone else?"

He has to tell the truth, so he does. "I told Doctor Chesterfield."

"Could he have warned her?"

"Yes—if, as Ms. Vasquez points out, it's possible to warn a dead person."

"We will have to ask him. Now, about whether the body in question is alive or dead, what do you think she is?"

"Just like the captain, I don't have the expertise to determine that."

"You're alive, aren't you? I think that makes you an expert in being alive, don't you?"

"Only as far as myself."

"What about death? In your work you come across bodies all the time. Is Ms. Murrow's body similar to or different from the dead people you've seen?"

"Well, she walks and talks, and they didn't. They couldn't. So I'd say different."

"But she reportedly has no pulse and did not breathe. Wasn't that also true of the dead people you've seen?"

"Yes."

"So you don't know whether Ms. Murrow is alive or dead, correct?"

He doesn't know what to say, primarily because he doesn't know the answer. So he keeps his mouth shut.

"Let me put it this way. The medical examiner said that she was dead, correct?"

"Yes, but—"

"Therefore, if she is indeed dead, then when you first arrested her, you moved a corpse in order to put it in jail. In short, *under the law*, at the time of the arrest you desecrated her mortal remains, did you not?"

This guy is getting to him. No, he's already gotten to him. He stands and clenches his fists. "NO!"

Reginald puts on a smug smile. "No further questions." He turns his smile on Faith, then sobers and addresses the judge. "Your Honor, in light of the evidence presented here today, none of which has been contradicted by physical evidence, the state moves that this case be taken to trial."

The judge says to Nick, "The witness is excused." Nick goes back to the defense table, and the judge addresses Faith and him. "Mister Silver, although the testimony in this case makes my head ache, what the prosecutor claims is accurate. There has been no physical evidence or testimony to prove that the charges are invalid. Therefore—"

The double doors to the courtroom bang open and a man shouts from outside. "Halt! You can't go in there."

A woman in a crimson jumpsuit barrels through the doorway, towing behind her a gurney with a black body bag on it. Her outfit reminds him of Meg's uniform, but there's masking tape over the place where Meg had had her name embroidered and another piece where the V1 logo was.

A big man in the same disguised uniform pushes the other end of the gurney. The woman calls out, "Faith Vasquez?"

Faith raises her hand. "Here."

The woman hurries to Faith and hands her a piece of paper. The courtroom erupts with a buzz of questioning voices.

The judge bangs his gavel and shouts, "Order! Order in the court!" He glowers down at Faith. "What is the meaning of this?"

Faith raises the piece of paper. "Excuse me, Your Honor. My witness has arrived. I believe she can clear things up. May I proceed?"

"What witness is that?"

"The woman at the heart of this trial, Megan Murrow."

The judge glares at Faith. "Is that a body bag, Ms. Vasquez?"

"I believe that is what it's commonly called."

"The courtroom is hardly a place for a corpse."

The gurney stops next to her and Faith goes to the bag. "Precisely our point, Your Honor."

The buzz in the court starts up again, but the judge bludgeons it into silence with his gavel.

Reginald objects. "There is no reason for an additional witness at this preliminary hearing."

The judge says to Faith, "As I recall, this witness is to rebut testimony solicited by the district attorney. Is that correct?"

"Yes, Your Honor."

"Please proceed."

Faith gestures to the bailiff. "Call Megan Murrow to the stand."

26: Nick and Meg

Faith starts to unzip the body bag, and Nick leaps out of his chair and covers the opening she has begun with his hands. "Stop!"

He points at the uncovered windows and glares at Faith. "Do you want to kill her?"

Faith swallows hard and backs away a step. "I forgot." She turns to the judge. "Your Honor, may we please have the drapes closed as tightly as possible?"

"For what purpose?"

Faith goes to their table and fishes out a piece of paper. "To block the sunlight, sir. My witness suffers from"—she reads from the paper—"'extreme polymorphic light eruption and photophobia.' She will suffer intense pain and injury if exposed to sunlight."

Reginald moves next to the gurney, his upper lip contorting as if he smells something rotten. "Objection, Your Honor. I object to these theatrics. There's no need for all of this drama."

The judge peers at him. "Are you certain?"

Reginald nods. "Absolutely."

"So then, Mister Prosecutor, you are familiar with what"—he looks to Faith—"what polywhatever—"

Faith reads, "'Extreme polymorphic light eruption.'"

"Thank you, Ms. Vasquez. That sounds horrible. So, Mister Smith-Arrow, you know about this condition and what sunlight will do to her?"

Reginald takes a step back. "Uh, no, Your Honor, I don't."

"I see no reason to take the chance of harming her. Objection overruled. Bailiff, please have the drapes closed. Tightly." He looks to Faith. "Would it help to dim the lights somewhat?"

"Yes, sir. It will make Ms. Murrow much more comfortable."

The judge leans back. "So, we are going to see this alleged cadaver in action." He smiles and rubs his hands together.

After the drapes are closed and the lights dimmed, Faith unzips the body bag and helps Meg sit up and swing her legs off the gurney. She hops down, then reaches back and retrieves her cat from within the bag.

Meg looks great. She is trim and professional in a khaki skirt and blue blazer over a button-down white shirt. She scans the room and spots Nick. Her expression remains cool. Faith gestures toward the witness chair, and Meg takes a seat, settling Patch into her lap. The disguised A.V.A. people wheel the gurney and body bag out of the courtroom, but then return and take seats at the back. Good, Meg isn't stuck here until after dark. Assuming that she will be free to go when she's finished.

Nick is dumbfounded that she's taken such a huge risk. And, he hopes, he is about to be eternally grateful to the human being he once sentenced to certain death.

~

Given the time it took for the A.V.A. Rescue Squad to haul Meg down there after they stopped at her apartment so she could change, it has been a while since she drank any V1. She doesn't have a pulse, but if she did, it would be pounding as she sits at the table. She has a few rolls of Death Savers in her purse because she doesn't know how long this will take. It's entirely too long already—she must be crazy, exposing herself to the whole world like this. But she couldn't live, as it were, with herself if she let Nick be railroaded, no matter how she feels about him. And it's not all that clear to her how she does feel about Nick. At this point, she guesses the best way to sum it up is "approach-avoidance."

The amazement on his face when she came out of the body bag was kinda fun. He hasn't stopped staring at her since. She doesn't mind, and she still likes his face, and his eyes. She's reminded again of their first meeting and the instant attraction she felt then. Another no-fly zone for vampires. Impossible, she knows, but it would have been nice.

The woman who is Nick's lawyer sticks close as Meg goes to the witness chair. The judge, a nice-looking man with white hair, addresses her. "You are Megan Murrow?"

"Yes, sir."

Reginald stands. "Your Honor, surely the court is not going to simply take this person's word for that. She could easily be an actress look-alike the defense has hired."

Nick's attorney—Faith is what Nick said her name is—addresses the judge. "Your Honor, the defense is well aware of this issue. Not only do we find the prosecution's suggestion that we would strive to deceive the court repugnant, but we have witnesses who are fully prepared to establish that Ms. Murrow is who and what she says she is."

The judge says, "Because this court does not wish to spend time without that certainty, we will postpone her testimony until then." He tosses a sharp-eyed glance at the prosecutor.

"And, yes, it was repugnant to suggest that the defense is behaving unethically." To her he says, "Ms. Murrow, please take a seat at the defense table."

Thrilled at not having to endure the third degree just yet, she hurries to a chair that Nick pulls out at the table. Faith's chair is between her and him, and that's fine with her. Patch seems content to sit in her lap.

"One more thing, Ms. Murrow. The cat. Why is it here?"

"For his safety, Your Honor. He suffers from the same, er, ailments that I do. I know he's safe with me, but I don't know if he is at home because of the way the police keep barging into my apartment."

He nods. "Very well." To Faith he says, "Your evidence of identity, Ms. Vasquez?"

She slips a piece of paper from her folder and takes it to the bench. "Defense Exhibit A is a certified copy of the fingerprint sheet made when Ms. Murrow was arrested and incarcerated in the Hollywood Community Police Station."

Reginald has a bit of a sneer in his voice. "I have no objection to the exhibit, Your Honor, but what are we supposed to do with it? Have her hold up her hands and we compare?"

As the judge accepts the paper, Faith rolls her eyes at Reginald. "Please call Mister Thomas Arnold to the stand."

The bailiff fetches a reed-like, bespectacled, middle-aged man from the witness room. He carries an attaché case, which he holds on his lap when he takes the chair. After he's seated and sworn in, Faith gets right to it.

"Who is your employer, Mister Arnold?"

His voice isn't much more than a whisper. "The Los Angeles Police Department."

"And your role there?"

"Fingerprint analyst."

"Have you been doing this for long?"

"Twenty years."

Faith addresses the bench. "Your Honor, we wish to have Mister Arnold take Ms. Murrow's fingerprints now and compare them with those on record."

The judge waves his hand in approval. "Please proceed."

Faith comes to her and gives Patch a quick scratch on top of his head. "With your permission, Ms. Murrow?"

What the heck, they already have her fingerprints, so the hole she's digging for herself isn't going to get any deeper. Yet. "Yes, go ahead."

The fingerprint guy comes to the defense table, opens his attaché case, and takes out a pad of blank paper and an ink pad. With smooth precision, he rolls the fingertips of her right hand, one by one, in the ink and presses them to the paper. The prints look perfect.

He gives her a cloth. "This will take the ink off, miss." He lingers for a moment and gazes at her face. His eyes tighten as if he's trying to see into her. But his expression is warm, not hostile. "Are you well?" He gestures at her hand. "You seem ... chilled."

She nods. "I do have a condition that causes sudden drops in body temperature." She gives him a smile that she means. "Thank you for your concern, but I'm all right."

He nods, then takes a magnifying glass from the case and returns to the witness chair with it and the prints he's just taken.

Faith goes to the bench again. "Your Honor, if I may have the fingerprints previously entered into evidence?"

The judge hands them over and she gives the sheet to the expert. "What is the name of the person whose fingerprints are on this?"

He reads, "'Megan Murrow.'"

Faith nods. "Please compare the two sets of fingerprints, Mister Arnold."

Squinting through the magnifying glass, he compares each of the prints on the sheets one by one, and then does it all over again. At last he looks up. "The prints on both sheets are identical."

Faith smiles and holds out her hand for the papers and hands them to the judge. "May I enter into evidence defense Exhibit B, the fingerprints taken here in the courtroom this morning?"

"Objection."

"Overruled."

The judge accepts the papers, and Faith turns to Mr. Arnold. "So, judging by the fingerprints of that woman sitting there"—she points at Meg—"are the fingerprints on the original report in the arrest record from the same person?"

Mr. Arnold says, "Yes."

"No further questions, Your Honor."

The judge asks the prosecutor, "Do you wish to cross-examine, Mister Smith-Arrow?"

The sneaky-looking man at the other table gulps a couple of times. He reminds her of a cat coughing up a hairball, luckily a thing that never happens with a vampire cat, since they don't shed. She gives Patch a rub on his shoulders, and he rewards her with a soft purr.

The prosecutor finally spits out, "Not at this time, Your Honor."

The judge excuses the witness, and Nick's lawyer is ready. "Please call to the stand Doctor Elma Johansson."

The bailiff escorts Mr. Arnold back into the witness room and emerges with a striking blond woman in a white suit. She carries a black valise like the ones you see doctors carry in the movies. Once the woman is sworn in and seated, Faith goes to work by establishing Dr. Johansson's experience as a general practitioner with a practice in North Hollywood.

Then she gets to the nitty-gritty. She points at Meg. "Doctor, have you previously met or seen the woman sitting there with a cat in her lap?"

She gives Meg a good look and then shakes her head. "No, I have not."

"Judging by what you can see from where you sit, does she appear to be a physically normal human being?"

"Without examining her more closely, I have to say yes."

"From what you see, if you were to examine her, would you expect to find a heartbeat?"

The doctor smiles. "Of course."

"What about breathing?"

"Well, she'd have to be breathing, otherwise she would be dead. She's petting a cat, so she is clearly not dead."

Reginald says, "Objection. There is no—"

"Overruled," Judge Washington says. "We wish to hear this witness."

Faith addresses the judge. "Your Honor, there has been evidence offered that Megan Murrow is both dead and alive."

Dr. Johansson whips her attention back to Meg. She leans forward and narrows her eyes, and Meg feels the doctor's focus on her intensify.

"We have asked Doctor Johansson here to do an examination to determine the facts regarding Ms. Murrow's moribundity."

The judge leans forward. "I could not be more curious, and Ms. Murrow's state of being is certainly germane to this case. Proceed."

"Doctor, would you please examine Ms. Murrow in regard to her heartbeat and her breathing?"

"Of course." The doctor takes her black bag to the defense table and takes out a stethoscope. Meg opens her blazer so the doctor can listen to her chest.

She places the little round diaphragm right over Meg's heart. She listens, and then her eyes widen and her eyebrows rise and her forehead creases. She listens for longer than five heartbeats and then shifts the diaphragm to the other side of Meg's chest and listens again. She frowns and shakes her head, then puts it against her own chest. After a moment, she nods.

The doctor takes Meg's wrist and puts her fingers where she would ordinarily detect a pulse. She frowns at that, too.

"One more thing." She pulls out an electronic thermometer and presses the tip to Meg's forehead. After she looks at the reading, she puts the thermometer to her own forehead and examines the result. "You are room temperature."

Meg doesn't have anything to say to that.

"How do you feel?"

She takes a breath. "Okay." She looks around at all the eyes staring at her. Another breath. "Actually, I'm a little stressed right this minute, but otherwise okay."

"Thank you." The doctor restores her instruments to her bag and returns to the witness stand.

Faith goes to her. "Doctor, what are the results of your exam?"

"Astonishment."

27: Patch and Nick

Meg eases her grip on my neck fur. I'm not saying it was tight, but if I were a breather cat, I'd have choked to death ten minutes ago. Snuggled in her lap and leaning against her belly, I feel her core muscles soften. I wasn't as stressed as she was, but there is relief for me, too.

Nick's lawyer finishes up with the doctor. "Doctor Johansson, tell us if the woman you just examined is alive or dead."

You know, that's a really good question. As far as I'm concerned, sitting here watching and thinking, I'm alive even though I'm pulse-challenged.

The doc gazes at Meg, and then she shrugs. "I really can't say. I guess that, since she moves and speaks, I'd come down on the side of alive if I had to. But then I'd have trouble reconciling the fact that her body is the same as a corpse in terms of vital signs."

That's another one of the crappy parts about being a vampire kitty-cat; other than being an active fellow, I'm no different from roadkill.

Faith says, "I have no further questions, Your Honor."

The judge asks the angry-looking guy at the other table if he has any questions. He gets a no and tells the doctor, "You're excused, Doctor Johansson. Thank you."

As the doctor leaves for the witness room, Faith turns to us. "I call to the stand Megan Murrow."

Meg's grip on me tightens again as if I'm some kind of security blanket. That's okay, because sometimes she's mine. She carries me with her and has to let go with one hand to place it on a book when she swears to tell the truth, but her hand is soon back to holding a handful of me when she takes a seat beside the big desk the judge sits at.

Nick's lawyer says, "Ms. Murrow, there has been evidence introduced that you are dead and that you are alive. The law states that the deceased's wishes regarding disposal of their remains are to be honored. If you are currently dead, how do you wish for your remains to be disposed of?"

Meg's eyes widen, and then she sobers. "I prefer to keep them with me, because I currently have a use for them."

The judge snorts and almost stifles a grin that quivers around the corners of his mouth.

"There has been testimony that Detective Silver took your remains from the county morgue. Is that true?"

Meg thinks for a moment, then shakes her head. "No. He gave me a ride home, but I wouldn't call that being taken."

"Was it his idea to take you home?"

"He suggested it, and then his captain told him to do it."

"So you are now residing in your home?"

"No. I'm staying away from there."

"Why is that, Ms. Murrow?"

"My understanding from conversations with Detective Silver and with Doctor Chesterfield—"

"The medical examiner?"

"Yes. They let me know that Captain Numm is, well, after me and wants to bring me in."

"And you have a problem with that?"

"I am a law-abiding citizen and want to cooperate with the police, but if I am taken from my home anytime it is daylight, I will suffer great harm because of my affliction with extreme polymorphic light eruption and photophobia."

Wow, I'm impressed that she can remember that, much less say it. And it sounds so medical and official. Almost as if being a vampire is a disease. Which, considering that the vee-bug started with a virus that turned into a parasite, I guess it is.

Faith says, "Detective Silver has been accused of warning you that police were on the way to pick you up, and that's why you were not there when the police arrived. Is that correct?"

"No."

"Why weren't you there?"

"I was at my place of work, the American Veggie Association. I drive a delivery van and have to prepare ahead of time."

"Are there people who can testify that you were there?"

"Yes. I spoke with Sarge, another driver."

The traitor detective signals to the attorney, and she says, "May I have a moment with my client, Your Honor?"

"Granted. Just keep it brief."

She goes to Nick, listens to him, looks back at us, and then nods. When she returns, she says to Meg, "Ms. Murrow, you mentioned that Captain Numm is 'after' you. Do you know why?"

"He"—she points at Nick—"that detective, arrested me for the murder of Flint Ascot, the movie star."

"Ms. Murrow, did you kill Flint Ascot? I remind you that you are under oath."

"No, I did not."

"Where were you when the murder happened?"

"I don't know when it happened. The only two places I go are my home and my work. Oh, and I was also having meetings at the Disney campus."

The lawyer's eyebrows rise. "Screenplay?"

Meg nods. Then says, "Yes."

"Thank you, Ms. Murrow. No further questions at the moment." She says to the judge, "I would like to recall Detective Silver to the stand."

The judge looks to the nasty guy at the other table. "Do you have any questions for this witness, Mister Smith-Arrow?"

"No, Your Honor."

The judge says, "Proceed, Ms. Vasquez." Meg and I go to our chair. Nick keeps his focus straight ahead when he passes us on the way to the witness chair.

After Nick sits and the judge reminds him that he's still under oath, Faith says, "Detective Silver, what did you tell me a few moments ago?"

"That I would like to withdraw my statement regarding the charge of murder against Ms. Murrow."

"Why is that?"

"I no longer believe she had anything to do with the crime. For one thing, a second murder that exactly followed the pattern of Mister Ascot's killing happened while Ms. Murrow was securely locked up in the Hollywood Community Police Station. It could not have been a copycat crime, because the first murder had not been reported by the press."

"On what evidence did you arrest her?"

"Something that I also now feel was entirely inadequate. She had delivered a juice product to the victim a month prior to his death as part of her regular delivery route."

"That sounds a little on the circumstantial side. Is there any physical evidence that connects her with the murder?"

"With the victim, yes, but not the killing. Her fingerprints were on a bottle containing a beverage in his refrigerator."

"That sounds incriminating."

"The trouble is, because she delivered other refrigerated beverages to Mister Ascot in the past and stored them in his refrigerator, she could have touched the bottle then. But the murder took place at a different location, not at the victim's home."

"So you want to withdraw your statement regarding suspicion of her for the death you were investigating?"

"Correct."

Reginald stands again. "Once again, I object, Your Honor. What does all this about another crime have to do with this hearing? The detective is the one charged with crimes here."

The judge raises his eyebrows at Faith. How does she deal with this?

She says, "This goes to several issues, Your Honor. It can be argued that the arrest of Ms. Murrow was the inciting incident in the string of events that led to Captain Numm leveling charges at Detective Silver. Had there been no arrest, the captain's persecution of her would be totally unfounded. She would not have been in the jail where she was taken for dead. She would not have been brought to the morgue. She would not have been labeled a dead person in the first place, a fundamental aspect of the charges against Detective Silver."

"Objection, Your Honor." Reginald approaches the bench. "This simply has no direct bearing on the issues at hand."

The judge says, "I'm inclined to agree with you, so the objection is sustained." He gives Reginald a stern look. "On the other hand, Mister District Attorney, if I were you, I would give serious thought to having the charge against Ms. Murrow dropped. Ms. Vasquez makes a good case."

Wow. Nick has really done us a solid with this one. My feelings about him dial down from sheer hatred to mere distrust, a significant decline.

Faith says, "Your Honor, because Megan Murrow can be legally considered alive, then the charge against Nicholai Silver for desecrating a corpse is invalid. Because Meg Murrow has declared that she wants her remains to remain with her, that charge is similarly invalid. Because Meg Murrow voluntarily left the morgue with Detective Silver, who was under orders from Captain Numm, the charge against him for removing her remains is invalid. Since he did not warn her about her impending arrest, the obstruction of justice charge is equally invalid. I move that all charges against Detective Silver be dismissed."

Except for Meg and me, everyone there seems to be holding their breath as the judge gazes at us. Then he nods and raps his gavel. "So ruled. Case dismissed."

Meg stands and we go toward Faith.

Reginald races up to the bench. "But, Your Honor ..."

The judge aims his gavel at Meg and me. "Mister District Attorney, I believe you have some work to do regarding the unsupported charge of murder against Ms. Murrow, is that not correct?"

Reginald's shoulders slump. "Yes, Your Honor." He turns, then goes to Faith and proves that he's not a complete ass by offering his hand for a shake. "Good work, Ms. Vasquez."

"Thank you."

When he leaves, Nick steps to her. "*Thank you* seem like such paltry words. Great job, Faith."

Meg says, "That goes double for Patch and me."

Faith scratches me under my chin. I definitely like this woman.

Meg turns to Nick. "For the second time, Nick, I find that I'm in your debt. Thank you."

"Coming forward the way you did, I'm the one who's thankful. Listen, can I—"

A shout comes from a room off to the side. "SILVER!" A man built like a box charges up to Nick and pokes a stubby finger into his chest. "You traitor!"

"Just doing my duty to tell the truth, sir."

"Your duty is to the law! Your duty is to me!"

I brace myself for this guy to start foaming at the mouth.

He rants on. "But not anymore! No. As of now, you're fired. I don't give a damn what the police union will say, you are gone from the Los Angeles Police Department!" He turns away and then swivels back around and pokes with his finger again. "And if they somehow, God forbid, find a way to keep you on the force, I will make it four kinds of living hell for you."

As if finally becoming aware that everyone in the room is staring at him, he downshifts to a more businesslike tone. "When you leave here, go to the station, clean out your things, and give your case files to Murphy."

Nick's face is both angry and sad.

Some days you get peanuts, some days you get shells. But usually not both on the same day.

The captain turns away, then stops so suddenly, he tips forward. He wheels back and aims a finger at Meg. "That's her! Hey! That's her!" He searches the room. "Bailiff, arrest this woman—we have an APB out on her. She's wanted for murder!"

A tap from the judge's gavel catches everyone's attention. The district attorney nods and goes to the captain. "Actually, Captain Numm, we are dropping that charge. She is free to go."

The captain clenches his teeth, his fists, and finally his entire body. He vibrates, his cheeks puff out, and his already red face reaches a fine hue of crimson. Unfortunately, he doesn't explode. He blasts up the aisle and out the courtroom doors as if propelled by hyperfart thrust.

Meg grins all the way across her face. She's free! Nick's reaction is different. Thunderstruck, I'd call it.

He goes to her and starts to reach for her shoulders, but she stiffens, and he drops his hands. "Did you know there was an APB out on you?"

She nods.

He sweeps a hand around to indicate the courtroom. "Why did you take the risk?"

"It wasn't right. I couldn't live with that."

"I have no words. You are one brave human being."

She laughs, a sound that brings joy to my fuzzy little heart. It's been a tough few days. "I think bat-shit crazy is the more accurate description." Meg carries me to the back of the courtroom where the Rescue Squad waits with the gurney. Both Sayed and Gloria are beaming.

Gloria says, "Good going, Meg. Until today, this was just a job. Now, well, I'm proud to be on your team."

Sayed smiles. "Where to now?"

Meg lifts her nose in the air, adopts a wonderfully snooty tone, and says to him as if he were her limo driver, "Home, Jeeves, home."

Sayed chuckles as he opens the body bag.

~

Even though the trial is over and Nick is a free man, he's not a cop anymore. That's all he can think about as his mind hops from despair to depression and back again. He's not a cop.

He doesn't know what to do with himself. Oh, he'll apply to other places, but they'll check him out, and he'll wager he'll be persona non grata five seconds after Captain Numm fulminates what he thinks of him.

It isn't far from dawn when he stops pacing in his apartment and decides to change into his other "self" and go for a run. Getting in touch with his animal nature always clears his mind, which has now started flip-flopping around Meg and what she is and what she isn't and what she's done and what she hasn't done and what he's done and what he should have do—

Enough.

But her face keeps appearing in his mind's eye, along with a warm feeling that, if she weren't a vampire, would mean ... something impossible that he can't think about.

It's not a long drive to the Hollywood Reservoir. It has areas that feel almost natural, especially on a miniature peninsula that sticks out into the lake. The tip is forested and is an island of peace and quiet in the midst of always-churning Los Angeles.

After he *shifts* and leaves his things in the car, he trots down the road toward the trees, his claws loud in the quiet as they click on the asphalt. Soon, the clean scent of water refreshes him. A nice, cool drink at the shore sounds exactly right. He might even jump in for a swim.

Then another scent, bloodlike, wisps at him. It's not fresh blood. It becomes stronger the farther out he gets on the peninsula. It's the smell of Patch and Meg. And the masher murder victim. Vampire.

The odor leads him to tire tracks that go toward an open area populated by scrub bushes. And there it is, another giant red hockey puck of bloody flesh and bones. This one is thicker than the last, but otherwise looks the same.

He races back to his car, *shifts*, gets dressed, and calls Manny. The medical examiner is groggy when he answers. "Yeah?"

"It's Nick. There's another masher murder out here at the Hollywood Reservoir. I figured you ought to know about it."

Manny's voice is immediately sharp. "Who else did you call?"

"Nobody yet. I figured I'd call Murphy and disturb his sleep."

"Will you stick around?"

"Got no reason to, and I don't need the captain any madder at me than he is."

"Do me a favor. I can be there in ten minutes. Wait for me. You're the only one besides me who's seen this before, and I could use your insights."

"What about reporting—"

"I'll call it in after we've had a look. Anonymous tip."

"Okay. I'll be here."

After Nick gets a flashlight from his car, he paces near the mess on the ground, more black than red in the predawn light, trying to ignore the bloody smell. Finally, Manny arrives. He shuffles up, a cup of coffee in one hand and a flashlight in the other, his jaws opening and closing with a bad case of the yawns. They stop as soon as he plays his flashlight over the mound of remains. "How does the killer do this? Why does he do it? Why is it round? What has the power to crush a human body this way?"

Manny's questions are all good, though Nick is also wondering how human this body is. Will it go up in smoke like the other one? He runs his flashlight beam over bits of clothes, crushed and broken bones, and red meaty stuff. The light catches something that's too perfectly straight to be a bone. When he gets close enough, it turns out to be a long, pointy stake.

The sun will soon crest the nearby trees and shine here. "Manny, take a look."

Manny joins him and crouches down to study it. "Looks the same, doesn't it?"

"Yeah. Did you ever figure out a cause of death for the first one?"

"Couldn't, not with all the mashing that was done." He stands. "No way to tell if the stake had anything to do with it."

Sunlight touches the edge of the remains, and they step back to watch while it crosses them, the red stuff steaming and smoking into ashes. He'd say they have another former vampire here.

Oops, can't think that way. He's not a cop. He doesn't have anything here.

Now that the red gunk is gone, it's easier to examine the bones. Manny gets a pair of tongs from his van to fish out the stake and shows Nick the top. It has D.V.L. stamped on it. It goes into an evidence baggie.

Nick circles around, peering into the tangle of bones, Manny going the other way. When he rounds the bones and is almost to him, Manny points. "Something shiny in there."

With the help of his flashlight to dispel shadows, Nick makes out finger bones splayed out with a ring on one finger. When Manny gets it out using his tongs, it's a big ring, gold with a ruby stone. Nick has seen it before. Score one for Meg; it looks like the Devils bagged a certain newbie vampire. He likes the irony of it being one of their own. The ring goes into an evidence bag.

"Tell Murphy to look into a guy named Hunter. Vincent Hunter."

"You know him?"

"Know of him. He's one of those D.V.L. crackpots. A murderous kind of guy."

He gazes at the bones. "At least he was. I've got—I *had*—an APB out on him for that homeless man with a D.V.L. stake in his heart."

Manny takes out his phone. "Thanks, man. I knew you'd be a big help."

Somehow his words don't lift Nick up as he heads for home.

Home alone.

Meg's face smiles into his thoughts again.

28: Meg and Patch

Back home in her apartment after having been cooped up with Patch in a room at the A.V.A. and then in a body bag twice, Meg now understands her kitty-cat's need to get outside and roam. She's bored with television—everything on it is so dull compared with her current life. Which, she wishes, was a whole lot less interesting. She can't focus on how to salvage her writing career long enough to stop veering off to everything that has happened.

But tonight is a night to celebrate. She's safe at home, she did the right thing, the charges against Nick were dropped, and it looks like she'll be out from under the baleful glare of Captain Numm. Since champagne is now out of her realm of possibilities, she heats up a couple bottles of V1 for Patch and herself.

She doesn't usually give Patch a whole bottle at once because he seldom drinks all of it right away, but he gets one tonight. He might want the leftovers for dessert later, and she's taking the night off. She's ravenous for some reason—perhaps all the pressure and stress—and comfort food is in order. For her, that means a second bottle of V1 juice.

After the sweet "pause" that follows a liberal helping of blood, she's energized ... but still lacking. She almost feels human again, but *almost* doesn't cut it tonight. She peers out the living room window at the swimming pool. Since it's after midnight, the pool is empty with the lights off and likely to stay that way.

God, she wants to FEEL something! She drinks another bottle of V1, and she swears she has near-normal body temperature after the V1 spreads through her. She rubs her bare arms, and the feeling is delicious. She wishes she could indulge more often, but even with her A.V.A. employee discount, V1 juice is far too expensive, and now she has lost that, and her income is zero.

But tonight ... When she opens the front door, cool night air wafts across her face and arms, the breeze caressing her skin. She steps outside—most of the apartments around the pool are dark. The lack of pool lights creates a cozy sense of privacy, but there's enough moonlight to highlight the water's surface with soft shimmers.

Patch comes out with her and sniffs the air, then strolls alongside the pool.

Carpe diem. She goes back inside, takes off her clothes, and digs out her bikini. She has the bottom halfway on when she flashes back to skinny-dipping as a kid, the water flowing over her skin the way the air does tonight. The bikini goes back in the drawer.

Thanks to the California sun during the day, the pool is between warm and cool, and it feels as if she's enveloped by liquid silk when she eases into it. Taking her time, she strokes the length of the pool, and the smoothness of the water streaming over her skin makes her shudder with pleasure. Such a little thing. She misses the little things. They're what make up life, aren't they, all the little things adding up.

Patch sits beside the pool, no doubt thinking humans are crazy for getting all wet. She doesn't care—she feels alive for the first time since she was turned into a vee.

The yappy little dog goes off. *How about some peace and quiet here?*

The dog's yapping winds down, but Patch's ears swivel toward the back corner of their building. He stands and faces it. Something's coming this way, but she doesn't hear footsteps. There's no time to dash into the apartment, but why should she bother? She's up to her neck in the water, and as dark as it is, no one can see that she's naked. She's content to watch.

Then Patch sucks in a breath and hisses when a huge coyote pads around the corner. A memory drifts up from the night the Devil attacked her. A coyote getting between her and the Devil, growling at him. There's a blurred image of her knocking the animal out of her way as the blood hunger drove her toward her prey.

Another image comes to mind. The coyote sitting a few yards away, a knapsack on its back, watching when she finished with the Devil and let him go.

Now it goes to her living room window and peers in through the gap in the drapes.

Patch slinks close to the edge of the pool, and then he growls, long and low.

The coyote spins and stares at the pool. She could swear it's thinking, making a decision. Then it trots to a tall shrub and eases into the deeper darkness of its shadow. It works its front legs until the knapsack is on the ground, and then it lies down.

And then the impossible happens. Its skin bulges as things move under it. The coyote's slender legs thicken and lengthen, and its fur retreats into pink skin. In less than a minute the changing stops and a slender, naked person lies by the shrub. The creature stands and reveals the narrow hips and broad shoulders of a man.

His back to her, he reaches into the knapsack, pulls out a pair of briefs, pulls them on, and turns to face her.

It's Nick. He smiles. "Surprise."

Holy shit. *Surprise* is a pitifully inadequate description of the cascade of thoughts crashing through her mind, amazement leading the pack. Patch must be freaking out—no, when she checks him, he's just sitting calmly as if he's seen this before.

Nick says, "I was out for a run and somehow I ended up here." He strides to the pool. "That looks like fun. Mind if I join you?"

She has apparently lost the capacity for speech as her mouth continues to gape. She guesses he takes her silence for consent, because he slips into the shallow end of the pool and comes toward her.

She regains her tongue when he's a couple of yards away. She holds up a hand. "That's close enough."

He stops and looks to Patch. "Hey, cat."

Patch says, "Mrrrah."

Nick turns back to her. "Nice night. The water feels good."

What is he doing there? "I take it this is not an official call. You aren't exactly in uniform."

"If you remember the captain's last words to me, there is no more 'official' or uniform."

Oh, yeah. She thinks of Nick's passion for his work. "I'm sorry about that. It wasn't right, what he did."

He shrugs. "Consequences. Consequences for things *I* did that weren't right. I should never have arrested you in the first place, and I'm sorry for that."

"You were doing your job, I guess." She doesn't feel sympathy for him, but she doesn't think his intent was malevolent, either.

"I'm also sorry that I couldn't warn you about the cops coming for you. It was a great relief when I learned they couldn't find you."

Her chin comes up and she glares at him. "Why didn't you let me know they were coming?"

"I was ordered not to. It was my duty. It was the law."

She lets out a snort. "The law? How about justice?"

"They're the same th—"

"They are NOT the same thing. I went to that court and risked my hide to help you because what was happening to you was unjust. If all that mattered was 'the law,' I could have happily watched you be *legally* tried and convicted for things you didn't do."

He stiffens. "I followed the rule of law—"

"This is not about the rule of law, it's about justice. It's about the right thing to do."

He twists his mouth in a grimace of discomfort, but he doesn't give way. Apparently, he's as stubborn as she is. "I swore an oath to be true to the law." He raises his brows and spreads his arms as if to say *don't you understand?* "How else do we know what's right? Following the law is our best guide."

"In my experience, your guide sometimes loses its way."

He sighs. "Then what is our guide?"

"Don't hurt people. Try to help the best you can."

He grits his teeth. "We have to be true to the law, not live according to bumper-sticker slogans."

How can he be so insulting and obstinate? It pisses her off, and she splashes water at him. "Being true to *justice* should be the goal. History is filled with bad laws that were unjust—that hurt people. When you see injustice being created by the law, should you then still obey it?"

"We have to obey the law. Otherwise we're savages."

"Yeah? Slavery was once 'the law.' The people who ran the Underground Railroad to help slaves escape were criminals in the eyes of 'the law.' But in the eyes of justice? Not so much."

He raises his hands in surrender. His voice is soft, his gaze too. "I am deeply sorry for the harm I've done you. If I can make it up to you in any way, I want to."

Her gaze settles on his hands, and hers twitch under the water. They want ... *she* wants human touch. She closes the distance between them. Her shoulders rise above the water, and she doesn't care if he can see that she's naked. "Hold out your hand."

He does. She lifts hers and takes his.

Oh.

His warm skin on hers sends a rush through her. She closes her eyes and savors it.

He says, "You're warm."

If she steps closer, her breasts will do more touching. They want to.

She steps closer, and they do, grazing his torso. She lifts her head and gazes up at him. He's so tall. And so warm. Her fireplace.

He leans down, and it feels like he's heading for her lips.

She tiptoes, heading for his.

Oh no.

She puts her hands on his chest and pushes back until she has to tread water. This can go nowhere. "Thanks for the apology. Now, if you don't mind, I'd like a little privacy to enjoy my swim."

"Megan."

The soft way he says her name gives her a shiver.

"Couldn't we, I don't know, I'd like to—"

Temptation threatens to heat her emotions to a boil. "No. It would be stupid. And dangerous."

"I'm not with the police anymore. You're safe now."

"I'm not thinking about me."

"Nothing has happened."

"So far." Thinking of the night at the observatory, she says, "You've seen what can happen, haven't you? It was you at the observatory."

He nods, then shrugs. "Maybe I'm willing to take the chance."

She doesn't know why she cares enough about this guy to be concerned for his safety. "Listen. You and me can't be." She pulls the bandage off her cheek and swims back to him, close enough that he should be able to see.

He winces when she points at the rip in her cheek. "See this? It will never heal. Never, ever. And this is nothing. What if I break a bone? It would never ever heal."

His shoulders sag. She guesses he gets it. A sharp pang of disappointment appears out of nowhere as if this were an argument that she doesn't want to win, but she brushes it aside. "Now, please leave me alone."

Nick straightens, and his gaze is fond. "If you ever need me."

He trudges out of the pool, steps into the shadows, then strips out of his wet underwear, modestly facing away from her. He does have a nice butt. Which goes along with the rest of him. Her nipples tingle, but she tries to ignore them. She doesn't succeed.

With quick efficiency, he wrings out his briefs and stuffs them into his knapsack. Once he has the knapsack on his back, he lies down, contorts and shrinks and expands and furs back into a huge coyote.

One last blue-eyed look at her and he trots away. The yappy dog explodes again. After quiet returns, a mournful coyote howl cuts into the night. Into her heart.

Yeah, her too.

~

I watched Meg swim furiously for a good half hour after Nick left. I suspect she burned up a lot of blood, because now she's sound asleep in the bedroom. She found *The Cat in the Hat* on television for me before she lay down, but that's been over for a while.

It's hard not to think about the detective being some kind of werecoyote. But he likes Meg, and I guess that explains him trying to defend her from the Devil at the observatory.

Not that she needed defending. Yeah, the nutjob managed to put that gash in her cheek—it broke my heart to hear Meg tell Nick about what injuries are like for vampires—but the guy got what he had coming.

I can still see the hole closing in his throat after Meg exercised her pitiful excuses for canine teeth on him. Maybe it's thinking of feeding that brings on a whimper of blood hunger in my mind, so I head for the kitchen, glad that she didn't put away my V1 leftovers.

As I lap up the blood—not as good when it's cold, but the hunger needs it—I think about Meg's injury. If only it could close up like the hole in the Devil's throat did.

Wait a minute. There isn't a hole in my throat where Meg tore into it when we first, uh, met ... and there's no hole in her throat from when she was bitten ... Holy moly!

My hunger is satisfied enough so that I don't need all of the blood in my bowl. The lethargy is coming on, but I fight it. After dipping a front paw in the blood to soak the fur,

I three-leg it into the bedroom and manage a clumsy leap onto the bed.

I'm in luck, she sleeps on her back. Which is okay because she never snores. I hate snoring. I dab my bloody paw on her cut, careful to fill the wound with fresh blood, and then sit back to watch while I lick my paw clean.

Nothing happens. Ah, well, it was worth a try. I step closer to lick the blood off of her face, but her skin is changing. Just like the Devil's neck wound, the blood around the wound is absorbed and the gash on her cheek closes. A minute later, it might as well have never been there.

I'm flexible enough, in the way cats are, to pat myself on the back. Then I curl up next to Meg and purr myself into a catnap.

29: Meg

Meg smiles. It feels good to have Patch at her side and be driving her delivery route again. She's looking forward to falling into a nice, boring routine. It took some convincing to get the A.V.A. to reinstate her.

What did it was that if she was exposed, it would be as a hero vampire for saving Nick. Marvin had never considered the value of *positive* stories about vees. He finally decided that, if their discovery happened, having one ready to tell wasn't all bad. She has moved back home, and things have been quiet so far.

She's not giving up on writing, though. Movies may be off-limits now, but a novel isn't, and you can do whatever you want in a novel. No vambies required. She glances at Patch. Maybe it would be fun to chronicle their adventures as vampires. How about a blog? She'll call it vampirekittycat.com.

A glance into the rearview mirror tells her that her cheek is actually healed. She still can't believe it, but she's happy to go with it. Who says no to a miracle?

She pulls into the driveway to Doc Lovely's house and stops before the wrought iron gates. They are the only opening in a ten-foot wall covered with bright green bougainvillea flush with red blossoms. It gives the place a lovely floral touch while guarding it with thousands of thorns. Nobody's climbing that wall, and the gate is just as tall, with sharp points on the iron bars at the top.

Slipping out of the van, she uses the intercom to let Doc know they're there. He says, "Great! I have a prospective client joining me right now, but come find me in the house after you've finished your delivery and we'll take care of that cut."

A click from the speaker lets her know he's gone before she can tell him the good news. No matter—it will be even more fun to see his reaction when she shows him her healed cheek.

The gates swing open. When she gets back in the van, she checks her face in the rearview mirror for the seven thousandth time to reassure herself that it's real. As she traces the place the cut used to be, she says to Patch, "Why me? Why should I be the first vampire ever to heal? And how?"

Patch shoves his head against her arm. "Mrrowf."

She scratches his neck. "I guess I'll never know, but I don't care. I don't need to know, I'm just glad to be whole again."

Now he shakes his head and looks her right in the eye. "Mrrr."

Nutty cat.

She drives into the grounds of Doc's place, brightly lit by floodlights, the gates closing behind her. The lights make her wince, but it's tolerable. His home is lovely, of course. A circular drive loops around in front of the house and connects with a four-car attached garage. His home looks like it should be on a plantation in the old South—two-story and white with six tall columns across the front. Twenty-foot, blooming magnolia trees fill the air with perfume and make the palm trees that border the driveway feel out of place.

There's an older Honda parked near the front door. Doc stands in the doorway, smiling at the woman who reaches out to shake his hand. She moves with such grace that Meg squints to make out her face—it's the dancer! "Patch, there's the woman who did the white kitten in *Cats*. Oh, I'd love to get her autograph."

Patch says, "Mrf." He's a fan too. They'll have to give it a try if they have a chance. The woman goes inside, and the door closes behind her.

On one side of the main house is an attached outbuilding where Doc has his clinic and the storeroom with two industrial-strength refrigerators, both having locks on the handles. One of them is where he keeps his V1 juice. There's a white worktable between the refrigerators. On delivery days, he leaves the key to the V1 fridge on a hook for her. She figures the other one holds drugs he needs for his practice.

The delivery can wait, though, because she's excited about showing Doc her cheek, and it'll only take a second, and maybe she can meet the dancer. She takes Patch out of his seat and he trots alongside her as they go through the clinic door and then into the storeroom where another door connects to the house.

The door is unlocked, and they slip through. She's never been inside the house, and the place is as opulent as the outside. Her feet sink into white carpet, and she wishes she was barefoot. Voices murmur somewhere ahead, down the hall, so she heads that way, Patch by her side.

The first doorway they come to is open to a study, the walls lined with bookshelves that flank an eight-foot fireplace on the far side. All of the books are perfectly vertical, with no gaps for missing books. An open rolltop desk is perfectly clear except for a nicely posed fountain pen on the surface. The pigeonholes are all perfectly empty.

The Hollywood Unmurders

The wooden furniture gleams. Perfectly. She bets there isn't a single speck of dust anywhere, even hiding under the desk.

Two framed movie posters hanging above the fireplace stand out. One features the doctor's grandmother Jade Lovely, starring with Glenn Ford in *Framed*, and the other stars his grandfather Max Lovely in *Singing Guns*. But there's something off about the posters that she can't quite make out from the hallway. Since the doctor seems to be engaged with his client, she slips inside for a look-see.

As she approaches the fireplace, the first thing that draws her in are his grandmother's crystal-green eyes, glowing out of the poster the same way they do on-screen. Doc's eyes are just like his grandmother's. But there's a dart stuck in her forehead, and another in the cheek of his grandfather's image. When she gets to the fireplace, it's clear that his grandmother's face and that of his grandfather in his poster are pitted with countless holes, the kind darts make.

A painting in a frame on the mantel is of a teenage boy with crystal-green eyes, a big nose, buckteeth, and a weak chin. The painting also has dart holes in it. The shape of the face reminds her of Doc, but Doc has a cleft chin of steel to rival that of Kirk Douglas, an aristocratic nose, and perfect teeth. He is more beautiful than his grandparents, and she suspects people come to Doc for plastic surgery because he is such an example of male gorgeousness.

Leaving behind the mystery of the darts, she strolls past mementos from their movie careers that decorate the study in exhibits around the room. She stops to admire a mannequin displaying the voluminous pink-and-roses ball gown that Jade wore in a remake of *Gone with the Wind*.

Next to the rolltop desk is a grouping of a saddle, spurs, a holstered six-shooter, cowboy boots, and a white cowboy hat with a feather in its hatband. They have to be from Max Lovely's star turn in *Smoldering Sagebrush*, hailed as an instant classic Western—although "instant classic" has always felt like an oxymoron to her.

When she moves back toward the study door, the distant voices come nearer. Darn! If Doc finds her here, he'll think she's snooping. She should have just gone and found him instead of sneaking around. She picks Patch up and stands behind the mannequin.

She can see the doorway, but the angle is such that anyone walking down the hall that way won't see her and Patch. She hopes they're going to the clinic, not this room.

Doc's mellifluous voice becomes clear. "Let me give you a quick tour of my clinic. Although I do operate in hospitals, I have the finest equipment right here and the best staff available on call. It gives my clients the privacy they desire."

The dancer says, "I'm not too worried about that. I just want to look young again."

"Oh, you will, my dear. Have you seen the photos of Stella Golden in last week's trades? That's my work. Not only can I erase the years more completely than any other surgeon, but I can guarantee that your new look will never fade if you follow my regimen."

Their voices are right outside, and Meg peeks around the mannequin. Doc and the dancer walk past the doorway. She'd felt sorry for the woman when Flem told her she was too old for the part in Meg's movie—now her ain't-gonna-happen movie. Looks like the dancer is going to remedy her age problem. Well, she couldn't have come to a better surgeon.

The dancer says, "What is this regimen, Doctor Lovely? Is it strict?"

"Oh, call me Adonis, won't you?"

Their voices fade, and Meg decides to sneak out the front door and come into the clinic with his order as if they'd just arrived. Maybe she can get an autograph and show Doc her cheek at the same time.

As she pauses at the study doorway to let them get out of sight, Doc says to the dancer, "The first part of the regimen is that I've created a revolutionary new treatment that changes your body chemistry so your tissues don't age. The new look my surgery gives you will stay that way for the rest of your life."

"That sounds almost too good to be true."

He chuckles. "It does, doesn't it? I'll confess that there are side effects. We'll go through everything to make sure you understand. I warn you that the regimen can be on the strict side at times. For example, the changes in your body chemistry and metabolism require one hundred percent avoidance of daylight, which is the second primary component of my regimen. Exposure to sunlight will completely destroy your new look."

Jeez, you'd think he was talking about vampires.

She says, "I don't know, that sounds very restrictive."

"Oh, my other clients have found ways around it. It's not a big problem, especially in Hollywood, where everybody sleeps until noon. The third part is a special diet, also because of the changes in your body chemistry. You will not be able to ingest ordinary food, but I have created a sustaining potion that will take care of one hundred percent of your nutritional needs."

A potion? No other food? Don't tell me ...

Doc Lovely guides the dancer through the door to the storeroom and the clinic. He laughs. "As a part of my full disclosure, you should know that the treatment causes a condition similar to Renfield's syndrome. This is hard for me to believe, but people afflicted with Renfield's behave like vampires." He chuckles. "They even drink blood."

"Ewww, that's disgusting. I could never do that."

There's a smile in his voice when he says, "Of course you couldn't, it would be silly to expect you to drink blood. Although it is possible that you might sometimes feel that you want to, in truth all you will ever need is my Elixir to satisfy those urges. It's only fifty dollars a bottle, delivered to your home, and you'll never have to go to a grocery store again."

Patch looks up at Meg. "Mrrr?"

She whispers, "Yeah, that's what he said. Elixir."

Doc says, "Here, let me show you." The jingle of a set of keys sounds, and then a soft whoosh. The sound a refrigerator makes when you tug it open.

The dancer says, "My, that's a lot of Elixir. It's a pretty red color."

"My clients love it. I have a very good supplier."

Meg carries Patch down the hall the other way and goes out the front door to her van. She busies herself with loading up a dolly with the Doc's standard order of bovine V1 while Patch supervises. He's good at that.

As she pushes the dolly toward the house, the clinic door opens and Doc Lovely ushers the cat dancer out. "Well, you think it over, my dear. I'm booked for the next couple of weeks, but after the surgery heals, the change in your body chemistry procedure takes only one day."

The dancer says goodbye and gets into her car before Meg can call out and ask for an autograph. As the woman drives toward the gate, Doc waves to Meg. "Hello. Good timing. Bring that in and then we can take care of your wound. I'll be in the clinic."

He disappears, and she wheels the V1 in and takes it to the storage room, Patch trotting ahead. He's done this delivery with her often enough to know the routine. The padlock on the other refrigerator is open. After she fills the empty shelves in the V1 refrigerator, a peek inside the other one shows rows and rows of red Everlast Elixir. She checks the ingredients list, but it shows only "liquid protein solution."

She takes the dolly back out to the van and braces herself for talking with Doc. Although she's really happy to be showing him how she has healed, she's perturbed about him turning unwitting people into vampires and selling disguised V1 to them. But how does he change them? He's not a vampire, so he can't turn them himself. Does he have a pet vampire to do the biting?

Patch is still with her when she knocks on the doorjamb of the open clinic door. Doc Lovely stands beside a medical table, his back to her. "Doc? I've got some good news."

He turns to her and smiles. "Excellent. We can all use good news." Then he frowns at her. "Your cheek."

"That's the good news. It healed."

Instead of a big smile, his frown deepens into a scowl. "Impossible." He strides to her and grips her jaw, his fingers clamping down hard. He forces her head to turn one way and then the other. "Which cheek was it?"

She points, and he leans closer. He says, "It's perfect."

"Yeah. So I won't be needing that glue treatment."

Doc steps to a counter and gets a magnifying glass from a drawer. He brings it close and studies her cheek for a long minute. Then he steps back and gazes at her, his expression a cool mask, not the friendly Doc she's come to know. "Perfect."

He leans close to her, or should she say looms over her. His voice grates, not its usual silky smooth, when he says, "How did you do it?"

What is his problem? She can only shake her head. "I don't have any idea. I woke up this way the morning after I took a swim last night, and the cut was gone."

"A swim?"

"Yes. I had a craving for feeling alive, so I drank three bottles of V1 and then had a swim. But I don't think swimming had anything to do with it. I didn't go to bed for a couple of hours after I got out of the pool, and the cut was there when I conked out. When I woke up, it was gone."

Patch volunteers, "Mraaow."

"Aha. Three bottles of blood all at once!"

She has to disappoint him. "The A.V.A. has been working on this for years, and they've tried blood saturation. Even after drinking four bottles, there were no changes in wounds."

Doc returns the magnifying glass to the drawer and then comes back to her. He glares, his mouth turned down. He grips her upper arms and squeezes. She's glad she's on the numb side right then; otherwise it would hurt. If she weren't a vampire, there would be bruises. He says, "Don't you understand how important this is? Healing wounds in vampires? Maybe even broken bones? If only I'd had this when some of my clients ..."

He trails off, and then shakes her. "Tell me!"

Patch leaps to the tabletop, takes a big breath, growls, and then hisses mightily, his fangs sharp and ready. He crouches, ready to leap, his focus on Doc's face. She tells Doc, "He bites."

Doc gives Patch a look.

She says, "You need to back off."

He lets go of her and offers a smile that she doesn't believe is real. "I apologize. You know how hard I work to fix injured vampires. I may be overly passionate about it."

Yeah, she'd say that says it. Stepping back a pace, she tells him, "Listen, I have a delivery schedule to keep."

He reaches for her again, but stops when Patch directs another growl at him.

"All right. Now I understand. Tell me how you did it and I'll give you a thousand dollars."

What is he saying? That she's holding out the secret of her healing for money? "You've got me all wrong, Doc."

"Ten thousand dollars!"

"You don't get it. I'd give it away if I knew." She strokes Patch then picks him up. "C'mon, Patch, we've got work to do."

Doc leaves her alone when she takes Patch out to her van, but he stands in the doorway and stares at her. She's thinking she needs to get him taken off her route.

Back at the A.V.A. at the end of her rounds, she goes to the dispatch office to ask about moving Doc Lovely to another driver. She knocks on her supervisor's doorframe and is answered with, "Come in, Meg."

Hoping this won't take long because shimmers of pain are telling her she needs a hit of V1, she goes into Gloria's office. "I was going to talk to you tomorrow about a change in my route, but now's a good time."

Gloria, a chubby, warm, earth-mother type, isn't her usual smiley self. "I'm afraid I have bad news, Meg. We're not going to be able to have you deliver for us anymore."

There's a great word for what she feels right then—*flabbergasted*. If you whacked her in the forehead with a baseball bat, she wouldn't feel more stunned. "What? Why? I do a good job."

"You do. Or at least you did. But now we have a major complaint from one of your customers."

Uh-oh. "Who?"

"Doc Lovely. He didn't say what you did, but he was very angry on the phone and demanded that you be fired."

"So take him off my route. That's what I was going to ask you to do anyway."

Gloria holds her hands out, palms up, in a gesture of surrender. "I suggested that, but he insisted. And Doc is an important man who does so much good for us, I can't say no." She goes silent, then says, "It was him or you, and we need him more than we need you. I'm sorry."

"All right. I'll go see HR. I'm a good typist, or maybe I can help with marketing V1—"

A shake of Gloria's head cuts Meg off. "I've already asked them if there's something else for you, but he called there first. Either you're out of the A.V.A. completely or he is."

She holds out an envelope. "Here's two weeks' severance pay. It's the best I can do."

Meg doesn't know how she makes back to her apartment. She just ends up sitting on the bed, petting Patch, and wishing she could cry.

30: Nick

After Nick's first rush of triumph at having Captain Numm's charges dismissed, he thought he was on his way again. Not so. Instead, he dropped into something like the Pit of Despair from *The Princess Bride* movie. It took him a couple of days to crawl his way out of that slump.

He could look for a non-cop job, but that's throwing away what he's dedicated years to achieving. He does apply for a private investigator's license. Thanks to his time on the force, he meets all the experience and education requirements, and since he is no longer charged with any crimes, he clears the criminal history background check. He's not sure being a PI will satisfy him. He could move somewhere else and maybe join a police force, but he hates the thought of tucking his tail between his legs and running away.

He's spent much of the last two nights in his other form, roaming the hills to work off his frustration. But he's still as angry as ever. He'll run again tonight as soon as he gets ahold of Manny.

The other positive thing he's been able to do is talk to his union rep about an appeal. There's no way the captain is going to simply kick him off the force. After setting up an appointment with the union lawyer, his job now is to round up witnesses. It's late enough in the day that Manny will be off work, so Nick calls his cell phone. He picks up right away.

"Manny, I'm calling to ask if you'll be a witness for me when the union goes after Captain Numm for firing me without cause."

"You bet. I'm sure your lawyer can help, too. Will you ask Meg?"

Although Meg's breasts had a different message for him that night in the pool, she was perfectly clear about what she wants from him—no more. "I'm sort of unwelcome with her these days. Not to mention forever."

"Yeah, you were pretty much a dick. So you haven't talked to her?"

"What's up?"

"She asked me for help finding her a night job. She got canned at the A.V.A."

"Why?"

"She said it was a complaint by somebody on her route. He's giving her a hard time. He wants her do something for him that she can't."

"Any idea who he is?"

"I don't know the who, why, or what, but I am looking for work for her."

"Yeah, well, I could be looking for work real soon, too. My savings are on the shallow side."

"I'm sure the union will get your old job back."

But does he want it back if it has anything to do with the captain? Which it will, sooner or later. The LAPD is big, but the captain is moving up in the ranks. "Thanks, Manny. I'll let you know what comes next."

"Oh, there was another masher body found in the Bronson Caves last night."

He knows the place. It's not far from Lake Hollywood Park where the first masher was found.

Manny says, "Get this—in amongst the bones were the fragments of a glass bottle with traces of blood on them. This time, we got part of the thing into the lab before the sun got to it, and I've sent samples out for analysis."

Damn, Nick wishes he was on the case. "Was there a stake?"

"Yes. Another one with D.V.L. stamped on it."

"No more toaster murders?"

"Nope."

"Keep me informed?"

"No problem."

After they end the call, he can't do anything but pace and think about the murders he is—he *was*—investigating, so he packs up his knapsack and decides that the Hollywood Reservoir would be a good place for a run. Maybe his coyote sense can pick up something at the old masher crime scene there.

When he gets back from his run, he's glad for the physical weariness it causes—maybe he can relax tonight. He didn't find any new clues at the masher murder site, but there was still that it's-blood-but-not-regular-blood smell he thinks means vampires. He didn't have time to report to the captain his suspicions about the Devils being involved before he was kicked out, so he's assuming there's no effort to investigate them. He figures he'll have to do his duty and let somebody on the squad know—it won't be Captain Numm. The only thing he'd like to give him is ... Drat, his nonviolent nature won't let him go there.

On the other hand, if he were to be his other self and come upon the captain, let's say, after work, maybe he could ... No, that's a scenario better confined to a screenplay. He wonders how Meg is doing with her Disney deal. Maybe it can help her get through her unemployment problems.

After a long, hot shower, he pours a nice head on a cold beer and then digs out his phone to check for messages before settling in to a good mystery where the bad guy doesn't get away with it. There's a voicemail from Meg.

"Nick, I don't know if this is connected to the cases you were working on, or if you'll even be interested anymore, but I have information that could be related to what happened to Flint Ascot."

He jumps to his feet, sloshing beer. Even though he's listening to a voicemail, "What?" bursts out of him.

On the phone, a doorbell rings in the background and she calls out, "Just a minute." She says, "Nick, I think Mister Ascot was turned into a vampire when he—"

Loud pounding in the background. She mutters, "Hold on ..."

She knows Ascot was turned into a vampire? And when it happened? Don't leave him hanging.

Her distant voice comes. "Who is it?"

Her phone picks up a low murmur. It sounds like a male voice, but there's no way to make out the words. Then a click that could be the door opening. Meg says, "Leave me alone. I told you I don't know." Then she cries, "What are you do—"

There's a low grunt, then the rustle of something. Nick hears a thud, and then a door slams, followed by a yowl from her cat. Then there's scratching as if the cat is trying to get out. And then silence.

He disconnects and then dials her number. His call gets no answer and then goes to voicemail. He grabs his keys, gets his backup gun out of its hiding place, and runs for his car.

At Meg's apartment house, a mother and two grade-school boys splash in the swimming pool, the water glowing blue with the pool lights. He rings Meg's doorbell, but there's no response. Another ring. Nothing. He says to the mom, "Have you seen the young woman who lives here?"

"Meg? Who wants to know?"

He steps closer to the pool. "Police, ma'am."

"Good. I heard pounding down here a little while back, but I didn't see what it was. We just got into the pool a few minutes ago."

"Thanks." He hammers his fist on Meg's door. More silence, and then scratching down low on the door. He tries the doorknob, and it's not locked. He calls out, "Meg?"

All he gets is more scratching and then a loud meow from inside. With his gun in hand, he eases the door open. Patch dashes past him and streaks toward the parking lot. Crazy cat.

He calls again. "Meg?" Silence.

Nick enters and finds her cell phone on the floor near the door, still turned on. Going room to room, nothing else seems out of order. But her purse is on the kitchen table, and her laptop is open on the coffee table in the living room. He wiggles the mouse, and a job search website comes up.

"Mrow."

Patch is back in the apartment. Funny thing about cats, it feels natural to talk to them. He says, "Hey, where's Meg?"

The cat looks him in the eye and then jumps up onto the coffee table and paws at a magazine. *The Hollywood Reporter.* Patch keeps pawing, opening the cover and then going through pages.

Nick flashes back to his first interview with Meg, and he gets it. He grabs the magazine and flips through it until he comes to the article on Doc Lovely. Before he can say anything, Patch pounces on Doc's photo, rips it with his claws, and growls.

Then he makes eye contact again, leaps from the table, runs to the door, then stops and looks back at Nick.

Nick whips out his phone and calls a friend at the station to get Lovely's address, then dashes out the door. The cat is faster than he is, and gets to the car first. This time Nick doesn't try to shut him out. He opens the door for him, Patch jumps inside, and they tear out of the parking lot.

31: Meg

Once again Meg is glad she doesn't bruise when Doc Lovely dumps her on a hard floor somewhere. She lies there on her back, the bag he put over her head loose, but she still can't see, and shaking her head doesn't get her anywhere. The gag in her mouth would choke her if she were chokable. Her legs are free but her arms are bound to her sides, so although she could kick something if she could see it, she can't do much more than lie there.

He pulls the bag off her head, but wherever he's parked her is dark. Then fluorescent lights flicker on overhead and glare at her. There's no ceiling, and the lights are attached to rafters. They illuminate every corner and irritate the hell out of her skin.

Hands slip under her arms from behind, and she's half lifted, half dragged to a chair and plopped into it. A rope goes around her and she's tied to the chair.

Doc Lovely comes around and gazes down at her. He looks like he just walked out of a 1940s movie about Hollywood, dressed in dark slacks, a white shirt that looks like silk, and a crimson smoking jacket with black lapels, all accentuated with a red silk cravat at his neck. It would be perfect if he had a cigarette burning in a long black-and-gold holder clenched in his perfect teeth.

"Hello, Megan. I'm hoping we can work this out. I really don't want to harm your pretty self. There's far too little beauty in the world as it is, so I don't want to lose yours, my dear."

There's no point in trying to say something with a gag in her mouth, so she doesn't bother taking a breath and trying. Instead, she scans the place.

They're in a four-door garage, in one of the two empty middle parking spaces. At one end is Doc's red Mercedes convertible. On the other side of her looms an ominous black van, the kind with no windows in the sides or back, and what windows it has are so dark they look black.

In the space next to the one she's in, he has an artificial turf putting green and a tee where he can hit golf balls into a net. A wire basket full of golf balls sits beside the tee, and a stand holds a golf bag of gleaming clubs. Her dad would have killed for a setup like this during the long winters in Illinois. She never went for golf—even Dad used to say that it's a great way to spoil a nice walk.

The place is perfectly clean and tidy, unlike any garage she's ever seen. No oil stains mar the concrete floor. There are windows, but heavy drapes cover them. Garden tools are hung on a wall in a pleasing pattern—they gleam, not a sign of dirt on the shovel or the hoe. A workbench holds neatly arranged tools alongside a mini-refrigerator. She does a double take when she spots a rifle in a gun rack mounted above the workbench. Four trophies featuring rifles decorate a shelf beneath the gun.

A 55-gallon steel drum sits a few feet from her chair. Poised a foot or so above the drum is a circular metal plate at the end of a mechanical arm. The disk looks to be a perfect size for fitting into the drum beneath it. It's attached to some kind of cylinder, and there's a big lever on one side. The drum sits in a metal pan wider than the drum's base.

"Here," he says, "let me make you more comfortable." By that he means taking off the gag.

When her mouth is free, she says, "I'd be a whole lot more comfortable if you untied me."

"I saw that you noticed my varmint gun." He goes to the workbench and strokes the barrel of the rifle. "A .22-250." He lifts it and works the bolt action. He raises it to his shoulder and aims it at her. "Sighted in for accuracy as close to perfect as possible. Coyotes still invade the neighborhood, and I've found that they don't come back if I shoot them." He indicates the trophies. "It's a single-shot rifle, but I don't miss."

She can't help but think of a certain coyote she knows, one who happens to also have a really nice derriere.

Doc comes back to her and smiles. "So. Untie you? Sure. All you have to do is tell me what you did to heal your cheek. Not only will I set you free, but I'll pay you twenty thousand dollars and tell the A.V.A. that I made a terrible mistake and hope that you'll return to delivering V1 to me."

"We seem to have a communication problem here. I'll try one more time. I. Don't. Know. How. It. Happened. I went to bed with a gash in my cheek, I woke up and it was gone."

After a slow shake of his head, he says, "Let me show you something that might help change your mind about telling me."

Doc strides to the drum. "Although technically this is a trash compactor, I think of it as my extractor. Pay attention, dear Meg, because your continued existence will end right here if you don't tell me what I want to know." He pats the side of the drum and it makes a hollow sound. "But you will still contribute to my success."

She doesn't have any notion of what this nut is talking about. But the more he talks, the longer she has to think of a way out of there. "You mean your success in turning movie stars into vampires?"

"Ah, you figured that out, did you? You can share in the credit, since your V1 juice has been so helpful. Although I think my notion of an everlasting elixir is so much lovelier than what the A.V.A. calls it."

He studies her. "But no, by my success I'm referring to creating more beauty in the world with my surgery and the fact that vampires don't change." His eyes widen. They glitter. "It's my passion, my purpose."

The guy is certifiable. "A noble goal, Doc, but I don't get how you turn people into vampires, since you're not one yourself." She looks around the garage, but they're alone. "Do you have a pet vampire tucked away in a dungeon to do the biting for you?"

He laughs. It echoes. It's creepy. "No, sweet Meg." He pats the drum again. "I manipulate my clients' body chemistry by infusing an, shall we say, essence that this little beauty makes for me. See the holes at the bottom?"

Now that he points them out, she does. One-inch holes run around the base of the drum. There's a red residue around the holes.

"I've been studying your kind since I started doing pro-bono work at the A.V.A. It's true that you don't bleed when cut because you have no liquid blood flowing in your veins, but that doesn't mean there's no blood in you. I have learned from examining tissue samples that vampires are, essentially, made of blood-filled cells that the microparasite uses to power body structures and functions. It's when these cells begin to empty that the blood hunger strikes."

This isn't news to her. The vee scientists who work for the A.V.A. figured that out a while back. It hasn't led to a cure or anything, but they're working on it. If she gets a chance, she'll ask them about her miraculous healing. Meanwhile, it won't hurt to keep Doc talking. "Amazing! But I don't get how you do what you do."

He taps the circular metal disk poised above the opening to the drum, and then rests a hand on the lever that attaches to the frame. He indicates a pair of buttons, one red, one green. "With a push of the green button, my extractor creates a crushing force of four thousand pounds of pressure." He presses it, a compressor a few feet from the machine starts up, and the round metal plate inches down toward the opening of the drum. He stops it by pressing the red button.

"You're a writer—I'm sure your vivid imagination can foresee what would happen if, for example, a vampire was in this drum. When I, er, compact the vampire, its essence flows out the bottom and into the pan."

Horror doesn't begin to describe the sick feeling that rises in her.

He ambles back to the workbench, at ease, in control. He picks up a thing she recognizes—one of the long, sharp wooden stakes from the Devils. "I'm a compassionate man, so I didn't want them to suffer needlessly. I tried chloroform, but it had no effect. I tried to put them out of commission before the extraction with one of these." He presses a fingertip against the knifelike tip of the stake. "Unfortunately, it seems that a stake through the heart doesn't immediately knock out a vampire."

Yeah, that's true. The end doesn't come until blood hunger hits and the heart with a hole in it can't pump blood to the rest of a body. She saw it happen to a vampire with a bullet hole in his heart. The vee-bug consumed him when blood pumped out of the hole instead of into his veins.

The way Doc is preening, she doesn't have to ask him why he's telling her all this. She twists at her bindings, but they don't loosen. She needs to keep him talking. "Vampires?" Oh, no—Sarge was asking her if she'd seen Andy. "Where do you get vampires?"

Doc smiles. He goes to the mini-refrigerator on the workbench, opens it, and takes out a bottle of V1 juice. "Thanks to the A.V.A., it's easy. I go to a park late at night, set an open bottle of blood by a tree, and then hide on the other side with my trusty rope at the ready. A vampire soon appears, and they always guzzle the entire bottle. When they sink into the lethargy, it's easy to tie them up and bring them here. You can figure out the rest."

He opens the bottle. The scent of blood wafts its way to her, and she has a desire to lick her lips. It's been a while since she last fed.

He returns to the mini-refrigerator and takes out a Mason jar filled with a dark red fluid. "After my clients' surgery is healed and they are as perfect as my talents can make them, I infuse them with essence of vampire and it renders my lovely work immortal."

Immortal, yes, but ... "But the problem is that vampires don't heal, do they?"

Doc shrugs. "Isn't that the irony? What makes their beauty eternal also makes an ugly cut equally everlasting. Or a broken bone."

Blood hunger flickers, the first twinge of the pain comes and goes. Maybe if Doc waits long enough, the blood hunger will take over and she'll be strong enough to break free. Then she'll treat him to some real vampire action. *Keep yammering, bad guy.*

Hold on. There was a white cowboy hat in Doc's study just like the one in the tanning parlor security tape. Tanning beds. Powerful light in an enclosed space designed to simulate sunlight. Of course. *Well, Nick, I've solved your murders—lot of good that does me.*

Keep him talking. "So you used a tanning bed to kill Flint Ascot."

His eyebrows rise. "Very astute, Meg. Although I'm not sure the term *killed* is appropriate for an undead person, but I certainly couldn't let it become known that one of my clients has a permanent gash on his forehead. Glue and makeup aren't an answer for someone who will be seen in extreme close-up, their faces twenty feet tall on a movie screen." He shrugs. "I know my measures may seem, let us say, harsh, but those are the demands of perfection."

He goes back to the empty drum and taps it again. "You see why I need your secret for healing. And you can be a hero—you'll save lives. What happened to Ascot won't happen again when I have the ability to heal vampire flesh and, I assume, bone."

"Why did you use a tanning bed to murder Mister Ascot instead of putting him in your masher and taking his 'essence'?"

"Oh, no, destroy my beautiful work in such a messy, ugly way? Aesthetics matter in all things, including murder. But homeless vampires? Who cares, and their essence is quite functional."

Doc returns to her side, leans in, and studies her cheek. "Hmm. I wonder if your ability to heal will be passed on in the essence I squeeze from you. Maybe I don't need you to tell me your secret method after all." He straightens. And smirks. "Wouldn't that be a lovely ending? You couldn't tell anyone about me, and I will have what I want."

Even if she had a secret and told him, he'd still have to eliminate her.

Doc strides to his putting green and takes a putter out of his golf bag. Taking a ball from the wire basket and placing it on the "green," he says, "Perhaps we should take a little break and relax while you think about the cost of keeping your secret." He putts, and the ball drops into the hole. He reaches for another golf ball.

The pain flares hotter. Just a little longer and maybe she can break these ropes.

32: Patch

Nick drives like the Indy 500 is on L.A. streets, swerving, honking, flashing headlights, hitting the brakes and then flooring the gas. It takes all four sets of claws embedded in the seat to keep me from being tossed from side to side and front to back. There ought to be cat seat belts, you ask me. But I don't want him to slow down. Doc Lovely has Meg. I know what he wants from her, and she can't tell him that I'm the one who healed her cheek because she doesn't know. Who'd have thought my doing that was a bad idea?

Nick slams into the short driveway at Doc's place and skids to a stop before the gate, inches from its black iron bars. He leaps out of the car and presses the button on the intercom attached to a gatepost. Looking at the towering walls of bougainvillea thorns on both sides, it would be helpful if the good doctor buzzed us in.

Nick left his car door open, so I scoot out and jump up onto the hood. Nick jams his thumb on the intercom button over and over, shouting, "Doctor Lovely," but he gets no response.

He paces along the wall one way and then the other, looking up, searching, shaking his head. He comes back to me.

"I don't see a way to get in." He steps back and studies the gate and its sharp spikes on the top, just as high as the walls. They look even scarier than the bougainvillea thorns. But I've seen this guy jump in his other mode.

Nick gets on the hood of the car and leaps up to grab the bars of the gate as high as he can. It's an impressive jump, but he grabs the bars a good three feet short of the top. And then his hands slip and he's back on the pavement.

I growl at him. When I have his attention, I jump up onto the trunk of his car. Then up to the roof, sliding to its edge. Then back to the ground, and then back up onto the trunk. And then to the roof. Then I try to imitate a coyote howl. It sounds like cat yowl to me, but his eyes widen.

He steps back and gazes up at the gate. "Maybe I can."

Moving fast, he gets his knapsack out of the back seat of the car, then strips and stuffs his clothes and gun into it. He straps on the knapsack and backs up, to get a running start after he changes, I suspect.

I get as close to a yell as a cat can get. "Mrrrooowww!"

When he looks at me, I rear up on my hind legs and hold my front paws up. To my surprise, he smiles, though it is a grim smile.

"Sure, cat, why not? Maybe you can help me find her." He points a thumb at the knapsack, then holds his fingers out as if they were claws.

I say, "Mrrrf" and move to the edge of the car roof.

Nick does his werecoyote thing and transforms. When he's done, a huge, angry coyote looks up at me. I leap for the knapsack on his back and hook all my claws into the canvas.

Nick trots out into the street a few feet, turns, and races toward the car. He leaps to the trunk and to the roof, and then launches us up and over the gate.

We clear the spikes but land hard on the driveway inside. Coyote Nick yelps and tumbles forward into the lawn area.

I manage to release my claws from the knapsack and land gracefully on all four paws, as a cat should.

When Nick *shifts* back into human form, he cries out and clenches his right wrist. He groans. "Broken. Just great."

There he stands, naked, wearing a knapsack, with a broken wrist. Well, he's just going to have to keep up—I'm going to find Meg. I head for the door I know, the one into the clinic and the storeroom. Nick follows.

I paw at the door—uselessly. Man, do I hate doors. Even if I could reach the knob, I couldn't turn it. Nick joins me and uses those wonderful digits on his left hand to try the knob. It opens. I'm sure Doc Lovely feels totally safe behind his ten-foot walls of thorns. Well, we're gonna show him.

When Nick sees the clinic, he rushes in and rummages through drawers until he comes up with a big roll of wide white tape and a handful of tongue depressors. Clenching his teeth, he splints his broken wrist, wrapping it tight with the white tape. I'm impressed. I remember what pain feels like, and he hardly lets out a whimper. When he finishes, he wriggles the fingers of that hand and sighs. "That's better. It's mostly useless, but it doesn't hurt so bad. I hope I don't have to shoot anybody using my left hand. In fact, if that's the case, I'd do just as well throwing my gun at them."

He is able to use his right hand in small ways when he puts on his clothes, finishing with his jeans and then slip-on shoes. Leaving the knapsack on the counter, he jams his gun into the waistband of his jeans at the back and looks to me.

I know he doesn't expect an answer when he says, "Where to now, cat?" but I give him one. I say "Mrrrf" and trot into the storeroom with the two big refrigerators. The locks are open on both of them. I go to the door that connects to the house and wait for him.

Nick goes to the worktable. He opens a drawer and says, "Wow."

Curiosity being one of my primary instinctual directives, I leap up onto the table. Nick takes a bottle of rubber cement and a handful of rectangular pieces of paper out of the drawer. He picks one up and reads, "'Everlast Elixir.'" He scans it, and then says, "'Lovely Care Products, Los Angeles, California.'"

He opens the refrigerator where Meg puts the V1, and it's half full of V1 bottles. He opens the second one. It too is half full of bottles, but they have the Everlast Elixir label on them.

Nick looks grim to me. "Now I know how her fingerprints got on the Elixir bottles."

He pulls out his pistol with his left hand and approaches the door into the main house. When he opens it, I dash through and into the first room along the hallway. It's the study. Nick follows me and goes to a white cowboy hat. "This looks familiar."

He pulls a dart from the *Singing Guns* poster above the fireplace mantel. "Somebody doesn't like Granddad."

Meg isn't here, so I head back out into the hallway. We go upstairs first and hurry from room to room. I'm faster than Nick, so whenever there's an open door, I race in, alert for Meg. Nick sees that if I come right back out, she's not there, so he just goes to closed doors and checks inside. Working as a team, we're soon downstairs in the last room to search, the kitchen with its walk-in pantry, but it's empty.

There's a door at one end where the garage is and another with a window that looks out on the backyard. Nick opens the back door and steps out, and I follow. Automatic floodlights go on. A brick patio bordered by gardens stretches across the rear of the house. In a far corner of the fenced yard, there's a small building, a perfect hiding place. I start across the lawn toward it.

Nick paces me, then stops mid-lawn and looks from the house to the garage and back. "This is taking too long." He takes a deep breath.

33: Meg and Patch and Nick

Meg hopes Doc doesn't notice when she squirms and grits her teeth as the pain throbs in her. Her strength is growing. Soon she'll be strong enough to—

Doc looks up from his putting green. "Oh, my, are you uncomfortable?" He walks over, his putter over his shoulder. "I've seen this before when the—blood hunger, you call it?—hit my first client. She became quite ferocious. And strong." He strides to the open bottle of V1 on the workbench. "Luckily, I figured out what to do before she ripped me to shreds."

He brings the bottle of blood closer. The scent is irresistible. Her mouth opens involuntarily, and she strains toward the bottle. If she could salivate, drool would be cascading off her chin.

"Well, since it seems apparent that you are not going to share your secret with me, I think it's time to go to plan B."

A long coyote howl cuts into the silence. It's close, outside the garage.

She's heard that howl before, at the observatory and then at her house. She takes a deep breath and shouts as loud as she can, "HERE!" Her scream echoes in the cavernous garage. "I'M HERE!"

Doc laughs. "Answering the call of the wild?" He frowns. "It did sound awfully close." He leans his putter against the golf bag, fetches the varmint gun, chambers a round, and then brings the bottle of V1 to her. She can't help herself: she strains against the rope, her mouth opens wide. She tries to break the rope, but she's not strong enough yet. *No, don't feed me!* She NEEDS that blood.

Doc says, "It's time for your last supper. When the lassitude hits you, I'll put you in my compactor and begin your donation process." His face saddens. "It appears that there's a lot of pain when I crush my donors to harvest their essence. I wish I could kill you first so you won't suffer, but that's not possible."

There's another strike against being undead. She tries to turn her head away from the bottle, but the irresistible impulse of the vee-bug is too strong. He puts the bottle to her lips and she guzzles the blood down. She doesn't spill a drop. The pain vanishes, the feel-good part starts trickling through her body, and she slumps in the chair, her body enervated.

Doc unties her from the chair and removes the rope binding her arms. He drags her to the 55-gallon drum, her arms and legs flopping helplessly. He lifts her as easily as he might a sack of flour and deposits her in the drum. Her legs have no desire to hold her up, and she's small enough that she sinks down into the barrel, all but her eyes below the rim.

He pats her on the head, and then pushes the red button. The air compressor starts up. Doc peers at her. "I'm going to set this for the slowest speed so you'll have time to think while you're being crushed, and I can stop it when you decide to tell me your secret." He backs out of view as the round metal plate above her begins descending. "Just give me a shout and I'll stop it." He smiles.

And she's supposed to be the monster.

Crazily enough, what she thinks about is Patch. She hopes he'll be okay, somehow. Maybe Nick will ...

~

I race after Nick back into the house. Meg's voice came from the garage, and he goes to the end of the kitchen with the connecting door. Nick has his gun in his good hand and tries to open the door with the hurt one. The second he grips the knob, he moans, but then he squeezes and tries to turn it. He cries out and lets it go.

"Screw this," he says.

Nick steps back, faces the door, rears back, lifts a foot in the air, and delivers a kick next to the doorknob. The door flies open just like on TV and I dash into the garage. A black van blocks my way, but I run under it. On the other side, a few feet away, some kind of machine chugs next to a big metal barrel—Meg is in the barrel, the top of her head and her eyes visible. Doc Lovely spins toward me, a rifle in his hands.

Meg's eyes widen when she sees me. "Help!"

Doc whips his rifle to his shoulder and squeezes the trigger—but I dash back under the van before he fires. The bullet hits the concrete floor where I was and *spangs* up and into the side of the van.

Nick barrels through the door behind me and runs to the front of the van. I join him right when he levels his gun at Doc and yells, "Freeze!"

Meg calls again. "Nick! In here!"

When Nick's focus darts to the barrel, Doc sprints to a workbench, grabs a small box, and runs behind a red car at the other side of the garage. Nick fires at him left-handed, but it goes so wide that a rear window of the car shatters as Doc rounds the front and ducks down out of sight.

I scramble up onto the hood of the van to see if I can see Doc, but he's crouched too low, so I leap onto the roof. Yes, there he is. He takes a bullet from the box he grabbed and puts it into the rifle.

Nick shouts, "Meg!" and runs for the metal drum—from atop the van I can see her struggling, but moving sluggishly. Just as Nick nears the drum, Doc pops up from his hiding place and aims his rifle.

I take a deep breath and screech a warning. Nick looks around and sees Doc. He dives for the garage floor just as a rifle shot cracks. Nick rolls and crouches behind a huge golf bag.

Meg shouts, "The compressor! Stop the compressor!"

That must mean the machine chugging near her. There's nothing I can do from here, but maybe I can get to Doc so Nick can deal with the machine. The rafters are a makeable jump from the top of the van, so that's where I go.

Nick is sure that Patch's warning saved his butt, but what is Doc Lovely doing to Meg? The compressor she wants stopped connects to a cylinder above her. A round metal plate is inching down toward the interior of the drum. The size and shape of the drum would hold a masher body. He can't think about that, not now.

Meg shouts, "Dammit, body! Move!"

He braces to stand and run to her, but he catches movement out of the side of his eye and drops back down behind the golf bag just as a shot sounds. There's a metallic *thwack* when the bullet hits a golf club.

Doc says, "Damn. My favorite driver."

Nick aims his gun at the compressor left-handed. He has to be able to do this. He fires a shot, and it sparks off the concrete a foot from the machine. It has to be stopped. There's nothing to do but keep trying.

Squeezing off each shot as carefully he can, he misses, and misses, and misses until there's one round left. He moves the revolver to his right hand. God, it hurts to grip it, but he's a great shot with that hand. Steadying it with his left hand, he aims at the spot where the hose connects to the compressor, squeezes—

Blam! Doc's shot tears the pistol from his hand. He's lucky his trigger finger doesn't go with it. The compressor keeps on chugging, and he's paralyzed by pain from his broken wrist.

Doc calls out, "Ready or not, here I come."

When Nick leans against the golf bag, a putter propped against it clatters to the floor. It isn't much of a weapon, especially against a gun. He eyes the compressor. The metal plate is inches from descending into the drum—and crushing Meg.

Meg shouts, "Nick! The red button!"

Got it. There's a red button on a control module. Gripping the putter in his left hand, he lunges out from the golf bag. A shot cracks, and the bullet creases his back. Laying out in a dive, he swings the putter at the button with every bit of strength he has.

His left arm is a lot better at clubbing than shooting. He smashes the button, and the metal plate stops coming down.

The steel barrel holding Meg starts rocking to and fro, so he rolls and gives it a kick. It sways back and then topples toward him, hitting the concrete floor with a huge clang that resounds through the garage. The click of the bolt on Doc's rifle sliding home seems loud in the sudden silence. The open top of the drum is toward Nick and his gaze meets Meg's. She shoves with her feet and squirms. Her head and shoulders emerge from the drum.

Doc steps from behind the car and stops maybe twenty feet from Nick. On his good hand and knees, Nick scrambles toward the bucket of golf balls.

Grabbing for a ball with his left hand, he also spills the bucket, sending balls scattering behind him. He jumps to his feet and throws the ball at Doc. Doc sidesteps and the ball misses by a mile, of course, and bangs off the Mercedes behind him.

When Nick reaches for another ball, Doc aims his rifle at Meg and says to him, "Now *you* freeze, mister, unless you want me to put a bullet in your little friend's face."

He drops the ball. Doc smiles at him. Holding his gaze, Nick backs away from him and away from Meg, who is getting to her knees. Doc has to turn his way—and away from her—as he transfers his aim to Nick.

Doc says, "Stop right there.'

Nick stops.

Meg wobbles and almost falls, then steadies herself with her hands on the floor and works to stand.

Doc says, "Who do we have here?"

"Detective Nicholai Silver, LAPD, and you're under arrest for the murders of Flint Ascot and Stella Golden."

Doc can't see Meg get to her feet, but he can. She grips a golf ball in each hand. Doc laughs. "Let me see. I observe a bandage and splint on your right wrist, and you have no weapon, is that correct? Oh, and I also have a lethal weapon aimed at your center mass, right?"

Nick doesn't answer, but he stares as hard as he can into Doc's eyes, trying to pin his gaze to him.

Doc says, "Somehow I don't feel as though I'm under arrest." He grins. "What do I have wrong?"

Meg winds up.

Doc's smile reminds him of the curve of a crocodile's mouth. Doc lifts the rifle to his shoulder and aims at Nick's face.

Meg throws, and the golf ball clips Doc's leg. As he turns her way, she throws again and nails him on the side of his head. He staggers back, but then he regains his balance and swings his gun to hold it on Meg. "Well, Meg, I guess we're just going to have to do this the hard way." He whips the gun back to Nick before he can launch into a charge. "I'm very well practiced with this weapon, and I can reload before you get to me." There's that creepy smile again. "But if you want to be a hero, be my guest."

He edges sideways, away from Nick and closer to Meg. He tells her, "Set that barrel up and get back into it or I'll shoot your, er, hapless rescuer."

Nick shouts, "Don't do it! He has to kill me anyway."

Doc shrugs. "And, as a result, I'll have a wonderful supply of human blood to use as bait. My, how propitious." He turns the gun back to her. "The drum, Meg, now."

A wild screech sounds from above Doc. He looks up.

Patch flies down from a rafter, yowling, legs spread wide.

He slams his fifteen pounds of brawny cat into Doc's uplifted face. His momentum and weight topple Doc backward as Patch sinks his front claws into the sides of Doc's head.

With Doc flat on his back, Patch digs his hind claws into Doc's chest, opens his mouth wide, hisses, and then holds his open jaws and gleaming fangs inches above Doc's nose.

Doc reaches for Patch with one hand and Meg shouts, "See those fangs? You ready to become a vampire?"

He freezes, then lets his arm down to the concrete floor and lies still, staring up at Patch.

In the long silence that follows, Nick drifts toward Meg, and she him. They come together, his arm goes around her shoulders, hers around his back at the waist. They simply hold each other and gaze at Doc Lovely ... and Patch, perched on his chest.

~

I'm *so* tempted to bite Doc Lovely and deliver the vee-bug. Why shouldn't I?

Meg comes over and squats down beside us. She says to Doc, "How would you like to spend a little time in your extractor?"

Doc's muffled response, which is buried in my furry chest, could be "No."

She says to me, "Patch?"

I don't move my fangs, but I do cut my eyes to the side. She says, "Bite him." She stretches her jaws wide and air-bites.

Nick shouts, "No! That would be murder." He joins us and looks down at Doc and me.

Meg turns to him. "Murder?"

"Well ... assault, maybe?"

Hmm, a dilemma that calls for catlike cleverness.

Ah, I know what to do.

I shift off of his face and lick Doc's nose with my raspy tongue. And again. And again. Again.

My taste buds perk up when the taste of fresh blood arrives—it's a minuscule amount, but it's there. And so is the vee-bug. I lick one more time for good measure.

I sit up on Doc's chest.

Meg says, "Aww, come on, Patch, give him a little nip."

Nick says, "I might have to arrest him if he does."

She glares up at him. "After what Doc was going to do to me? He was going to crush me in that ... that thing."

Nick studies the drum. "The masher murders." He steps closer and says to Doc. "You are very soon going to be arrested for multiple murders."

Doc's mouth and face twitch in mini-spasms as the vee-bug does its thing. I step off of his chest and sit by his side to watch. The twitches turn into tremors that spread over his body as the vee-bug invades. His nose, not visibly bleeding, nonetheless heals.

I look up at Meg's soft, "Oh." She understands. I say, "Mrf" and go to rub against her.

She stands, picks me up, and holds me to her chest. "You did it. Patch, you're my hero."

Turning to Nick, she says, "You, too."

Doc's quivering stops and his mouth moves. His eyes widen—they look panicky, darting from side to side. His mouth flaps again. The man's a dummy.

Nick looks to me. "You didn't."

So arrest me. I say, "Mew."

Doc looks down at his chest and then puts both hands on it. He puts a hand over his heart. His look of panic is eaten by a look of horror.

Meg says, "You have to breathe to speak."

Doc gasps in air and says, "What have you done to me?"

Nick says, "Not half of what we're gonna do." He stoops and picks up the rifle, works the bolt and examines the chamber, then rams it home. "Locked and loaded." He gazes at Doc. "Let's see ... We can start with assault with a lethal weapon, attempted murder, assault on a police officer, murder ..." He grins. "That ought to do it."

He looks to Meg. His eyes widen. "What ..." He does a double take, steps closer to her, and touches her cheek where the cut was. "It's gone."

She smiles. "Yeah." Her smile downshifts into a scowl aimed at Doc. "That's why Doc kidnapped me. He wants to know how I did it." She kicks Doc in the ribs with the toe of her shoe. "One more time, Doc—I don't know how it happened."

Doc says, "A million dollars. Let me go and tell me, and there will be a million dollars in your bank account tomorrow." He turns his attention to Nick. "You, too."

That earns a snort from Nick. "So what should we do with you now?"

She looks at her watch. "We're not long from dawn. If we want to get Patch and me out of here before sunrise, whatever it is needs to be quick."

Nick scans the area. "Tie his hands behind his back with that rope."

Doc says, "No, please." His eyes look like they want to cry. "You have to understand! I was just trying to make them forever beautiful."

Meg fetches the rope and tells Doc to roll over.

He doesn't move. Nick jams the rifle barrel into Doc's chest where his heart lies. "I understand a bullet hole right here won't kill you outright. That comes later."

Doc rolls over and Meg ties his hands behind his back. Nick strolls through the garage examining things. He bends down and looks at the red gunk on the holes at the bottom of the 55-gallon barrel. "You know, this barrel is the size and shape of a mangled vampire body found in Lake Hollywood Park." He turns to Doc. "But why?"

Meg says, "He crushed vampires in that to get our blood and used it to turn his clients into vees. There's a bottle in his refrigerator."

Nick circles the black van and stoops to check out a bumper sticker. "Hey, Doc. We have a witness and tire tracks that will place this van of yours at the Lake Hollywood murder scene. Nice touch, using a D.V.L. stake to put the blame on them."

He goes to the workbench and checks inside the refrigerator. Then he examines a wooden stake on the bench. "And you have a nice set of equally incriminating D.V.L. vampire stakes here. Just like the ones we found in three crushed bodies."

Meg says, "Nick, we need to go. We have to have enough time to drive to the A.V.A."

He pulls out his cell phone and grins. "There's somebody I feel an urge to humiliate." He dials, and then there's a considerable wait. At last, he says, "Yes, I know what time it is, Captain. Thanks to the assistance of the woman you wanted dead, I've captured the killer of Flint Ascot and Stella Golden and three other people. Take down this address. You'll find the perp tied up in his garage and plenty of evidence all around." He dictates Doc's address and then ends the call.

Doc Lovely rolls onto his back. "You can't do this. Do you know what will happen when they take me outside?"

Meg puts on a shocked expression. "Oh, my! That would be terrible." She looks to me. "Wouldn't it?"

I echo her sentiment. "Mrow." I wish I could watch.

Nick grins. "Just tell them you're a vampire. I'm sure that will work."

Meg gives him a look—telling Nick that didn't work so well for her. But then she smiles when he winks at her. He says to Doc, "We're just following the rule of law, Doc. Maybe this time it will lead to justice."

He holds his hand out to Meg. "Let's go."

She picks me up and holds me to her with one hand while she takes his with the other.

34: Patch and Meg and Nick

I stretch out on the couch next to Meg when she plops her laptop on the coffee table and fires it up. It's been a relaxing week of no drama—nobody trying to snuff either one of us, no murders, no cops, no giant coyotes, no nothing. You might think that would be boring, but you've got to consider what would be boring to a creature that normally sleeps sixteen hours a day. Right. Virtually nothing. If ever a species evolved to be perfectly suited to a life of leisure, it's us soft, furry, adorable cats.

I'm not a complete slacker. Late-night prowls are still fun, and I haven't seen anything resembling a coyote this week. I do miss riding along with Meg on her A.V.A. delivery route. After the uproar about Doc Lovely being a murderer, they took away her job again, and she lost her employee discount on V1 juice, so that's doubly hurtful. She's working with that nosey Manny guy to find night work. Although I think his interest in her body is disturbing, he did offer to help her with the rent. Meg's proud, though, and she turned it down. She still has some of the cash the A.V.A. gave her when they kicked her out.

A photo appears on her screen—the face makes me think of a rotten pear. She gasps. "Oh my God! It's Harvey Flem on the front page of *The Hollywood Reporter*. Get this, Patch."

She reads, "'Harvey Flem, former Disney producer, canned for sexual harassment.'" She scrolls through the article. "Hey, I think it was us. Says here a video of him exposing himself to a writer was sent to management." She smiles at me. "Couldn't have happened to a worse person, there being no worse person." She gets a thoughtful look on her face. "Except Doc Lovely."

I like the way writers think and how they say things. I also like licking, so I initiate a bath, which is about as wild an activity as I'd like right about now. Or ever, for that matter.

Her phone rings, and my supersharp hearing picks up the melodious voice that comes after she answers. "Hey, Meg, Jeanine here. Did you see *The Hollywood Reporter* article on Flem?"

Meg laughs. "Just did. I may print it out and frame it. So you sent my video to a decent person?"

"Ninety-nine percent of the people at Disney are decent. They are also interested in creating good entertainment, which is why I'm calling you. Got a minute?"

Meg hops up and moves into the kitchen. She likes to pace when she talks. I continue licking. Maybe she'll come back with a bowl of V1 for a treat.

Not thirty seconds passes before she squeals, and I mean squeals. "Squee! Yes! Oh, yes! Twenty thousand? Oh my God."

There's a little more conversation and then she says, "We can be there tomorrow night, whenever you say."

Meg listens, then says okay nine o'clock and ends the call. In the midst of a good round of paw-face-paw-face washing, the microwave turns on. That's soon followed by Meg bringing in a bowl of blood, a mug of the same in her other hand.

"We're celebrating, Patch. You and I are going to work with Jeanine at Disney to make our movie. And they're paying me a twenty-thousand-dollar advance for the script plus a salary as an associate producer when they start to make the film."

Her smile is huge when she sets my bowl on the coffee table. I'm glad to join her in a drink, but I refuse to celebrate spinning a dancing musical tale of vambies. I turn my nose into the air.

"It's gonna be my original concept, Patch. We get to tell our story our way."

Okay, so maybe stardom is still in my stars. I step onto the coffee table and lap at the warm blood in my bowl as Meg drinks hers. It hasn't been that long since we last fed, so this hit will bring extra energy and feeling. Maybe I can get a good scratching from Meg while my skin is sensitive enough to truly enjoy it. Soon enough, we settle into our lassitude and enjoy a peaceful moment.

When we rouse, Meg calls up a document on her laptop, and I recognize the script she's been working on for months. There's a little smile at the corner of her mouth as she scrolls through it, stopping every once in a while to type something.

Then she shuts down and takes out her cell phone. She eyes me for a moment, then keys a number. After a pause, she says, "Nick? This is Meg."

Oh, no. Not again. I glare at her as well as my fixed features allow, which is mostly composed of lowering my head so that I glower up at her from beneath my brows.

She listens and then smiles. "I have something to celebrate. Maybe we could do something? Tonight?"

This calls for sterner measures—I still don't trust that guy. I mean, he's a weird kind of *dog*. I walk to her, take a breath, and hiss.

She laughs. "Oh, that's just Patch being cranky. Listen, I'm a little stir-crazy tonight. Can we meet somewhere?

The observatory? It should be deserted by now. It's almost midnight."

Her smile tells me his answer.

I am not happy about this.

~

Meg gets Patch and herself to the observatory a little early, but it's a beautiful night, so they leave the car and walk to the side that looks out over Los Angeles. Patch hops up on the half-wall barrier and she leans against it. She knows it's a cliché, but the lights look as if all the world's riches in jewels are scattered before them, reaching to the horizon.

The breeze up here feels good on her skin, like a caress. She's glad for the sensitivity that comes from the extra blood and for wearing a tank top and shorts. If she were Patch, she'd purr.

Her hands are fidgety tonight, so she busies one of them with petting Patch. It's as if she's nervous about meeting Nick, but that's silly—she can't be nervous, because there can be no relationship with that man.

That breather.

That *food*.

Though the observatory is closed, the outside is lit; there are spots of light between shadowed places, but there's no one else there. Looking around for Nick, it occurs to her that she doesn't know whether to look for tall, good-looking Nick or huge-coyote Nick.

Either way, she doesn't truly understand why she called him tonight. After all, he nearly got her killed and then he betrayed her. So this is somebody she should call to celebrate?

On the other hand, there's that fireplace heat thing. And he did save her life at least three times.

Yeah, she's going to call it a *life* instead of mincing words such as *undead*. Screw that. She's alive. Dammit, she will continue to be a human being, which includes having friends. They haven't been in L.A. long, and even though there are some nice folks at the A.V.A., she hasn't made any friends yet. About the only thing the people at work have in common besides being vampires is that they're all writing screenplays.

With that extra helping of V1 before they came, she'll be all right when Nick is here. Now that she thinks of it, though, having to be certain to take that precaution is a sure sign of trouble ahead. What if they do become friends? They'll go places together, right? What if the car breaks down miles from anywhere and the blood hunger hits her? There are only so many rolls of Death Savers you can reasonably have on hand.

Images of her tackling that big Devil guy and gnawing on him flash on her mind's movie screen, and then she superimposes Nick's face on the guy. With her chewing on his neck.

That's no way to treat a friend.

As much as she'd like to do this, she can't.

"Come on, Patch, we need to go." Patch gives her a look but hops down and trots alongside. The muscles in her back relax—she hadn't realized how tense she is. A cool sense of relief comes with the decision she's made. She'll still be lonely, but Nick will be safe.

The little bit of joy in her that had flickered at the prospect of seeing Nick dies. But this is the right thing to do. There are times she wishes she wasn't so hung up on doing the right thing.

"Hey, going somewhere?" Nick steps out of a shadow. He's in his human form. "Sorry if I'm a little late." He looks good, more at ease than he's seen him since, well, since they first met and he was being deceptively charming. His jeans, sandals, and black T-shirt with a *Law & Order* logo on it are much friendlier than his usual rumpled suit.

She immediately understands what *discombobulated* truly means. She has a pulse still, and it picks up speed. Her cheeks feel warm, and she wonders if it's possible that she's blushing.

"Going somewhere? Yes ... no ... I—"

"I have something to celebrate too." He gives her that sweet smile of his. "So I was glad you called."

There's a cast on his right wrist, but he's not using a sling. It's pristine white, and she points to it. "Nobody willing to sign your cast?"

He lifts one shoulder. "Who would?"

"How about me?"

He smiles. "Well, I want to be careful about what kind of sentiment goes on it. And we've had our, uh, issues in the past."

Okay, fair point. But she's not a vindictive person, though how would he know that? All she can say to that is "True. But I wouldn't—"

"Wow." His gaze looks past her and he strides to the wall. "I forget how beautiful this is when I'm neck-deep in the crap that goes on during the day."

Patch headbutts her leg and then starts toward the parking lot, but she stays put. There's nothing wrong with having one last conversation with Nick before calling it quits. He's safe tonight. She joins him. "So tell me what you're celebrating."

"Well, it could be that the union got my job back."

"That's good news." Wait—*could be?* "They didn't?"

"They did."

"Then wha—"

"I'm not going back." He pulls a business card from his pocket and hands it to her. There's enough light to read, "Nicholai Silver & Associates. Private Investigation."

She looks up at him. His gaze is sober, as if he's anxious about her reaction. She feels good for him, so she beams and says, "Oh, cool!"

He breaks into a huge smile and then laughs. "Yeah. I can still help people, but I'll be free to do it right." The smile returns, smaller and softer. "I thank you for getting me to understand what that is."

There's a swell of emotion in her throat—she's proud of him. And of herself, too. But that's not all ... dammit, that extra blood has her feeling a little too much alive to be indifferent to the warmth coming from him. Her arms rise as if of their own accord, heading to embrace him. Her gaze goes to his face, and she wants a kiss.

A forbidden kiss. She forces her arms down, but can't make herself turn away.

~

Nick had hoped Meg's response to his news would be like this, though there's no reason a vampire's opinion should matter. But that of a smart and lovely young woman does. She gets it, what this means to him. Does that also mean she gets him, the person, too? He wishes she would. He knows anything between them is impossible, but since that night in the pool he hasn't been able to keep her out of his thoughts.

Patch leaps up onto the wall and positions himself between them, and that's a glare he's sending Nick's way. Oddly, Nick is sort of glad to see the peevish hairball. Maybe it's because the cat is a part of what Meg is ... and he did like how Patch handled things when they fought Doc Lovely. Hell, it's more than likely he'd have at least one bullet hole in him if it weren't for Patch. He holds out his hand, his fingers a few inches above Patch's head, and waits for permission to scratch.

Patch looks up at the hand and then sits, effectively moving his head out of Nick's reach. Okay, he can live with that.

Unsure of where to take this, he says to Meg, "What did you want to celebrate? Did you get your job back?" He remembers how important her paychecks were to her.

Now her smile lights up, and the glow of Los Angeles below them dims. "No. Something better." There's excitement in her voice and her body when she tells him the story about the asshole producer and what she did that led to his demise and her new gig working on her movie.

He applauds at the end. He's proud of her, and he wishes a hug was in order, but he doesn't think so. But he gives her his biggest smile and raises a hand for a high five. She hits it, and her hand feels a little bit warm.

Then she sobers and turns to look out at the view. "I have to be honest with you. I was leaving when you stopped me."

She glances his way, and his eyebrows ask why.

She raises her chin and she looks him in the eyes. "We can't be friends."

His eyebrows turn into a frown that says oh no.

She takes a deep breath and sighs. "Because I'd be a danger to you." She strokes Patch. "Patch would be, too."

"I can take care of myself."

She looks up at him. "Do you remember what happened the last time we were up here?"

Oh. That. She took out a guy who was bigger and stronger than Nick. And turned him into a vampire.

But maybe it would be worth it. "What's the worst that can happen? You turning me into a vampire? You're doing okay."

She shakes her head hard enough to make her hair swish from side to side. "Okay? How okay is it when you'll never have a glass of wine with a friend? Or share a bowl of rocky road ice cream?"

Meg gazes at him. "If you were a vampire and heard someone outside cry for help in the daytime, you couldn't do anything. You couldn't even look out the window."

That hits hard. That's the point of his life, to help people.

She looks out at the city again, the corners of her mouth turned down. Patch seems to understand how she's feeling, because he goes to her and rubs his head against her. She puts an arm around him. Her voice is a whisper when she says, "I can never have a child."

That melts him. He reaches to give her a hug, but Patch turns to him and lets out a low growl. Nick settles for a hand on her small, soft shoulder. He was right. She is warm to the touch tonight, just like she was in the swimming pool.

"One more huge thing," she says. "I'm not alive, and you are."

"You're more alive than most of the ... breathers I know."

She chuckles when he says "breathers."

"And we can just be careful."

She turns to him. "We can't be *perfectly* careful. And what if I, or Patch, accidentally turns you? Vampires don't change. Maybe you couldn't do your coyote thing anymore."

He takes his hand back. Okay, that's a shocker. He *likes* that part of himself, and it gives him an edge. Now it's his turn to stare out at the city, going through the what-ifs of an "accident."

Her little hand settles on his arm. It's warm. And gentle. She says, "I'm sorry. Sorry for both of us. I think we could have been great friends."

He does too.

Back to the what-ifs. He gazes out at the city as if an answer were there. Manny is a kinda-friend, but they don't hang out. Because of Nick's condition, he's never gotten close to anyone. You don't want to freak out your friends with the beastly side of your nature.

But Meg knows about his coyote mode, and she doesn't seem to care.

Screw it. What's most valuable in life? Doing a good job? No. Money? No. Running around like a wild animal? Maybe … No. It's people, and he doesn't have any of those, other than his parents, and they're far away.

Turning to take her in, he warms to everything he sees, her face, her lips, but mostly to the intelligence and concern in her eyes.

A part of him desires a lot more than friendship, though that can't be. But he wants her in his life. Holding out his hand for a shake, he says, "Friends?"

Her eyes widen.

Patch says, "Mrf?"

~

When Nick holds his hand out to Meg, I look to her face. Surprise appears there first. It's followed by one of those smiles she gets when she reaches for me to hold me. It's pleasing to see her pleased.

Meg says, "We need to talk about the coyote in the room."

Nick takes his hand—his paw?—back and runs it through his hair. "I can't really explain it. My mom was pregnant with me when she and Dad were camping not too far from Area 51. They were big fans of UFOs and aliens. She found a very large coyote in a trap. When she freed him, she scratched her arm on a cactus. She told me that when the coyote gazed into her eyes, she felt like she was with a person, not an animal. He licked her wound clean, and then trotted off."

"So what were you when you were born?"

I'm wondering the same thing. A baby, or flea bait?

"A regulation baby. The coyote part didn't come out until puberty."

I'm remembering that it was a full moon when I first made the coyote's acquaintance. Meg must have had a similar thought. "What happens when there's a full moon? Do you eat people?" She pets me. "Or cats?"

I say, "Mrrrow."

He laughs. "No, the full moon doesn't affect me. It's always under my control." He looks at me. "As for cats, they are not a menu item for me in any form."

Good to know.

Nick says, "So. Friends?"

She scowls at him, then shakes her head. "I can't. I ... I like you, a lot, and it would mess me up seriously if I were to accidentally make you a vampire. You can find yourself other friends."

He gazes out at L.A.'s glittering carpet of diamonds and rubies and emeralds. He sighs. "No, that's not gonna happen." He turns to her, leans forward.

It takes him a while, and there's a catch in his voice when he finally says, "I feel like I grew up alone, at least after this coyote thing happened. There was, literally, no one like me. I was the ultimate 'other.' You say it's dangerous to be your friend. Well, at least you know what can happen and why. I don't."

"You seem okay to me." She smiles. "And you make a great coyote."

His frown sinks her smile. "Yeah? What if I *shift* and can't change back? That's possible, as far as I know, mostly because I don't know anything about being what I am. Do you think friends would like hanging out with a carnivorous beast that can't talk and would like to eat them? What about work? How would I earn coyote food? Do I hunt?" He glances at me. I shiver at the possibility. He turns back to her. "Like I said, I'm alone." He settles back, and his next words are not much more than a whisper. "And I think you are, too."

Hello? That's sweet, but AHEM! I step forward and give him *the glare*. "Mrrrow."

A smile lightens his face. "Okay, so you're not *totally* alone." He reaches for my head as if to scratch me, but I haven't given him permission yet. I add a squint to *the glare*.

He sobers, takes his hand back, and says to her, "Don't tell me you don't feel like an 'other,' like someone—or some*thing*—that doesn't fit, can't belong."

A deep breath and a sniffle come from Meg. I look back at her. Her eyes glisten as if she has tears. Her face is as sad as I've ever seen it.

I step to her and give her a good headbutt. The smile she gives me doesn't touch the sadness in her eyes, and she holds me close.

"What did you do when you first changed into a coyote?"

His gaze drifts to the distance, as if he's searching for a thought. "I hid in a closet until I figured out how to change back." Nick turns back to Meg. "Other than my mom and dad, you're the first person who's ever seen me change. Or even know that I can."

Meg's chuckle is bitter. "Thanks for thinking of me as a person." Her hand strokes my back as she says, "I'm so weary of hiding. I can go out among breathers at night, but I'm still hiding. I fake breathing just to pass. I can be with ordinary people, but not really, not ever. What makes it hard is that was once my life, too—breathing and bleeding and warm and cold and loving. Now? Now, if I'm too late in feeding on blood, I will think nothing of ripping out someone's throat." She shudders.

It's her turn to gaze out at the stars below. "Anyone would be crazy to want to be a vampire's friend."

"I don't know about that. Maybe two"—he points at me—"or three 'others' can add up to something together." He grins, and his eyes get that twinkle. "How about Fur, Fangs & Fem Private Investigation and Storytelling Inc.?"

Mrf! If I could laugh, I would. Meg inhales with a snort and her laugh is happy. And free. She gazes at Nick. "You're crazy."

He sends a shrug her way. "Nothing new there." He holds out his hand to her again. "So, crazy friends?"

She gazes down at me. I give her my best you're-asking-me? look. Meg releases me and looks Nick straight in the eye. Well, sort of straight, him being a foot taller.

She cracks a smile and takes his hand. "Okay."

Well, there's a twist.

Still holding his hand—and not petting me—there's honey in her voice when she grins up at him and says, "I like knowing I'm not alone."

Once again, what does she think I am, chopped liver? Why, I oughta—

Nick holds his hand above my head. He looks me in the eye. "Friends?"

I look to Meg. She nods to me. Okayyyy ... I give his fingers a headbutt and allow him to scratch behind my ears. His touch is almost as good as Meg's.

Ahhh.

Meg turns her gaze back to the lights below. "The fight with Doc Lovely keeps coming back to me. Being in that awful barrel." She wraps her arms around herself. "Nightmares aren't supposed to be real."

"I'm sure Doc Lovely felt that way at the end."

"The end?"

"Manny let me know what happened when Captain Numm arrested Lovely."

Her eyes widen, and she puts a hand to her mouth. "The sun?"

Nick nods. "Just like the toaster murders. Bones and ash. The captain is saying it was spontaneous combustion, which is more ridiculous than Doc being a vampire."

"Even though I hated him for what he wanted to do to me, I don't feel good about that."

Nick nods. Me, I've mostly left it behind. *Now* is always my universe.

She says, "It was ... scary. Still is. And when I remember it, I need ... I sure could use ..."

Nick's voice goes soft. "Something like this?"

He stops petting me, puts his arm around her shoulders, and hugs her to him.

She rests her head on his chest. Her eyes glisten again. "Yeah. Exactly like this."

I call foul. Unfair competition. Hugs simply aren't in my repertoire. And, from the looks of it, headbutts are not an adequate alternative.

Meg sighs. "Thanks." Then she leans back and looks up at him. "Do you think that sometime ... that is, when you're a coyote ... I wonder ... could I pet you?"

Then she reaches up and runs her fingers through his hair. His reaction is the closest thing I've heard to a human purring.

Wait a minute! This is going too far.

But then her hand leaves his head and scratches the side of my neck. His hand joins hers, but on the other side, and they scratch both sides of my neck.

Stereo scratching.

It is to purr.

Dear Reader

A thousand thanks for reading my book—it is to purr. If you enjoyed my story, please consider telling your friends and posting a review on your blog or at Amazon.com.

And my typist, Ray Rhamey, would be glad to talk with book clubs about my tale. He seems to think that there are themes in it, stuff like prejudice, bigotry, greed, and being an outsider. Whatever. You can contact him at ray@rayrhamey.com.

The prequel to *The Hollywood Unmurders, Support Your Local Vampire Kitty-Cat*, is a stand-alone story that introduces Meg and Patch. There's action aplenty with satire for seasoning as they struggle to survive and thrive as newbie vampires. You'll find it at Amazon.

Patch

About my typist

My typist, Ray Rhamey, asked me to tell you a little about him. Since he's been a good associate, what with the catnip and typing up my story and all, I'm happy to oblige.

Ray is quite catlike, independent as hell and really loves to have his back scratched. I think he was purring when this picture was taken.

His wife, Sarah, reminds me of a Siamese cat—elegant and beautiful. Ray has four fine offspring, too: Abby, Molly, Becky, and Dan. They're also catlike, especially on the independence part.

He has made his living with this writer thing he does for quite a while now. He did a long turn in advertising as a copywriter and then a creative director. I hear that his sense of humor bubbled up in a lot of his creative work, which was capped by the droll Budweiser TasteBuds commercials he did that people saw on *Saturday Night Live* back in the Eighties.

But he left advertising and did screenwriting for a while—kids enjoy his television adaptation of The Little Engine that Could. Then he moved on from that.

Here's where Ray is less like a cat than, say, a cat—he doesn't sleep most of the day. No, he keeps trying stuff.

He's invented a board game that he says is more fun than Scrabble.

He makes me tired. I want a nap.

Ray tells me that he's always been drawn to storytelling. It was only natural that he turned to writing novels after his screenwriting period. He has read a couple of them to me, and they're darned good—they were the primary reason I agreed to let him help me with telling my story. If you get a chance to read one, you won't be disappointed, even though they're not funny. There's one—*Gundown*—that really makes you think, if you're into that kind of thing (thinking, that is).

Digging into the craft of writing novels to tell his own stories led him to doing freelance editing of book-length fiction, and that led him to create his blog on writing compelling fiction, *Flogging the Quill*. I'll be honest, some of the things I learned from him helped me do this book ... okay, that's a plug, but, hey, I'm biased. Full disclosure.

Anyway, his blog led to him teaching writing workshops at writers' conferences and publishing his book, *Mastering the Craft of Compelling Storytelling*. Even though he lives in the Pacific Northwest, he's got fans all over the world, and I can see how much he enjoys being a member of the writing community and helping other writers. But I don't hold it against him as long as I get my full share of his time.

Speaking of which, now he's doing editing and book design full time at crrreative.com. He designed my book.

I wonder what's going to happen next, what with Meg and Nick getting all touchy-feely. Stay tuned.

Keep on purrin'.
Patch

Novels by me I think you will enjoy

In small-town Bloomsburg Illinois, newbie vampires Patch, a calico tomcat, and Meg, a pinkish human being, are targets for vigilante vampire hunters. Patch and Meg come out of the coffin to campaign for sheriff so they can stop the vampire killers.

On the way to election day, Patch is kidnapped, tried for murder (hey, it was one of those yappy little dogs), there's betrayal at the American Vampire Association, a bloodthirsty preacher has vampicide on his mind, and Patch and Meg are hit with a deadly double-cross.

Support Your Local Vampire Kitty-Cat is serious fun in the way only satire can be. More than that, it's the story of a cat and a young woman who struggle with a curse that is destroying their lives.

Join Patch in a tale rife with action, humor, and what vampire life, so to speak, is really like.

Paperback books and Kindle ebooks are available on Amazon.com. A search that includes my last name will find them.

Final Fire is the story of a woman, a healer, who loves deeply ... and has lost.

Of a man whose beloved child is deeply troubled ... and he doesn't know how to help her.

Of a child lost in a whirlwind of psychic abilities.

Of a people with an ability to heal, to extend life, or to kill without a touch.

Of a madman who creates a plague to destroy the human race to avenge the death of his son.

Of a Homeland Security agent whose rabid hatred of terrorists leads her to despicable acts.

The Magians are amidst us. A mutation gives them control over natural life energy to extend their lives, to heal ... or to kill. Their kin have been burned at the stake as witches, so they live apart from the rest of humanity in small scattered clans. But their genes course through the populace, and many of us unknowingly share their heritage.

Homeland Security is pursuing Rhianna, a Magian healer, because they see terrorism in the manifestation of her ability. On the run, she learns that Drago, a Magian clanmaster, will

launch a fatal plague that will wipe out "ordinary" people, billions of us, as vengeance for the murder of his son.
And battle is joined ...

Paperback and Kindle editions available on Amazon.

The air was as still as it was hot—only the whir of a grasshopper's flight troubled the quiet. Jesse felt like an overcooked chicken, his meat darn near ready to fall off his bones. Mouth so dry he didn't have enough spit left to swallow, Jesse croaked, "That guy tryin' to kill us?"

Turns out the answer is "not yet." A ranch hand is murdered and bad things start happening to Jesse, just an average kid working on a ranch the summer of 1958.

And then there's Lola ... the boss's daughter is a firecracker of a girl, and her bold ways send death their way.

It will take all of their heart and courage to survive.

Paperback and Kindle available on Amazon.

In the time it takes an average person to read this novel, three Americans will die from a handgun bullet.

In today's America there is no hope of preventing those killings. Dealing with gun violence is mired in a cultural logjam—as things are, nothing will change.

But what if gun makers could make billions if states made lethal firearms illegal? They'd make it happen. And what if we had a way to defend ourselves without using lethal firearms? We'd make it happen.

In *Gundown*, guns are still everyday killers. Ordinary people have no defense—except in Oregon, where reforms have self-defense on the rise and guns that kill are banned.

But gun advocates fear losing their rights. Hank Soldado, Army veteran and ex-cop, is a good guy with a gun. He accepts an assignment to stop the gun-reform leader.

Going undercover to get close to his target—the closer he gets the more he's drawn to the man's vision for a way to turn America's murderous gun impasse into gun-free self-defense, security, and safety.

Then treachery strikes to destroy that vision, and Hank becomes the only one who can save it—a man who has a lifetime of guns in his blood.

Paperback and Kindle editions of these novels are available on Amazon and through your local bookstore. I hope you'll give them a look.

And I'd appreciate it if you could post a review of *The Hollywood Unmurders* on Amazon.

Thanks for reading.

The Hollywood Unmurders

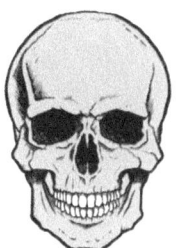

www.ingramcontent.com/pod-product-compliance
Lightning Source LLC
LaVergne TN
LVHW041623060526
838200LV00040B/1404